The Ripper's Apprentice

Lambeth 1891; haunting the shadows of the slum alleys and the bright din of the saloon bars, the dark and silk-hatted figure of a psychopathic killer watched his victims with infinite patience. One after another, the street girls of the Waterloo Road woke to the agony of slow death by the cruellest of poisons.

The absurd figure of 'Fred' proved to be a criminal of erratic and sadistic genius. He left no clue beyond a series of taunting letters, demanding money with menaces from some of the most famous people of the day – and daring the police to 'Catch me, if you can'.

Against the vicious brilliance of this multiple murderer Scotland Yard's Inspector Swain (of *Belladonna*) and Sergeant Lumley must pit their wits. In a final derisive gesture, the murderer offers to unravel the crime for a payment of £30,000. Before the case is over, the name of one of Victorian England's most famous sons and that of a Prime Minister's grandson have been sullied by it. To the last moment – and the last sentence of the novel – the psychopathic killer keeps the nerves of his hunters strung taut.

The novel is based upon a Victorian murder case of 1891-2 and derives from the author's documentary 'The Ripper's Apprentice' in his successful BBC series *The Detectives*. It has been suggested that the 'apprentice' was also Jack the Ripper himself.

The sombre squalor of the Victorian streets of London is made vivid. Donald Thomas is distinguished as a biographer and a poet, but his studies of Victorian crime have also brought distinction (for reviews of *Belladonna* see back panel of this jacket). Here he has used his knowledge and his gifts to terrifying effect.

DONALD THOMAS
THE RIPPER'S APPRENTICE

MACMILLAN

First published in Great Britain 1986 by
MACMILLAN LONDON LIMITED
4 Little Essex Street London WC2R 3LF
and Basingstoke

Associated companies in Auckland, Delhi, Dublin, Gabor-
one, Hamburg, Harare, Hong Kong, Johannesburg, Kuala
Lumpur, Lagos, Manzini, Melbourne, Mexico City, Nairobi,
New York, Singapore and Tokyo.

British Library Cataloguing in Publication Data

Thomas, Donald, *1934-*
    The ripper's apprentice.
    I. Title
    823'.914 [F]   PR6070.H59

    ISBN 0-333-40850-0

Typeset by Bookworm Typesetting Ltd.

Printed by Anchor Brendon Ltd.

Author's Note

The following novel is based upon the investigation of a series of murders in Lambeth during 1891-2. Such public figures as Lord Russell and the Hon Frederick Smith were involved precisely to the extent described here. The characters of the murderer, his associates, and his victims are drawn from historical reality. However, the personalities of the investigating officers have been consolidated in Inspector Alfred Swain and Sergeant Oliver Lumley.

The fact that the most bizarre incidents of the case are taken from real events does not make them more credible in fiction. Yet the conduct of the killer in his life and letters, as well as the irregularities of burial described in Chapter 16, are matters of record.

Despite the greater notoriety enjoyed by Jack the Ripper in 1888, the Lambeth murders were no less unnerving and perhaps more grotesque. They revealed for the first time the nature of a newly defined criminal personality – the psychopath.

Small wonder that the shadowy figure of the Lambeth slums acquired the nickname of 'The Ripper's Apprentice'.

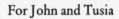

For John and Tusia

1
Madhouse Cell

August 1890 – the first entry
Any prisoner with the strength to urinate has a limitless supply of invisible ink. Offensive though this expedient may sound in polite ears, the secret is old as Egypt and papyrus.

Without its aid, how could I share with you my memories of pleasures past – my private visions of the future delights which the world owes me?

Who 'you' may be, I do not greatly care. It is enough that someone reads these hidden lines. You make me immortal. I speak from the grave and you hear me.

Do I truly have my sinister ambitions? A man locked away as securely as I have been? Indeed I do! The world must hear of me again, I promise. The headlines shall be bigger than the last time – such as you never saw. And, of course, I have learnt from my mistakes. I shall not fall for the same trick twice.

To business, then.

This week is the ninth anniversary of my arrival here. A propitious moment to begin this 'true confession'. For some time I have trained myself to observe my own behaviour with dispassion. I find I am steadier and more rational than in the first years of captivity. I know the worst and have grown contemptuous of it. No longer do I quail each time a warder snarls. Nor do I despair at the filth ingrained in every steel bar and block of stone.

I eat my slum-gulleon and scarcely notice the stink of it.

Nine years gone, then, and the rest of a life sentence to serve. The moral frauds who plan our correction in this place will insist that such a fortress of brutality can break any man.

Not me, good people! Nine years or ninety will leave me just as I was. Unless, perhaps, so much of your brutal attention has made me stronger still.

Do not misunderstand me. If you could see me now, you would agree that I have cultivated a manner which is as obliging and obsequious as my guardians could wish. The chaplain, Mr Rossiter – that pennyworth of perambulating ear-ache! – finds me soulful and penitent. Over his shoulder last week, I read a scrap of what he had written about me.

'Promise of moral amendment,' it said.

Moral amendment! No sooner was the fool out of my cell than I well-nigh danced and sang at my little triumph. That night the world within my skull was bright and busy. I lay in the darkness after the nine hundred steel doors of the cell-house had been locked. I was deaf to the groans of the long-term convicts all about me and to the quiet weeping of the fresh fish. I celebrated the memory of doing away with such painted creatures as the world was better rid of. How exquisite to me was the rare anticipation of similar pleasures which the same world still owes me!

September 1890
And now, about this secret writing of mine. How do I do it? There was not room to explain the matter in my last entry.

The means of transmitting my memoirs beyond the prison walls proved so simple that I hardly dared hope it would succeed. I hit upon the idea of penning my invisible script between the lines of that dutiful family letter which every prisoner is permitted to send once a month.

It must astonish you to see how much can be squeezed between those lines of penitential blather over which the gaoler casts his censoring eye.

I tried a few modest experiments before making my first proper entry.

You can imagine the fears and anxieties I felt. There are punishments administered by the warders here which are unknown to the law or the world at large. My cell is next but one to the bath-house. I have heard the screams of men adding an obbligato to such favourite retributions as the 'water cure' and the 'humming-bird'. Were my secret writings to be discovered, it would be a mark against the warders in the governor's book. I have no doubt how they would reward me. Men have died while wired up to the 'humming-bird'. Despite my fortitude, I should be heard a long way off.

My fears were unnecessary, as you see. The secret writing remained invisible to my captors. After one or two attempts, I knew that I could commit my thoughts to paper in perfect safety.

Why should I take such a risk in order to record thoughts and memories already well known to me? That, of all things, is the most difficult to explain.

I have an itching in my brain which drives me to make known all that I have done and what I propose for the future. It greatly soothes that irritation to celebrate my wishes in this form. It is no more unusual than the poet who cannot be content with the verses in his mind but must let them boil over on to paper and give them to the world.

All the same, I am the first to admit that these memoirs of mine are not likely to be read by anyone. Who would bother to warm the shoddy prison paper at his fire in hopes of seeing a second row of rusty script appear? I would do it, of course. But, then, I must be set at liberty to accomplish it.

Sometimes I amuse myself by picturing a descendant of mine, yet unborn, who tosses these pages on the coals as so much useless lumber. How I chuckle to imagine the astonishment in his eyes while he watches the paper burn! For an instant, before its leaves blacken and crumble into ash, the heat of the fire will make the secret writing plain.

What deaths and scandals will shimmer in the flame!

Rosie Barnes, a blackmailing little tramp, wedged naked on the seat in the wooden lean-to. Dead with a wash-bag over her head and the empty chloroform bottle on the floor!

Arabel Faulkner, who lived by swearing out paternity summonses, staring up from the table in the morgue with the most astonished expression ever seen on the face of a corpse!

Helena Stack, would-be extortioness, gasping out her last with her knees in her belly. She seemed about to pass from this world to the next in a gymnastic caper!

And four others, who deserved all that they got and a good deal more.

All mine, good people! Prove it if you can. You never will, I promise you. . . . Not without my assistance, I took such care of them, you see.

So much for the past, the dear dead past. But am I not changed now? Do I not, as the Reverend Mr Rossiter notes, show 'promise of moral amendment'? Am I in earnest when I assert that far from ending my business with the Rosies and Arabels and Helenas of this world, I have only just begun with them?

I am sane and in earnest. Presently you shall see for yourself. Do you care if the city is rid of such creatures, the insolent purveyors of their flesh? Does anyone care? Do you not, on the contrary, heave a private sigh of relief? Come, no hypocrisy now! In all honesty, will you not wish me luck in my future endeavours?

My mirth ends as soon as it began. I know that these grey pages are most likely to rot with damp or burn unseen in the iron cylinder of a stranger's stove. No one will watch as the heat coaxes my secret into the light of day.

Unless, of course, I should escape from here.

October 1890
'Hell-o! Hell-o! Mary had a little lamb, its fleece was white as snow!'

These words, Mr Rossiter tells me, were the first to be recorded on the phonograph by the egregious Mr Edison. I have tried them over and over. Perhaps I shall adopt them as my clarion call.

You see how well we get on together now, Mr Rossiter and I?

Last month, in the last word of my memoir, I spoke of escape.

Escape!

From the time of a man's arrival here, the day when his head is first shaved and he puts on his zebra-suit, escape is the stuff of his dreams, the favourite topic of whispered conversation. This mirage of liberty is all that has kept many a poor fellow from madness or the grave.

Have no fear, not a man has escaped from here. That is why the guards care nothing for these fanciful whisperings. They know how strong are the walls, how punctilious their security.

12

There have been attempts, to be sure. Brave attempts. Such incidents are talked of long years afterwards, until they grow into prison legends.

Were I to escape – which I intend to do – I should be unique in this.

As in so many other things.

November 1890
The Reverend Rossiter's kind and beaming eye upon me prevented my adding much to last month's memoir. God blast him to hell!

Now, however, I am left alone and so can return to the matter of my escape.

Were you to stand a mile off and take a survey of this prison, the problem would be clear at a glance.

From a distance, you might mistake the building for one of those massive battlemented castles of the Middle Ages set in a vast and open plain. The walls are quite forty feet high, their ramparts patrolled by blue-uniformed guards with repeating rifles under their arms. Detachments of armed warders keep a constant watch on the gates to east and west.

But how, to begin with, would one get out of such a cell as this?

I have occupied the present one for nine years and a few months. It is eight feet long and four feet wide. Most of the space is filled by the iron bed-frame with its straw mattress, pillow, and blanket. My furnishings consist of a wooden bucket, a drinking-crock and a stool. During the day I am forbidden to sit on the bed.

There is no wood in the structure of the cells, only stone and steel. Like the other lifers, I occupy a place on a corridor without exterior windows. My view of the world consists of a segment of the landing seen through the bars of the cell door. Light comes from an incandescent electric lamp in the ceiling which is turned on from outside at half-past five every morning and turned off again at nine o'clock in the evening.

In such a place as this, you could not otherwise tell time from eternity.

There is no way out but through the bars of the door. Our

13

gaolers know this well. Each morning the chief warder's patrol passes down the corridors of the cell-house. One of the guards strikes every bar on every door in turn with a hammer. If the steel rings true, all is well. The least cutting or tampering is betrayed at once by a dull resonance.

So much for the cell door.

Sometimes, of course, one leaves the cell.

Every morning at half-past five, the light in the ceiling comes on and the whistle blows. Shackled in pairs, we march in lock-step across the yard to collect breakfast from the ration-tables. As chance may be, we pass the day in the prison quarry or making chairs in the workshop. Always under armed guard.

At night they return us here, one by one. When inside his cell, a man must clutch the bars of the door so that his hands are constantly in view until the warder has turned the key in the lock.

Men have tried to escape from here during the working day. To be sure they have. Not one has succeeded.

Windy Dick and a dozen of his cronies rushed the guards on the east gate with 'navy revolvers' made up from gas piping to look like the real articles. The guards opened fire before they got near enough to hold up the post. Four men died. Windy Dick and the rest surrendered.

My lanky friend Speckled Jim – a spry young housebreaker – hid among boxes of shoes made in the prison shop. He rode half a mile in the van before they heard him.

They gave him the 'water cure'. Ice water at 'town pressure', one hundred and fifty pounds to the square inch, was hosed on him that winter day. Two ribs cracked and his bowels ruptured.

Speckled Jim was a game young chap. Absconding from a wash detail, he found a coffin in the bath-house. A prisoner, executed that morning, was inside, awaiting burial in the prison garden. Jim hid the corpse in a laundry basket, under a pile of dirty shirts, and took its place in the coffin. His plan was to emerge, terrify the prison gardener who digs the graves, and make off through the governor's quarters where there were no guards. While he lay waiting in the bath-house,

14

the shirts were collected and Jim was caught.

They made the 'humming-bird' sing for Speckled Jim. Four warders stripped him in the wash-room and put him in a metal tub. They put a blindfold on him and strapped his arms behind his back. His feet were hoisted on a pulley-rope so that he sat in a V-shape. The chief warder applied the electric battery to him, beginning on the spine and working down. You could have heard Jim bucking and dancing in the tin tub a block away as the charges went through him. His very bones hummed loud as the metal.

They checked his pulse from time to time in a lackadaisical fashion. He was still lunging and capering when they took the battery away. But it was only the battery. Jim had been dead for a while. Perhaps it was the shocks that made his pulse seem to beat. He died of natural causes, as they call it here. Heart failure.

That night, after Jim's heart gave out in the tin bath, the duty warder spoke to me as I held the bars of the door while he turned the key.

'Nothing gets out through these bars,' he said quietly, 'nothing that's bigger than a rat!'

I sometimes think he was giving me a hint. In his words I saw the solution to my problem.

I had only to become a rat.

December 1890

A rat. The irony of it will be lost upon those who never tasted life in a cell-block.

A prison rat walks on two legs.

The warder's rat is his favourite convict, who earns titbits by betraying his companions in small matters.

Prisoners sometimes have their own rats. Lust being as common in the gaol-house as in the world, many a long-term jocker will have his punk among the small fry. The little creature is known as his master's rat.

To adopt the ways of such lower vermin would be of no use to a man in my situation. A warder's favours are trivial by comparison with the reward I sought. Therefore, I should be no man's rat unless he could assist my grand design.

I thought carefully and watched my chance. It was more than a year ago when I saw what I must do.

I would become the chaplain's rat.

January 1891

At first sight the thing appeared ludicrous.

In all prisons there are men who curry favour by frequenting the chapel and putting on a hang-dog look of remorse. That would not do for me at all. Such expedients never won a man his freedom. I wanted nothing unless it was to be outside these walls, a free citizen in possession of all his rights again.

How best to accomplish this?

After seven or eight years of making so little progress with me, the Reverend Rossiter was ravenous for some note of remorse in my confessions. Little by little, I began to show the most gratifying signs of contrition. That alone would not win my freedom, of course. However, most clergymen hunger for the sweets of repentance. I put them to the Reverend Rossiter as one feeds a small expectant rodent through the bars of its cage.

You may be sure that I fed these titbits to him one by one. I was careful never to surfeit him. On each occasion there was some further delicacy, merely hinted at, which I held over until the next time. His visits to me grew more frequent in their regularity.

Mr Rossiter is the type of philanthropist who loves talk of women – being possessed of a wife himself who is cold as stone. His pleasure in talking of fallen creatures and their rescue is as keen as that of those who caused them to fall in the first place. He fondles and mauls and worries over them in his mind quite as eagerly as the most ardent sensualist. Women of that kind had been my undoing. Hence, I became to him a most agreeable companion.

Yet he possesses an obvious, if rather foolish, look of virile, straight-backed decency. He would climb into the ring and box the devil, man to man, according to Lord Queensberry's rules. I could see that, for such a man, my repentance would be welcome. But repentance alone would not spring me from here. Mr Rossiter – rot his priggish soul – would congratulate me on having seen the light of religion. And then he would advise me to serve the rest of my life sentence with courage – take in on the chin, like a man.

Oh no, thank you very much! That was not at all what I intended!

So, I was gradual. I took infinite pains with him. Never seeming to trespass on his tolerance, I abandoned the servility proper to a convict and began to talk to him straight – just as if we were new-found friends. I grew skilled in this, always sensing the moment when familiarity was dangerous. Then, at once, I would draw back, reminding him of my dark crimes and the tortures of conscience from which I now suffered.

Sir Henry Irving could have taken lessons from me.

My patience was sorely tried by this dog-collared nincompoop and yet I never lost hope.

My strategy was to confess freely and contritely to the murder of which I had been convicted, while protesting my innocence – on my knees and with eyes brimming – of those deaths which they had never been able to pin on me. I did not deny that the little fool Rosie Barnes had died of chloroform, wedged in the lean-to privy at the back of my premises. Yet what had I to do with her? There was no jot of proof to show my hand in her death. Less still could it be shown that I was the man who had put her in the family way.

He listened gravely. Then, to my astonishment, he conceded that I had been much maligned by public gossip over her death.

I did not deny that I had known Arabel Faulkner. So had a hundred other men. To be sure she had blackmailed me as the father of her unborn child. She had made the same threat to most gentlemen of her acquaintance. She died of a drastic medicine, taken to rid herself of the unwanted burden. Was I to be blamed? Not a court in the land had found evidence upon which to try me.

I concealed from the Reverend Rossiter my sincere opinion that the world was well rid of such tramps as the Misses Barnes and Faulkner – and that it should have awarded me a pension for life.

I went further. I explained to him that the rumours aimed against me in the cases were the work of those who had been responsible for debauching such young women and who sought to shift the blame. In the case of Helena Stack, I called their bluff. It was *I* who demanded an investigation and legal proceedings.

When the authorities demurred, I wrote an open letter naming Pyatt, the chemist, laying the girl's death at his door. What happened? It went to court. My innocence was shown and Pyatt's responsibility proved.

I thought for a moment that I had fed Mr Rossiter too much of my innocence. So I confessed hastily and contritely that I had prepared a potion for the victim whose death brought me here. But that mixture was intended to subdue and not to kill old Daniel Stott. It was not I but his promiscuous young bitch of a wife, Julia, who overdosed the old fellow and sent him to hell. Still, what business had he, at sixty, marrying a chit who might have been his granddaughter?

I did not put the matter in quite these terms to Mr Rossiter, you may be sure. How, then, was I to excuse myself of murder?

If there was one thing which went straight to the heart of this cassocked simpleton, it was decency combined with nobility.

Very well, then, I would be decent and noble. It costs nothing.

February 1891

Because I confessed so readily to my part in old Stott's death, the Reverend Rossiter seemed prepared to believe that the other accusations against me might be slander after all.

Still, the wretched Stott was dead. No two ways about it.

With all the earnest decency I could muster, I made my confession to Mr Rossiter.

Young Julia Stott came to me, I could not deny it. After one or two visits, I fell passionately in love with the creature. Yet she was the wife of another man and so, at first, my nobler feelings strove to extinguish this flame of illicit desire.

I had almost conquered my infatuation – I assured Mr

Rossiter of that – when Julia revealed to me her terrible secret. Her elderly husband – a railway supervisor – was a brute who beat her often and used her ill. His violence was made worse by some predisposition to epilepsy for which no treatment had been ordered.

Julia's wide-eyed appeal moved me profoundly and quite overcame my scruples. I tried at first to be only her protector but, almost without knowing it, became her lover too.

Mr Rossiter nodded slowly at this admission, as if he quite understood and forgave me!

I had persuaded a chemist of my acquaintance to make up a soothing potion for old Stott. I could not deny that strychnine was one of its active ingredients – yet each dose was too small to harm him. My accusers swore that I must have added a further quantity of the poison to the mixture before it was given to him.

But no one saw me do it! It was never proved!

Julia alone was responsible for giving the old fellow his sedative tonic. I was never within a mile of him.

Imagine Julia, I murmured, with her soft sunbrowned body, her dark silken hair and wide eyes. She was desperate in her plight. The old wretch who had bought her on the marriage market ruled her by the fist. Could one not understand and pardon how, in fear and despair, the young woman might pour the entire bottle into his drink to be rid of him, once and for all?

I swear that Mr Rossiter's chin hardened and his blue eyes glittered with anger on behalf of the outraged girl. I, who had provided the means of old Stott's destruction, began to appear in his view like Sir Galahad himself.

A less skilful actor than I would now have begun to justify himself, to proclaim his innocence in any part of Stott's death.

I did much better than that.

On my knees I groaned in my guilt. Though mine was not the hand which poured the poison, yet I had provided it. Though I was twenty miles away, I would willingly have done the deed to save that poor girl from such a brute. I was guilty in thought, however innocent in deed.

Talk had begun. I described how Stott was dug up from the

cemetery and the cause of his death discovered. Who could blame Julia, in her terror of the gallows, for trying to shift the blame on to me? I assured Mr Rossiter that I had forgiven her everything. I listened in silence while she swore to the court that it must have been I who added a lethal quantity of strychnine to the bottle. The poor girl's fear for her neck quite overcame her love for me.

Raising my moist eyes to Mr Rossiter, I vowed that I loved her enough to take the guilt upon myself. At my insistence, my lawyers did not contest her evidence too vigorously. The court saw that I had, in part, consented to my own condemnation. I had lived for Julia, I would die for her. Yet my judges were uneasy, plagued by a certain doubt. Hence my life had been spared, to be spent in this torture of perpetual confinement.

No tragedian of modern times ever acted his part better than I, kneeling on the stones of my cell that afternoon. Mr Rossiter was so moved that he could not speak. He laid a firm but gentle hand upon my shoulder and left without another word.

March 1891
That night I lay in a mood of the greatest anxiety. Had I overdone it? Did I protest too much? What if he should question those who might tell a different story? But, you see, I had anticipated that. I did not deny my guilt. I groaned and wallowed in it, while showing that it was nothing like guilt at all.

My greatest problem was that he might make a charitable visit to Julia Stott. That fat and self-regarding young slut might certainly have observed me topping up the bottle of tonic! I do not think she did, but one cannot be sure. I relied on the probability that, after so much scandal, she would have moved away and changed her name. Ten years had passed. She would not easily be found.

Of course, I would find her if I could. What satisfaction there would be in rewarding her by such a hiding as might make old Stott seem the soul of gentleness! I do not forgive easily. Especially when the offence is committed by such as

20

she. You will understand that presently.

By great good fortune, the judge and the prosecutor in my case have both shuffled off this mortal coil since my arrival here. A good riddance to the pair of them! So their tongues will not be able to answer me back.

I lay in the darkness of the cell-house, listening to the stirring and moaning of the men around me. The soft footfalls of the patrolling warder sounded in the corridor at regular intervals, down and back ... down and back ... down and back ...

Whatever happened, I knew I was clean away with three of my little jobs. Rosie ... Arabel ... Helena! The proof, like the little drabs themselves, was dead and gone. I thought of Mademoiselle Barnes wedged naked in that lean-to. She looked ridiculous rather than dead. In my new mood of optimism I began to see the funny side of it all and laughed until I could feel the prison bed shaking with my paroxysms. The warder must have thought me buffeted by private grief.

April 1891

I was so careful after my first little success with the Reverend Rossiter. So *very* careful. I did not press my case. When he spoke of it, I recognised my guilt quietly and admitted the justice of my sentence.

A few weeks later, as a matter of routine, I was interviewed by the governor. My demeanour was modest and unpresuming. Unlike the rest of the illiterate crew who make up the prison population, I made no complaint of having been hard done by, nor did I demand a review of my sentence. I confessed only one small resentment. It saddened me to be locked away in useless idleness, when I might have been free to serve humanity in however menial a capacity.

That, I thought, was a neat stroke.

For weeks – yes, *weeks* – I waited in silence and with patience to see what would be done for me now.

Nothing! Absolutely nothing! It appeared as if all had been in vain.

I did not despair, however. Not me. Despair never helped a fellow in such a fix as mine.

21

There was a moment of hope which almost persuaded me that matters continued to develop nicely. In one of our conversations – we had talked of Shakespeare and the improving effect of great literature – Mr Rossiter remarked that chatting to me was quite like conversation with a friend. As if I were not a convict at all.

Whoopee! Perhaps . . . Perhaps! . . . The Grand Perhaps!

Whatever hope this raised was dashed in a few days. A fool who thought he could escape, made his bid and failed. They wired him to the humming-bird and gave him the works. This time, I think, they meant to send him all the way. And so they did. Another case of heart failure.

The trouble was, of course, I had heard his yells. Twenty feet from the wash-house, how could I be deaf to them? If they were to let me out now, there was no knowing what stories I might tell the world.

Another year of slum-gulleon, then! Stink and dirt!

God blast the whole pack of them!

May 1891

I saw, of course, where I had gone wrong.

I had prepared the ground well, but that was not enough. It was going to take something special to get me out of here. The powder was stacked and the fuse laid. I needed the spark. It seemed to be the one thing I could not provide for myself.

I am fit for freedom, of course. I have shown them that.

They needed a pretext for my release.

Almost anything would do.

June 1891

There came a Sunday. Twelve hours alone, locked in my cell.

I was sitting on the little stool reading Captain Marryat.

A warder known as 'Champagne Charlie' for his tall and affected elegance strolled up to the bars of my door.

'Stand up and hold the bars with both hands,' he said in his usual snappy way. 'There's a message from outside. Your father's dead. All right?'

He began to walk away. I stood there, holding the bars and trying to remember what my father had looked like when I last saw him. It was years ago. The news brought no great welling up of grief. In this place, the outside world has no existence. Life and death out there make no odds to us here. I doubt if I had even thought of my father the past month or two.

Champagne Charlie came back. He tapped the steel gently with his truncheon.

'Hands off the bars again,' he said. 'Back on the stool. You'll soon get used to being an orphan. Happens to every man. Prison won't treat you any different.'

Now that was where, it seems, he made a mistake.

July 1891

The day after my 'bad news', Mr Rossiter fairly smothered me with consolations and good advice!

I bore up bravely. Of course I did.

There was no sense in whining for permission to attend the funeral under guard. For some reason, never explained to me, the old man had chosen to return and die in his native Glasgow. It was the last thing I should have expected. Glasgow!

All the same, I permitted the Reverend Rossiter to comfort me in my loss.

It occurred to me that there was an opportunity in all this which ought not to be overlooked. So I did not weep for myself, nor even for the dear departed. No, sir. My only tears were shed with great care for my poor dependent family.

I confided to Mr Rossiter that I was the eldest, the only one with a head for business. As such I should be looked to for advice and support. It would have been my duty to manage the funds and investments which my father had left. Alas, in this moment of their greatest trial, my dependants must look to me in vain!

Now, there was no reason for him to doubt me. My very worst enemy cannot accuse me of fraud or of any underhand dealing with money. It is wrong to suppose that a man who commits one crime is easily capable of the rest. In this prison, embezzlers look with contempt upon burglars. A man who slits a fellow's throat for money seethes with moral indignation against a rapist. At the first opportunity a boiling vat in the kitchen goes spilling over him.

So, whatever my other failings, Mr Rossiter quite rightly saw in me a man who could be entrusted with the management of the family wealth. And so I could. I might cheat through necessity but it would never give me the pleasure – the sheer pleasure – which my other little japes have brought me!

Mr Rossiter returned to me next morning. He had spoken to the governor. So he had. And what had he said?

I could scarcely believe it!

With his tough-chinned, clear-eyed decency, he had pointed out my family's situation. He added a little coda on the bereavement which I had suffered. I was thoroughly contrite and filled with remorse for my part in old Stott's death, he said. Brimming at the gills with repentance.

There was even some doubt as to whether I was the one who had been primarily responsible for croaking the old man. It was, after all, Julia's hand which administered the fatal drink. Ah-ha!

If they had all been quite certain that I was the sole villain, I should not be here now, I suppose. Nine years ago they would have had me dancing on air with a rope round my neck and my head comically on one side.

All this, in politer terms, Mr Rossiter put to the governor. In consequence, the matter of my sentence was at last to be put to higher authority.

Surely, surely my time had come? Mr Rossiter sat and talked with me about the world beyond the prison walls. How changed I should find it since my arrival here. How I must adjust my mind to it.

For some reason, which I cannot fathom, he believes that all men must be interested in sport. So, when the stock of conversation ran low between us, he began to talk to me about cricket.

Life, he said, was very much a matter of keeping a straight bat upon a sticky wicket.

I stared at him in amazement. I have put to death half a dozen people. How, then, should I be interested in cricket?

24

The last entry
The end of my memoir in captivity. Next week, they promise me, I shall be out of this place for good.

Why do I bother to make this last secret entry? It is because I have a horrid fear that I shall quite simply expire of excitement before the week is over and my last thoughts never be known.

How shall I explain myself – my frame of mind – to you, whoever 'you' may be? You are so unlike me that you cannot imagine why I should seek out another Rosie Barnes or Arabel Faulkner with whom to enjoy my little capers. Very well, I will explain.

It seems to me I lack the indifference to insult which other men have. A milliner's assistant looks at me with insolence in her eyes. A draggle-tail in a promenade bar turns her head with contempt from my appreciative gaze. Another gives me impudence or a coarse answer. I cannot leave such creatures alone. The red rag is shown to the bull and the challenge is accepted. I promise you I think of such a young woman for weeks afterwards and meditate my retribution. No lover ever felt such a thrill, such quickening of the heart, as I.

As a rule I can do no more than dream and wish. Yet my interest is solely in those women who have thrown down the gauntlet to me by their insolence or indifference. I would not give a 'Thank you' for the chance to wreak havoc on some mild maiden with downcast eyes.

Ah, but the others! The Rosies, the Arabels, the Helenas, the arrogant and self-regarding dross of the city streets! What satisfaction to apportion their desserts. They ask for them – I assure you, they really do. And at my hands they drink a bitter broth!

You see? You do not understand me. I knew it would be so. Who can comprehend another man's lusts without standing in that fellow's skin? Still, I have tried to explain my feelings. I have pleasure in ridding the world of those creatures whom the world can easily spare. Remorse? I have never felt it for an instant.

There, now. That was what I had to put on paper in case I

25

do not outlive the week.

So, after all the harsh things which the law has said of me, it has behaved in the most irrational manner. Because my father has died, my sentence is to be reduced from life to seventeen years. By a process of judicial mathematics, which I do not pretend to understand, seventeen years makes me eligible for release after ten. Yet the same law once thought me unfit to live in human society.

My ten years will be over next week.

Each night I celebrate with secret riot in my skull.

I did for Rosie Barnes – and shall go free!

I snuffed out Arabel Faulkner – and shall go free!

I booted Helena Stack to a happier land – and shall go free!

I croaked old man Stott – and shall go free!

I chuckle and feel almost virtuous at the thought of the two drabs and the blackmailing hussy. To have lived ten years in this place for coopering the lot of them is an outrage. I am not unreasonable. If mankind had sent me here for a year or two, I might have shrugged off the injustice. I am a good citizen. I pay my taxes and my debts.

Ten years in hell is quite another matter. The bill has been overpaid. Now comes the time for some adjustments in my favour.

I chalk up Rosie Barnes, Arabel Faulkner, Helena Stack . . . After what I have paid, I am owed at least half a dozen more.

I do not suppose that you – whoever 'you' may be – or Mr Rossiter, or the governor, or the gentleman whose name appears on my commutation, will see the matter in quite that way.

I, on the other hand, do. We must agree to differ.

All the same, I tell you this. I have learnt my lesson, by which I mean I have learnt the mistakes to avoid. You think I will be nabbed at my first attempt. I think not.

So, good people, as we go our separate ways . . .

Catch me. If you can!

2
Sweets from a Stranger

1

Sergeant Oliver Lumley of A Division, Metropolitan Police, stood well back in the railway arches and tried to be inconspicuous. A drizzling September evening veiled the tenements and warehouses of the Waterloo Road. In the early darkness the gaslight shimmered and flared in pools of gold on the wet cobbles. High above the street, on the brick arches which gave Lumley his concealment, the well-lit trains thundered through the dark in fiery pillars of steam, entering the great terminus of the South-Western Railway.

It was the Saturday-night market which had brought Lumley to the Waterloo Road, in his plain-cut suit, bowler hat and policeman's boots. From where he stood he could see most of the way from Waterloo Bridge towards St George's Circus. The scene was as crowded as a fairground with stalls and beggars, flower-sellers and ragged children. Tarpaulined drays from the railway goods yards jostled between the lines of stalls with two-wheeled hansom cabs and four-wheeled growlers. A procession of horse-buses bore aloft their bright tin placards for Oakey's Knife Powder, Holloway's Pills, and Reid's India Pale.

With more accuracy than elegance, Lumley opened his mouth and inserted the second half of a veal-pie slice bought from the cooked-meat stall a few minutes earlier. As his plump jaws worked upon it, he watched the figure of Eddie Eyeball shuffling along the pavement in cast-off military jacket and trousers, his white stick and tin cup to the fore. His nickname in the Borough came from an ability to roll his eyes up and present only their whites to a likely philanthropist.

'Penny for a man that lost his sight at Majuba Hill!' The cup rattled plaintively. 'Copper for a poor blind sojer!'

As he shuffled past the first of the railway arches, he turned his head and paused.

'Evening, Mr Lumley,' he said plaintively.

Lumley scowled at the thin, bent figure, the shock of hair rising waywardly as if in perpetual surprise.

'Keep moving on, Eyeball,' he said firmly, 'I shan't pinch you unless I have to.'

'You ought to count your blessings, Mr Lumley,' the beggar said.

Lumley crumpled up the paper which had held the veal-pie slice and dropped it on the paving.

'If there was any justice,' he said quietly, 'your eyes would get stuck like that one day and not come right again. Still, if you were to tell me where Maggie might be, the one they call 'Twitching Mag', I might drop a sixpence in your cup. If I found her there, that is.'

Eddie Eyeball shook the tuft of his hair emphatically.

'Seen her nowhere, Mr Lumley. Nowhere whatsoever.'

He was looking towards Waterloo Bridge where the horse-buses set down their passengers. By eight o'clock, clubmen and heavy swells, sporting gents and counting-house clerks were on their way south of the river, in search of a good time. From the fashionable promenade of the Strand they came to the warren of little streets which ran off the Waterloo Road towards the notorious rookery of the Southwark Mint.

Seeing his natural prey, Eddie Eyeball put new energy into his pathetic shuffle, closing upon the silk hats and chained waistcoats.

'Penny for one of General Frere's poor blind soldiers. . . .'

Sergeant Lumley turned, watching the long road to St George's Circus. On either side the stalls stretched along the pavement's edge, lit by the white glare of their self-generating gas-lamps. The little shops of the neighbourhood which sold wigs and powder, bonnets and cheaply printed novels, pale cigars and playbills, had put up their shutters and abandoned the Saturday-night trade to the stall-holders. The heat of the lamps and the stoves filled the shabby street with odours of roast nuts and whelks, burnt sugar and Yarmouth bloaters, the smells of a hungry city with wages to spend.

The crowd from the horse-buses was dispersing to the side streets and to Gatti's-Under-the-Arches. Down on the river level, Gatti's was something special even by the standards of the most easy-going music halls. The jokes were riper, the amount of flesh displayed both on stage and in the promenade bar was more alluring.

Now Lumley was watching one boy, dressed in a cast-off suit and a man's cap pulled over his eyes. The lad was standing at the confectioner's stall, playing with a piece of string. It was one of the oldest dodges. The fingers that wandered so aimlessly over the string would soon amble over the merchandise with a true sense of purpose.

Still looking south towards St George's Circus, Lumley eased his bulk up behind the lad. He took the collar of the jacket and hoisted the suspect until the boy was obliged to stand on tiptoe.

'Hands!' said Lumley quietly.

Unresisting, the boy opened his hands. Two lumps of pink nougat fell to the cobbles.

'Pockets!' said the sergeant gently.

The jacket produced one more piece of nougat, a spare length of string, and a shapeless lump of toffee.

Lumley sighed and lowered the culprit.

'Turn,' he said.

As soon as the boy edged round, Lumley cuffed him hard across the head. The youngster staggered into a passing market-porter and bounced off him.

'Right, my son!' said Lumley magisterially. 'We'll have less of that in future. See? Next time, I'll have you sent home for a leathering. I know who your father is.'

The boy backed away, his presence of mind returning.

'Then you know more than Ma and I knows,' he shouted.

Without waiting to see the sergeant's response to this derision, he turned and ran, swerving between the stalls and disappearing through the legs of the crowd.

Lumley resumed his natural dignity and withdrew into the shadows. From the little streets opposite, where parties of sailors and soldiers were gathering, he could hear the sound of a hurdy-gurdy and the shouts or screams of those who danced round it. Prostitution had not merely taken over the decaying Georgian terraces of Stamford Street and its tributaries. It traded with windows uncurtained and doors wide. L Division of the Metropolitan Police exercised a distant vigil over the area. Its officers even patrolled the little streets and riverside alleys, but not as a rule until the night's festivities had dwindled into silence. L Division was content to keep order in the Waterloo Road itself. The darkness beyond the grimy brick-Venetian of the York Hotel – 'Family and Commercial' – was ruled by another law.

Just then, Lumley heard the whoop of a hunting-horn and a 'View-halloo' from the southern end of the road. A smart olive-green wagonette with several passengers had rolled into the stream of vehicles, swerving and manoeuvring for position. The men in their loud check suits and shallow brown hats might have been barkers for Wombwell's Menagerie at the Crystal Palace. Above the rumble of wheels over cobbles, they were bawling out a chorus, like racing-men back from Brighton or Goodwood.

> Wot-cher, Ria!
> Ria's on the job . . .

The driver hauled at the reins to avoid one collision and almost precipitated another.

> Wot-cher, Ria!
> Did yer spec-yer-late a bob?

Cabmen and conductors shouted abuse, though much of it was good-natured. 'Flash' Fred Linnell, who drove with a girl on his knee, was known to the entire village. Sairey, the girl in question, was one of his dollies and a good worker too. The news in the Borough was that Sairey had done stunning for her keeper. She was too big and loud to be a beauty but she had a loyal following among the mild counting-house clerks and the rowdier men on leave from Aldershot.

> Oh, Ria she's a toff,
> An' she looks immensikoff . . .
> Wot-cher, Ria!

Beside Fred Linnell was the bandy and whiskery little figure of Lord Q., as they called him, fit for a portrait in the *Sporting*

Times or *Vanity Fair*. He seemed more like a bookie than a marquess in his russet tweeds. All the neighbourhood knew that for the past weeks Fred Linnell and his lordship had been inseparable companions on racecourse and in bawdy-house. It was said that Lord Q. had introduced Flash Fred to the society of the Café Royal and was soon to entertain him on the Ayrshire estate.

The wagonette drew up at some distance from where Lumley was standing. There was a second girl, not riding with the passengers but standing on the footboard as if they had given her a lift down the length of the Waterloo Road. Lumley felt a sense of satisfaction, the certainty of patience rewarded. In her brown cloak and boots he recognised the working costume of Twitching Mag. Under the cloak were pockets, into which the watches and wallets of the heavy swells disappeared by the art of her fingers.

As soon as the wagonette had rounded a corner, Maggie began to give her cautious inspection to the men about her. She was not a stunner, her features too bold and her face too round. Her fair hair was pinned by a tortoiseshell clip so that it hung in a limp strand down her back.

Maggie was grateful for the ride, Lumley had no doubt of it. The wagonette had carried her clear of the petty thefts at one end of the Waterloo Road, depositing her where her fingers could begin to 'twitch' watches and pocket-books, from fresh victims.

Lumley walked towards her slowly, keeping the line of the stalls between him and his prey. The glass double-doors of the York Hotel's public bar opened briefly. He caught a glimpse of chandelier-light clouded by tobacco smoke, a rich glow of bottles beyond the mahogany of the bar. There was a burst of laughter and a snatch of music before the doors swung to again upon the warm convivial scene. In another hour, beer would make the counting-house ninny a match for any trooper with a webbing belt.

Quiet as a shadow, Oliver Lumley's bulk moved between the roast-chestnut barrow and the fish-stall. He came up behind the girl and took the loose fold of the cloak on her shoulder in a grip which seemed gentle but proved unshakable.

33

His other hand patted the sides of the cloak and felt the hard outlines of small metal objects in its lining.

'Christmas come early for you this year, Miss Mag?' he asked humorously. 'Has it?'

The game was one they both knew well. The girl's instinct for escape was sure. She had only to get the crowd on her side long enough to evade the sergeant's grasp. Lumley struggled to hold her as she pulled to free herself and began to scream.

'He touched me!' she shrieked. 'The brute! He touched me!'

Lumley breathed hard as he held her.

'Him!' said a woman from the stalls, 'Tried it on a respectable girl! Get back your own side of the river, you dirty dandy!'

The man from the fish-stall came up behind them as a little crowd gathered. In his striped apron and straw boater he was a head taller than Lumley.

'Take your hands off her,' he said quietly. 'Get back your own side of the bridge and don't show yourself here again.'

Lumley, red with exertion, twisted his head round.

'Hold her, Jimmy Styles! She's as likely got your watch and chain as anyone else's!'

'Mr Lumley!' said Styles, beginning to smile but making no effort to assist. 'You caught a tartar there, Mr L. I shouldn't like to have your bruises for something!'

He took off the straw boater and wiped his forehead on his sleeve.

Before Lumley could reply, there was a sudden convulsive scream. It was not Maggie but another girl, who had just come out of the York Hotel bar-room. Lumley ignored it, holding fast to his prisoner. It would be a routine dodge of Twitching Maggie's to have a confederate ready to cause a diversion. As he got his captive's arms securely behind her back, he saw from the corner of his eye that the other girl was Nellie Donworth, one of Fred Linnell's hard workers.

Nellie lurched against the street wall of the hotel. One arm was clamped across her stomach, the other clawing at the stucco. She bowed and swayed like a drunkard but the shrillness of her voice carried a clear and terrible sobriety.

34

'Help me! Oh, help me! Please! Someone, for God's sake...'

She pitched forward on her knees, her head doubled down to the pavement as if in some grotesque obeisance. Like Maggie, Nellie Donworth was no beauty, a plump young woman with a frizzy fair mane and a round red-cheeked face. Lumley was uneasily aware that her screams were not of the contrived kind used merely to distract attention.

'Mr Lumley!' Styles was calling him now, 'Over here, if you please!'

He hesitated a moment. Nellie Donworth began to vomit in loud spasmodic retchings.

'Mr Lumley!' Styles' voice carried an anger of impatience. 'Over here! She's falling into a fit!'

With a vicious shove which sent Twitching Maggie sprawling, Lumley released his prisoner. His anger was a match for that of Styles. Then he turned and saw Nellie Donworth. She was lying on her side in the foul and slippery dew of the pavement, her body in a foetal curve with her knees pressing desperately against her stomach. The screaming had stopped and she was groaning as pain and terror tore at her.

Lumley stooped over her and saw a face that was white with pain, the hair plastered on the skin by a cold sweat of agony. He put his arm under her shoulders to prop her up but she flinched away from him with a cry of madness.

'Don't straighten me! For God's sake don't try to straighten me!'

Lumley drew back. He looked down at the girl, her body a cage of torment imprisoning her. The extreme horror of her suffering held his gaze. A series of convulsive cries broke from her, though Nellie Donworth's teeth remained clenched and her face set as if in an epileptic frenzy. For a moment or two he thought that she would die before they could lift her from the pavement.

'Get a shutter!' He turned to Styles, 'Anything we can carry her on!'

'She's one of Connie Crow's girls,' said a woman in the crowd, 'down in Duke Street.'

The pain diminished a little and Nellie exhaled in long

rhythmic gasps. Lumley knelt beside her.

'We shan't hurt you,' he said gently. 'Try and tell me what happened.'

The eyes which she rolled round at him were large with fear.

'It was him . . .' she panted, 'him in the dark clothes and tall silk hat . . . him that called himself Fred. . . .'

'Not Fred Linnell?'

'Not him!' Her teeth clenched suddenly on her lower lip but she fought for speech. 'Never saw this one before. . . He gave me some white stuff from a bottle to mix in the gin. . .It's like a knife in me. . .Oh, God! I shan't die, shall I?. . .Please. . .Oh, help me!'

Her head went back and the knees jerked against her stomach as the waves of pain surged through her. Lumley knelt there helplessly, hearing the dry contact of vertebrae and the wild cries.

'She's got the cramps,' said one of the women, 'that's all. Loosen her whale-bones and let her breathe a bit. She'll be all right.'

But Lumley had seen men and women die. He knew that Nellie Donworth was entering that last dark landscape of life.

'Good biz!' said one of the men reassuringly. 'Here's the carrier for her.'

Lumley and Styles lifted her on to the shutter, while she screamed and fought against the two men for the pain they were causing her. At last she lay still, her eyes glazed and her mouth drooling, as if she had slipped into a coma. But her voice was still audible, though faint.

'I'm sorry, Mr Lumley. . .so sorry.'

Another man and the woman from the crowd came forward.

'Catch hold on her,' said Styles sharply, 'else she'll throw herself off when the fit comes again.'

Almost at once her shoulders went back with the brittle sound of bones in contact and she crammed her knees into her abdomen. If her cries were feebler, it was exhaustion and not the shifting of the pain which made them so.

With four bearers carrying the stretcher and others holding

36

the girl down, the little procession set off into the rowdy length of Stamford Street. They passed the brightly lit and uncurtained windows, the open doors where girls in bedraggled finery and feathered hats squatted on the steps. The dancers round the hurdy-gurdy, the organ grinder with his mop of black hair and fierce moustache, stood back for Lumley to pass. Old women who held either end of a rope for ragged children to skip paused and watched them. Only the men in their shirt-sleeves, leaning against the lodging-house wall and smoking their pipes, seemed unmoved.

From the windows above, where young women of the nighthouses leant their elbows on the sills, came the volleys of neighbourhood wit.

'Nellie's had her whack early.... I wouldn't booze if it gave me the sick.... Ain't she got up dossy too?.... Dressed to death and kill the fashion!'

It was Jimmy Styles who looked up angrily at the open windows.

'She's not boozed! She's sick, real sick! Can't you see?'

From above him came a mocking 'Ooh-ah!' of disbelief.

At last they turned into Duke Street, the narrow cobbled way with its open gutters, lined by old and lowering houses whose tall fronts were dark with damp and decay.

'Run on up and open the door of number eight,' Lumley said to the young man walking beside him.

By the time that they reached the doorway, it was blocked, the bulk of a stout woman confronting them. She was a creature of florid cheeks and narrow eyes, the grey hair drawn back tightly from her forehead. Lumley recognised Connie Crow.

'You ain't bringing her in like that,' she said firmly. 'Leave her where she is. A girl that gets boozed first thing on Saturday can stay out. That's the first rule of Connie Crow's house. Don't think I'm going to have her fetching up over the carpets and leaving a mess for me to clean!'

'She ain't boozed, Miss Connie,' said a girl's voice from the shadows. 'She's hurt or ill. You can see her shivering. The sweat that runs off her is ice-cold with the pain.'

'Then hospital's the place for her,' said Connie Crow

emphatically. 'If I wanted my house turned over to a lying-in ward, I'd advertise the same and employ nursing staff. Clear off, the pack of you. . . .'

Her self-confidence faded as Sergeant Lumley stepped into the light.

'Mrs Crow?' he said, as if they might have been strangers. 'This young person lodges here and pays you rent. If she's to be refused admission now, I shall have the leisure to look into your business affairs a little. And if I shouldn't have time already, I'll make some.'

Connie Crow knew when to acknowledge defeat.

'Mr Lumley!' she said, the dead eyes staring from the raddled face. 'Well, of course, if she's *reely* ill. . .poorly. . .well, there isn't none of us wouldn't. . .'

'Thank you, Mrs Crow,' said Lumley and led the way up the bare wooden staircase to the girl's room. With the assistance of Styles and another man, he lifted Nellie Donworth from the shutter on to the mattress with its brass-railed bed-frame.

'Undo her whale-bones,' said the woman who had followed the shutter down Stamford Street, 'else she'll smother.'

Lumley ignored her and turned to one of his men.

'Go for Dr Lowe's assistant. Mr Johnstone. Hundred and twelve, Westminster Bridge Road. Sergeant Lumley's compliments. Criminal Investigation, A Division. Ask him to step over here sharp as he can. And, if he doesn't mind, perhaps he'd send for Dr Lowe in person.

He went to the window and watched the young man hurrying off down the squalid riverside alley of Duke Street. Lumley turned back while Connie and another woman removed Nellie Donworth's outer clothes and undid her stays.

'Seems to me she's brighter already,' said Connie optimistically. 'It'll pass. Like most things. All the same, she's missed her chance of making a fortune tonight.'

As if to contradict the old bawd's reassurance, Nellie emitted a wail of fear as the first ripple of a new pain quivered in her entrails. A moment later she was convulsed by the surge of agony which followed, throwing herself upwards, her spine

38

curved until it seemed ready to crack, her face set in the static rictus of a tetanic fit. The grin was immobile and grotesque as death itself.

'Hold her down,' said Connie brusquely. 'She'll be off the bed and on the floor otherwise.'

For half an hour, Sergeant Lumley watched Nellie Donworth's spasms, fearful himself as each one approached and yet unable to draw his eyes from the grinning tetanic mask of her face. Nothing in his childhood teaching about the pains of hell had equalled this. No flight of imagination could convey the reality, the young face contracted into lines of age at the riot of agony in the web of nerves, the hair matted against the cold dampness of flesh from which the blood seemed to be drained. Then there were the interludes, the five or ten minutes between the seizures, when the girl doubled her knees under her and hugged the pillows to her belly, whimpering with fright.

Lumley left it to Styles and the others to hold her down as the convulsions returned, the sheet wet with her cold perspiration. It seemed to him that in her last sufferings she met the pain as an enemy, her head and shoulders thrown back, the snarls of animal discomfort breaking from her. Yet it was blockage of her throat and nostrils which produced the bestial sound.

'She'll be better for that,' said Connie Crow foolishly after another such spasm.

At last the doctor's assistant arrived, a student from St Thomas's Hospital who had begun to walk the wards. Mr Johnstone was a plump youth with a fresh face and dark curls who looked at the girl on the bed and saw another convulsion gathering in her body. They held her down as best they could while he examined her. When he lifted his head at last they were surprised to see that he appeared as frightened as they. It was the first time that the people of the little streets had seen a member of his profession other than cool and assured in his dealings with them.

Johnstone looked up at Sergeant Lumley.

'Someone must go to St Thomas's, please,' he said quietly. 'Tell them the young woman is taken with convulsions and in great distress. She needs a doctor quickly and a growler to get her to hospital. I shall give chloroform to help her through the seizures. I can do no more than that.'

Before Lumley could ask, one of the men in the doorway turned and ran down the stairs with the message. The student opened his bag and took out a gauze mask, a domed shape which would fit over the patient's nose and mouth. While several of the women held Nellie Donworth still, he fitted the mask and began to drop the sweet spirituous chloroform on to it from a dark bottle.

After a few minutes the cries and groans stopped. Despite her semi-conscious state, the girl's convulsions continued in a grotesque dumb-show. Drugged and dying, her body braced and arched itself in the spasms, the breath snarling through her teeth. Then she would go suddenly limp in the grip of those who held her.

The next hour passed in a repeated sequence of seizure and exhaustion, a reek of chloroform and human odours filling the little room. The groaning began again as she stirred into full consciousness. Outside, in the dark little street, a group of men and women from the public bars and flash houses gathered in silence. Some showed compassion, others were lured by the sinister thrill of a girl who had been put to death for the pure pleasure of a top-hatted swell.

At last she seemed to rouse herself in a new surge of energy as the pain once more broke through the drowsy chloroform mist. Johnstone watched in dismay, knowing that the amount of chloroform needed to keep her under would kill Nellie Donworth anyway. She burst suddenly from her holders and threw herself over in a strange, contorted posture, her head dangling until it almost touched the floor, her stomach wedged over the side of the bed to find relief in the pressure of the mattress and the pillow which she hugged under her.

'Leave me!' she cried. 'For God's sake don't move me!'

In a moment there was another seizure but this time it was little more than a brief muscular contraction. Nellie Donworth made no sound, lying still at last in the final quiet of death.

Johnstone felt for her pulse and then looked up at the men

and women round the bed. He seemed, in his frightened glance, to beg their understanding.

'She's gone,' he said, 'I did all I could. I daren't have given her more chloroform. It wouldn't have saved her anyway. Nothing would.'

Lumley touched him on the shoulder.

'There's not a doctor could have done better,' he said gently. He turned to the onlookers. 'Now, if you please. Everyone out of the room and leave the poor soul just as she is.'

Johnstone led the way. The young man's fresh face was grey with his first experience of such a death. On the little landing he came face to face with a man in a neat worsted suit who had just come up from the front door. The newcomer was in his thirties and had the long calm face of an intelligent horse. He appeared, at a glance, to be a pattern of the pale and intellectual man.

'I'm Swain,' he said gently. 'Where's Mr Lumley?'

Though they were strangers, Johnstone seized at the hope now offered.

'Dr Swain?' he asked quickly. 'From the hospitals?'

'Inspector Swain,' said the newcomer in the same gentle voice, 'from the Criminal Investigation Division. I have a report of murder being attempted tonight on a young woman of this house.'

2

The young medical student was not the first to be misled by Inspector Alfred Swain's appearance. An assortment of criminals, great and small, had made the same error. In the London prisons, from Wandsworth to Pentonville, they brooded on the unfairness of such a deception.

Mildness and good breeding infused the steady gaze with which Swain scrutinised his suspects and the scenes of their crimes. Yet if he had a face like a horse, the inspector also shared with that species a willing intelligence and an aptitude for learning the tricks of a trade. In the tall skull under the thin fair hair, the strategies of the forger and the tactics of the thief had been categorised and stored for easy reference.

As it happened, murder was not one of Swain's specialities. Despite the literature of detection surrounding it, murder seldom presented a mystery. Nine times out of ten, the culprit was caught in the act, or surrendered willingly, or took his own life. Swain's superiors at Scotland Yard made better use of his talents. They set him to work on the truly sophisticated felonies of fraud and finance. Columns of figures and the system of double-entry book-keeping were more familiar to him than the victims of homicide.

Unlike that of some of his loud and earthy colleagues in the Inspectors' Office, Swain's upbringing had been one of doomed gentility. His father, a country schoolmaster, had eloped with the daughter of the manor house. The young woman died giving birth to their only son and the father followed her to the grave during the summer cholera when the boy was ten years old. Alfred Swain had inherited a few small debts, a shelf of books, and a habit of natural curiosity.

A cautious and self-educated bachelor, Swain liked to regard himself in a modest way as being a thinking man of his century. He sought pleasure in the Poet Laureate's *Idylls of the King* or, more daringly, in Mr Swinburne's *Poems and Ballads*. For self-improvement, he preferred Laing's *Modern Science and Modern Thought* or Huxley's *Lay Sermons*. Novels or story-books he suspected as a frivolity.

His superiors at Scotland Yard would have preferred a man who found recreation in the company of a four-ale bar and the shimmer of powdered flesh displayed on the music-hall stage. At length they had grown used to the inspector's intellectual aspirations. For some time the other occupants of the Inspectors' Office in the Criminal Investigation Division had treated Swain with easy-going ribaldry. Now he had outlived the jibes at his 'school-miss' book-learning.

On the night of Nellie Donworth's death, Swain had been sitting alone in the office, the only one of the Division available to undertake a preliminary investigation. He had been reading Tait's *Recent Advances in Physical Science*, a work popular ten years earlier, which he had bought for sixpence that morning from a market barrow. He was puzzling over the problem of why the observed orbit of the planet Mercury should differ from the calculated orbit by ten per cent, when the call brought him to Duke Street.

Sergeant Lumley's bulk blocked the doorway of the bedroom where he had taken up guard on the evidence. As Swain appeared, the sergeant in his dark suit and stout boots pulled himself up as if at attention.

'Well, Mr Lumley?' said Swain patiently.

'She's gone, sir,' said Lumley, his jowls colouring self-consciously. 'A few minutes ago, poor soul. Best thing for her. There wasn't nothing to be done. . . .'

'How, Mr Lumley?'

Lumley's brow wrinkled with an effort of comprehension.

'Poison, sir, it seems. A man she met and never knew before. He gave her something white out of a bottle to mix in her gin. Something to make her feel frisky. She won't be feeling frisky nor anything else again. The young student, Mr Johnstone, talked about convulsions. Tetanic convulsions, he said.'

'Strychnine,' said Swain quietly.

'Sir?'

'Rat poison, among other things. It produces death by convulsions and in extreme agony. It works fast, as arsenic works slowly. A few minutes very often.'

Confidence and satisfaction glowed in Lumley's face.

'No, sir. She was a good couple of hours.'

Swain nodded.

'Because the man wanted her to be. Mix the poison and you prolong the death agony.'

Lumley grimaced with disbelief.

'Deliberately, Mr Swain?'

Swain nodded.

'Just so, Mr Lumley. A man whose pleasure was in her ordeal.'

'Pleasure?' The twist of the sergeant's mouth made the word sound like an obscenity.

'Mr Lumley,' said the inspector gently, 'I shall make my notes alone. Meanwhile, I want no one to leave this house. See to that, please. If we have to deal with a maniac of that kind, it's possible that he came along here, pretending to assist, in order to enjoy the sight of what he had done to her.'

Lumley shook his head.

'She called him a swell, in dark clothes, silk hat, and moustache. There's only been ordinary people here, from the stalls and houses.'

'Just see to it, if you please, Mr Lumley,' said Swain coldly.

As the sergeant moved aside, the inspector entered the gaslit bedroom alone. Swain was accustomed to the presence of death in such cases of murder as had come his way. He felt neither repugnance nor fascination as he worked, only a natural peace. However violent the death, the calm which followed was what he sensed most acutely.

The mean little room which constituted Nellie Donworth's lodging was papered in a cheap flower-pattern, the pale colours darkened by age and the deeper ones faded. Pink rose-petals had turned brown and green leaves yellow. On the chipped varnish of the dressing table was a cluster of wax fruit – black grapes and yellow peaches – under a glass dome. A pair of candlesticks in light pink with blue flowers stood at either end of the narrow mantelshelf beneath the white glare of the lamp-bracket. Here and there, on chairs and stool, were the discarded slips and dresses, the crumpled silk and the feathered hat. A bottle of Gordon's Gin, reduced to its last inch as the girl prepared herself to earn her Saturday-night wage, stood by the soap-dish on the washstand.

The disorder of the bedclothes almost hid the body from Swain's view. They had left her as Nellie Donworth had thrown herself in her final spasm, head downwards on her stomach over the edge of the mattress.

To hope for conclusive evidence in such a place as this was foolish. All the same, Swain began to examine the contents of the room, the detritus of Nellie Donworth's existence. In building up a knowledge of her habits and associations was his only expectation of finding the man who had killed her. A sheet had been drawn over her lower limbs but, as he crossed the room, the inspector caught his first glimpse of the dangling face, gorged and wide-eyed. He turned his back resolutely and began to go through the contents of the dressing-table drawers.

In his mind he tried to imagine the stranger in the bar of the York Hotel. 'Fred', with his tall silk hat and his moustache. The swell who had picked out Nellie Donworth as his victim. Why Nellie Donworth? And why the white fluid in her gin, condemning her to terror, agony, and a death so atrocious that a mere animal would have been put out of its misery, as an act of kindness, long before the end?

Swain opened the first drawer. He thought of a criminal lunatic with his hands on a supply of strychnine. A man who put a girl to death with the same chuckling satisfaction as another might feel in playing a harmless joke on her. It was possible, of course, that the lunatic might try to poison men and women indiscriminately. Swain doubted it. The criminally insane generally showed a loyalty to their narrow obsessions. Fred, whoever he was, found satisfaction – perhaps even ecstasy – in poisoning girls of Nellie Donworth's kind. He was most unlikely to stray from the straight and narrow path of his sadistic compulsion.

The first drawer yielded nothing but ribbons of every colour and texture, combs of tortoiseshell and cheap metal. He opened the next and began to sift its contents.

Strychnine. There was enough strychnine in rat poison, sold by any chemist, to kill half London. How did Fred persuade the girl to mix the 'white stuff' from the bottle in her glass of gin?

Swain thought of Nellie Donworth alive. Plump and foolish, eager and avaricious for 'a good time'. There were half a dozen sham aphrodisiacs on the market, alleged to transport the girl and her lover to a state of total rapture. Cupid's Cup and Venus Vino. They were harmless, if useless. But how easy to make a foolish girl of Nellie's kind swallow the latest magic potion, promising sexual excitement regardless of the choice of partner. Swain had seen enough of the misery and loathing behind the hectic laughter to know how readily Nellie and her kind would anaesthetise their feelings during the necessary

45

labours of their profession.

In the next drawer he found two photographs, cracked at their edges, showing an elderly couple sitting impassively before a cottage doorway.

Nothing in the room would identify Fred. How many other girls would have to die, Swain wondered, before the killer either gave himself away or wearied of the sport? Three years before, in Whitechapel, five young women had died before Jack the Ripper tired of his pleasure with a knife. Fred, whoever he was, might be less easily satisfied. Inspector Swain was perhaps the only officer of his rank to have seen a memorandum from Sir Melville Macnaughten, Assistant Commissioner, identifying the Ripper as Montague John Druitt of King's Bench Walk, a barrister who had drowned himself in the Thames soon after the last Whitechapel murder. But what if Sir Melville was wrong and the Ripper was back?

With increasing gloom, Swain sifted the relics of Nellie Donworth's nineteen years. No one had seen the Ripper and lived to describe him. Fred, at least, was known to have a tall silk hat and a moustache. So did thousands of London's male middle class. Worse still, Fred might not be a Londoner. The South-Western Railway terminus was scarcely more than a hundred yards from the York Hotel. Fred might come from anywhere at all.

Looking up, he confronted his reflection in the dressing-table mirror, the glass tarnished and fly-spotted round its edges. Beyond his own pale reflection he saw the room and, inadvertently, his gaze settled on the wide eyes in the hanging, gorged face of the corpse.

Turning away to the chest of drawers, he opened the top one with an oppressive sense of futility. And then his heart seemed to stop momentarily with expectation. On top of the folded silk underclothes was an envelope. It was addressed to Nellie Donworth at the Duke Street house. Examining the postmark, he saw that it had been sent from the West End of London at noon on the previous day, Friday. The girl would have received it on Saturday morning. Twelve hours later she went to her last rendezvous in the bar of the York Hotel.

With great care he took the envelope from the drawer and

saw that it had been slit open along the top. Inside it there was a single folded sheet of paper. He drew it out, laid it on the dressing table, and saw that it was a message in copper-plate with nothing to indicate the sender's address, though there was a signature at the foot of the page. Swain read the letter and felt a still deeper sense of unease.

> Miss Ellen Donworth
> I wrote and warned you once before that Frederick Smith, of W.H. Smith & Son, and Earl Russell, were going to poison you. I am writing now to say that if you take any of the medicine given you to procure an abortion, you will die. I saw the so-called Hon. Frederick Smith, M.P., prepare the medicine, and I saw him put enough strychnine in it to kill a horse. If you take any of it, you will die.
>
> W.H. Murray

For a moment, the inspector stood in thought. Then he went to the bedroom door and opened it.

'Mr Lumley, if you please!'

'Sir?' Despite the usual pink flush of his jowls, even the sergeant was now looking yellow with fatigue. 'What about them out there, sir? You still want them watched?'

'Never mind them, Mr Lumley. Step in here and read this. If any of them does a bunk, we shall know which to look for.'

He handed Lumley the sheet of paper and watched the sergeant's face.

'It can't be sir!' said Lumley scornfully, giving the letter back.

'Unfortunately, Mr Lumley, anything can be, in our business. A man called Fred.'

'The Honourable Frederick Smith?'

'Yes, Mr Lumley. A pillar of good works and the Methodist Church, a Member of Parliament and head of the biggest booksellers in the country.'

'And *Earl* Russell?' Lumley asked. 'The one that inherited from Lord John Russell, the Prime Minister?'

Swain ignored the question.

'Have the goodness to ask Connie Crow if she knows

47

anything about this letter – don't tell her exactly what's in it. Ask if she knows about a letter that Nellie Donworth got this morning. If the girl read this, as seems likely, why the devil wasn't she more careful?'

Lumley went out and came back a few minutes later.

'Nellie Donworth didn't read,' he said smugly. 'Couldn't read. Never taught to read. She used to bring any letters to Mrs Crow or one of her chums among the girls to have them read over to her. There *was* a letter this morning but she never had the time to take it for them to read to her.'

'It's been opened, however.'

'Mrs Crow expected that. Nellie always opened the letters first. Sometimes they had money in. From gentlemen that admired her.'

Swain finished sifting through a drawer.

'In that case, Mr Lumley, our W.H. Murray is either the most evil and cold-blooded devil that ever did a girl to death, or else he knows who killed her and hopes to grow fat by extortion.'

'Frederick Smith?' Lumley's mouth twisted sceptically. 'Earl Russell?'

The inspector sighed and closed the drawer, retaining only W.H. Murray's letter in his hand.

'Can you imagine the man who did this, Mr Lumley? For the life of me, I can't. I've had dealings with a dozen men and women who went to the gallows. Some killed from fear and some for greed. Some even killed for love. But this... I've never known one who killed for fun. If my people could have got their way without killing, they'd be alive themselves now. But this one! He must pick out some girl in the street and watch her. Then he follows her to find where she lives. Taunts her with letters. He makes up his poison so that it won't kill her outright. She's to die in agony over several hours as surely as if he was torturing her to death with his own hands. And then he meets her, waylays her, and does it. You think about it, Mr Lumley. He must spend weeks watching, spying on the girl. He courts her from a distance, for all the world as if she was a lady from romance and he the lover of chivalry. The quiet persistence of the obsessive, Mr Lumley. The private

48

world of true madness.'

Lumley shrugged.

'Mad or sane, the sooner he's hung, the better.'

Alfred Swain said nothing.

In his mind he tried to reconstruct the portrait of the man who had killed Nellie Donworth. As he did so, he knew that the worst possibility was not that it might prove to be Frederick Smith or Lord Russell. However great the scandal, that at least would give him certainty and put an end to the matter. Much worse was the wraith which now haunted his imagination. He saw a misty figure, the dimly lit figure of melodrama. Silk-hatted and moustached, the killer stalked his victims through the shadows of the Lambeth slums. He put them to death without any motive beyond the pure pleasure of imagining their sufferings. It was murder of a kind which Swain had heard of but never encountered professionally – gleeful and hedonistic. The mad, exultant letters in which the destroyer proclaimed himself were of the type signed by W.H. Murray. The inspector was all too well aware of the manner in which the Whitechapel Ripper had employed them.

He closed the dressing-table drawer, his back turned to Lumley. Most men who killed, he thought, did so once, either in extreme circumstances or from necessity. Not this one. The Lambeth poisoner promised a joyful carnival of slaughter. If he remained free, there was no reason why the agony of Nellie Donworth should not be infinitely repeated among the young women of the narrow streets off the Waterloo Road.

He roused himself from contemplation, aware that Sergeant Lumley had spoken for the second time without acknowledgement. A van had stopped and the voices were louder in the narrow street below. Swain heard the cheap shell of the municipal coffin bumping on the narrow stairs.

3

Alfred Swain lived, or rather lodged, in a brick-built family house near the quieter end of Clapham High Street. It was close to the tram terminus, from which the horse-drawn omnibuses rumbled on their iron rails to Vauxhall and Brixton, Pimlico and Westminster. The broad and tree-lined High Street had a gentility which mirrored Swain's own modest prosperity. There was a Nonconformist church with a narrow spire, decoratively tiled, and a parade of smart pillared shops with sunblinds.

Though he was permitted to live out in lodgings, rather than in a section-house, Swain still required the approval of his superintendent for the home he had chosen. Five years before, that approval had been given. Since then, he had been the lodger and tenant of Mrs Ryland, a widow, who lived with her daughter Rachel.

Edith Ryland was spoken of as a handsome woman rather than a beauty. She was just over forty and the rather petulant plainness of her face was offset by the elegant piling and pinning of her fair hair. Between Swain, who occupied the attic floor, and his landlady there was a shyness as if each was aware of an unspoken and unresolved question affecting them both. Swain compromised by spending part of every evening after dinner, and an hour of Sunday after lunch, sitting with his landlady and her daughter in the drawing room. He listened to Rachel Ryland reading aloud from novels with such titles as *Laura Gay* or *The Sorrows of Gentility* and watched her mother crochet white table-covers and bed-spreads.

When Swain first came to the house, Rachel Ryland was thirteen, a diminutive version of her mother. As a child she had the smug pale-faced look of Edith but with her brown hair still tied in a tail at her collar. Sometimes they had fed swans on the common, Rachel's hand insistently thrust into his, its fingers moving with insinuating affection. A year passed and Swain sensed that their friendship was approaching awkwardness of the kind he had taken care to avoid in his dealings with Edith Ryland. He smiled less at the girl and spent more time in his own rooms with his books. There was an attempt at amateur science, which ended after the boiling over of a beaker containing sulphuric acid and iron filings.

'I'm not complaining, Mr Swain,' Edith Ryland had said gently, 'you know I'm not complaining. It's just that . . .'

Rachel's awkward phase continued and then, at sixteen, blossomed into something more alarming. Mrs Peckinpah, the neighbour, invited for punch on Boxing Day, had cornered the inspector and looked knowingly at Rachel Ryland.

'There's only one man for her, Mr Swain,' Mrs Peckinpah had assured him with a significant nod, 'and you know who that is, don't you?'

Swain treated the remark with polite scorn but the words remained with him. The years had passed and now the little girl who had clutched his hand as they crossed Clapham Common was eighteen. There came a day when he returned to the house while Edith Ryland was visiting her married sister at Streatham. Going up to his rooms, he heard a sound from what he thought of as his sleeping quarters. Opening the bedroom door he saw the solemn fair-skinned face of Rachel on the pillow, her body covered by the counterpane but dressed only in bodice and drawers.

As he drew her out and propelled her to the door, she did not struggle but remained rigid as a corpse.

'If you behave like this,' he had said gently, 'I shall have to leave – to live elsewhere. You must understand that.'

That was where matters stood when the unknown Fred administered strychnine to Nellie Donworth.

On the following day, after Sunday lunch, Swain sat politely in his chair. Edith Ryland, on the far side of the carved mantelpiece, talked quietly but constantly, never raising her eyes from the crochet-hook. With the exhilaration of family pride, she was describing how Henry, her married sister's eldest, had been confirmed in his clerkship at the City

51

and Suburban Bank. Swain tried to recall the appearance of the youth, a tall and scrofulous boy of Rachel's age who had once been present at tea.

Outside in the cool sunlit afternoon, the leaves of the municipal trees hung limp and acid-yellow on their branches. The autumn light gave a rich glow to the Ryland drawing room. It brightened the dark mahogany chairs and table, mellowed the blue and white Chinese vases, and danced in the cut-glass pendants of the gasolier.

Rachel, in her brown dress with leg-of-mutton sleeves, passed slowly behind Swain's chair. She sat down on the tawny carpet between her mother and the lodger, her legs drawn under her and her back resting against the edge of an armchair.

She looked up at Swain with a sulky glance that a stranger might have mistaken for hostility. Of late, she had taken to cutting her light brown hair short and straight in the manner of a 'modern' young woman. There was a challenge in her firm fair-skinned face which Swain found a little unnerving and yet distinctly exhilarating. He thought of the feeble handshake and pimply smile which constituted his recollection of Henry, whom Mrs Ryland seemed to consider a safe match in marriage for her daughter. Poor young Henry, Swain thought. He had all the qualities which would irritate Rachel into making his life a prolonged misery.

Rachel looked at him, graceless and determined.

'What's aconite?' she said.

She had, of course, been reading over his shoulder as she passed behind the chair. Swain guessed as much at the time. The report he had been reading that morning was still in his hands. It was a scientific analysis and comparison of the strychnine used by Palmer, the Rugeley Poisoner, and the aconite with which the late Dr Lamson had preferred to despatch his victims. So effective and yet undetectable was aconite that the judiciary had for some time forbidden medical witnesses to name it in court.

'Aconite?' Swain returned the girl's tight-lipped challenge with a mockery of his own. 'It's a vegetable extract.'

'A poison!' she said contemptuously, brushing the hair

back to the side of her forehead and turning away.

'Only in excessive quantities,' Swain said. 'A hundred different things will act as poisons if taken in excess. The point about aconite is that its presence in the body is very hard to detect. Most others are easy.'

Edith Ryland looked up from her crochet-hook at last.

'That poor girl!' she said helplessly.

By this time the death of Nellie Donworth was news all over south London, apart from Swain's account.

'She didn't die of aconite,' Swain said. 'That's certain.'

Rachel brushed irritably at the bothersome fringe again.

'How do you know?' she demanded, not even deigning to turn her face to him this time. 'You're not a doctor and there can't have been a post-mortem.'

'It was white,' he explained gently. 'She drank something white. That means strychnine, not aconite.'

'I really think,' Edith Ryland looped wool over a hook, 'I do really think, Rachel dear, that this is not the subject for a drawing room.'

Rachel said nothing. She stared into the empty fireplace as if the other two had not been present.

'My fault,' Swain said, 'entirely.'

Rachel swept at the short hair tickling her forehead.

'If you'd only let it grow,' murmured Edith Ryland, 'it would pin back so easily.'

'I much prefer it as it is.'

Mrs Ryland sighed.

'If you'll excuse me,' Swain said, 'I ought to do a little more reading. They'll expect a long report from me tomorrow.'

He withdrew and closed the door. His hand was still on the cool white china of the knob when he heard Edith Ryland speak in the same mild voice.

'You must not talk to Mr Swain in that manner, my dear. I won't have it. He's been so good to you, to us both . . .'

'Too good,' Rachel said moodily. 'He could sleep on ice and it wouldn't melt.'

'When we were alone,' protested Mrs Ryland, 'when you were a little girl . . .'

'I'm not a little girl now, Mama!' Sulkiness flared into

exasperation, 'I wish he could realise that. And you too.'

Mrs Ryland sighed.

'I wish . . .' she began, 'I sometimes wish you could learn to be more like your cousin Henry. Really I do, Rachel.'

'Cousin Henry!' Rachel's scorn was finely balanced between outrage and mirth. 'I'd rather be like Alfred Swain!'

'*Mr* Swain!' The first quiver of anger troubled Edith Ryland's placidity.

Swain, conscious of the impropriety of his presence and yet fascinated by the exchange, smiled as he took his hand from the china knob and tiptoed upstairs. There was a certain pleasure and expectation in knowing that he was not to be despised as greatly as the unfortunate Henry.

The address of the attorney-general to the jury in Palmer's case was a classic exposition of the characteristics of strychnine as a poison. Sir Alexander Cockburn had studied the subject for the 1856 trial until he was absolute master of it. Swain read through the transcript, sitting in the cane chair by the popping gas-fire and making notes in an orderly column. He had got as far as 'Tetanus by natural causes', when a bell rang downstairs and he heard Edith Ryland at his door.

On the doorstep of the house stood a uniformed and helmeted constable from the Wandsworth Police Station in Union Road.

'Mr Swain?'

Swain nodded.

'A Division, Scotland Yard, wired through for you, sir,' said the constable importantly. 'Criminal Investigation Department. Mr Lumley's apologies for disturbing you on Sunday afternoon but can you go to Whitehall Place now? He says it won't keep till later.'

Swain looked with mild curiosity at the man.

'I'm here to be disturbed,' he said gently. 'It's what they pay me for. Telegraph to them and say I'll be there in half an hour.'

A few minutes later, in his top-coat and bowler hat, he set off at a brisk stride for the cab-rank. The corner of the lace curtain at the drawing-room window moved a little. In a fleeting image, he saw Rachel's face, still a little moody but

54

distinctly self-pitying at his departure. For a reason which he had not time to analyse then, her discomfiture seemed to him like a reward long sought.

The nature of his work, the analyses of financial frauds and misappropriation, had secured for Swain a small room of his own near the Criminal Investigation Division's main office. It was distempered in the regulation colours, the lower wall green and the upper half white, with a black dividing band. Its one narrow window had a distant view of the river, interrupted by roofs and chimney-pots at the rear of Parliament Street. When he arrived there on this occasion, Sergeant Lumley was waiting at the door.

'Well, now, Mr Lumley,' Swain allowed himself only the mildest scepticism, 'what's all this about?'

He opened the door and Lumley followed him into the narrow room. The sergeant's fleshy jowls were a shade pinker with self-consciousness and the apprehension of one who knows he may have made an error of judgement. Swain sat down behind the little desk and Lumley stood at ease before it.

'Lord Russell and the Honourable Mr Smith,' Lumley said uneasily. 'Matter of interviewing them.'

Swain did not understand but his patience seemed infinite. 'The requests have gone in to Sir Melville Macnaughten,' he said quietly. 'To interview two such suspects on such evidence as an anonymous letter will require his authorisation. He is, I understand, a weekend guest of Lord Shrewsbury – until tomorrow. Or do you mean he has been called back?'

Lumley shook his head.

'It's the two suspects, sir. They're asking to be interviewed. As soon as possible.'

'Mr Smith and Lord Russell?'

Lumley stood his ground.

'We had enquiries this morning, sir, to see if a girl had been poisoned in Lambeth last night. Then came two messages, separately. Mr Smith and Lady Russell want to talk to the officers investigating the murder.'

'*Lady* Russell?'

The sergeant nodded again.

'Seems she's separated from his lordship and is now living apart from him in a suite at the Savoy Hotel. I didn't think you'd want the matter to wait.'

Swain stood up. He turned and stared out at the slate roofs.

'No, Mr Lumley, I wouldn't want it to wait. You shall pay a call on Mr Smith. I will see what can be got from young Lady Russell.'

'Savoy Hotel,' Lumley reminded him, envy and awe mingling in the words.

Swain went down to the telegraph room and sent a message to the Savoy requesting an immediate interview. One did not, he supposed, knock on the door of a countess unannounced, as if arresting a Lambeth pickpocket at Orient Buildings or Hercules Road. Almost an hour passed before there was a reply, on the authority of Lady Russell's private secretary, inviting him to come at once.

By five o'clock on the autumn evening a river mist had begun to gather, deadening the clatter of wheels among the plate-glass windows of the Strand. The new Savoy Hotel rose like a pillared Venetian palace in the vaporous afternoon, its seven storeys of concrete and steel fading in the murk. Unlike the older hotels of the area, the Savoy had a reputation for the fast and the raffish. That summer one of the guests had paid to have the entire courtyard flooded so that he and his friends might dine in floating gondolas at midnight.

From the tumult of the busy street, Swain entered the expensive silence of the Genoese Hall. Deep carpets hushed every footfall. From concealed recesses a new electric lighting flushed the walls and ornate ceiling. The square pillars of the lobby rose with the solemnity of a temple. To make one's home in such a place seemed to Swain as odd as living permanently in a cathedral or a theatre.

Discreet and taciturn, the assistant manager led him up the broad and carpeted stairway. In the corridors above the same silence hung as oppressively as the gathering mist outside. Swain's guide tapped at a plain, expensive door painted in silver grey. After a murmured conversation, the inspector was admitted to the cool electric radiance of a broad sitting-room. With the pale silk of its modernistic chairs and sofa, the grey

56

walls and clear light, it belonged in another century from that of Edith Ryland's drawing room of dark mahogany and fussy velvets.

Swain had never met a countess and he confronted the young Lady Russell without expectations of any kind. She was much younger than he had expected, perhaps no more than two or three years older than Rachel Ryland. In manner and poise, however, the difference between them was that of the mature woman and the awkward child.

Lady Russell rose to greet her visitor, the silk tea-gown flowing about her slim figure and the bangles sounding on her wrists. She looked, he thought, as if she might be about to perform Salome's dance. The neatness of her face and the skill with which it was painted gave her the look of a very expensive doll. The fair hair formed a halo of curls against the cool light of the electrolier.

'Mr Swain?' she enquired, her voice low yet richly modulated, 'Mr Swain from Scotland Yard?'

'Ma'am,' said Swain punctiliously.

Her movements appeared gentle and graceful, her lips parted in hopeful innocence, as she came forward and took his hand. Still holding the hand, she looked long and directly into his eyes.

'Please,' she said at last, 'please sit down, Mr Swain. It was so good of you to come so soon.'

Prudently, he chose the chair diagonally across the pale carpet from where the young woman had been sitting. It crossed his mind that she scarcely seemed to be of the same sex as the bedraggled creatures of Nellie Donworth's kind.

'Mr Swain,' she recalled his attention softly, 'I am greatly in need of your help. Tell me, if you can, whether there is any evidence in your hands which would convict my husband of murder.'

Swain sighed.

'Even if there were, ma'am, I should not be permitted to say so to you.'

She nodded, stood up and went across to the silver cigarette-box. While she lit the cigarette and returned to her chair, Swain considered the loss to the London stage. This performance would have held the attention of the most casual matinee audience at Her Majesty's or the Haymarket.

'I am told Mr Swain, that my husband is a murderer.' Her slim fingers curled tightly over the ends of the chair-arms, her gaze cool and direct. 'You may know that he and I no longer live under the same roof. I cannot say whether the accusation is true or false – but I mean to know.'

Swain nodded, as if he approved of her determination.

'Whom did he murder, ma'am?'

The girl – as he thought of her – evaded his question.

'It is true, is it not, that a young person has been poisoned in Lambeth?'

Only the denting of the white cigarette by fine nails betrayed her anxiety.

'It is.'

When she shifted in her chair, the thin silk of the tea-gown again suggested the flowing lines of a dancer – Salome's limbs.

'I am told, Mr Swain, that my husband murdered that girl. Unless I pay two thousand pounds, proof will be sent to the police. I could not pay, even if I wished. It is more than I have in the wide world.'

Swain glanced sceptically at the immaculate hotel suite, its pale silks and dove-grey decor, the silver boxes and subtle carpeting.

'How was the demand made?'

'In a letter, delivered this morning by the Sunday post and sent by the final collection last night. From south London at ten o'clock. I put it at once in the hands of my solicitor. George Lewis.'

Swain nodded again.

'Quite the best thing, ma'am. Sir George Lewis will bring it to the commissioner's attention first thing tomorrow, I expect.'

Her dark eyes showed a glimmer of petulance.

'You miss the point, Mr Swain! I know what George Lewis will do but I must have the truth of this matter now. For my own peace of mind. You know, surely, that Lord Russell was dismissed from Oxford for indecent conduct? He met my mother, Lady Scott, and through her he met me. We thought he had mended his ways. It seemed so. Could a young man from so noble a family be other than noble himself? How deceived I was! Once we were married, it was evident that he wished both my mother and me to be no better than his concubines. Last June – four months after our wedding – I was driven from his house by practices I will not describe to you. I am now preparing to petition the courts for a judicial separation.'

'But not to indict him for murder, ma'am?'

'Would he not indict me?' Her fingertips rattled on the chair arm. 'Does he not tell the drawing rooms of Mayfair that my mother and I have the morals of a pair of Choktaw Indians?'

She stopped at once, as if sensing that her appeal had become too strident to achieve its purpose.

'I will speak to Sir George Lewis,' Swain said.

'Speak to whom you please!' The collapse of temper into sulky resignation reminded him again of Rachel Ryland. 'You may hang Lord Russell at Newgate a dozen times over before I will pay a brass farthing to Mr Bayne! I ask only what I have a right to know as Lord Russell's wife. For my own protection.'

Swain had been about to stand up. He sank back into the soft chair with a sense of apprehension.

'Who is Mr Bayne?'

'H.M. Bayne,' she said impatiently, 'who signed the demand for money. The man who would blackmail me, if he could.'

'H.M. Bayne?'

'The man who knew Matilda Clover.' Her fingertips tapped again. For the first time, Swain lost control of the conversation.

'Ma'am?'

'Matilda Clover,' she said sharply, 'the girl in the blackmail note. The young woman Lord Russell is said to have poisoned in Lambeth.'

'The girl who was poisoned was called Ellen or Nellie Donworth.'

'Then why does this man Bayne talk of Matilda Clover?'

'I don't know,' said Swain foolishly, 'I've never heard of her.'

'That's absurd,' she said, 'you must have done!'

He shook his head.

'Your husband couldn't have murdered Matilda Clover because no one of that name has been murdered. All related crimes in the Metropolitan district were checked against the details of Ellen Donworth's death this morning. If Matilda Clover ever existed, I imagine she's still alive and well.'

An hour later Swain confronted Sergeant Lumley.

'Matilda Clover!' he said bitterly.

'And Lou Harris,' the sergeant said.

'Who the devil is Lou Harris?'

Lumley shrugged.

'The letter sent to Mr Smith accused him of murdering Matilda Clover and Lou Harris. Not a word about Nellie Donworth.'

'A letter signed by H.M. Bayne?'

'Better than that,' Lumley said, 'H.M. Bayne, Barrister. There's no such name in the lists of the Inns of Court. I checked that. And there's no Matilda Clover or Louisa Harris murdered, or missing, or even known to the police.'

Swain took the copy of the letter which had been sent to Frederick Smith by the Sunday post. He began to read with the foreboding of a victim in a practical joke. The copper-plate was a script taught to every child at school. It was like W.H. Murray's. Like enough to be his own hand disguised, or the work of a second correspondent who wrote as 'H.M. Bayne, Barrister'.

> The Hon Wm Frederick Smith, M.P.
>
> I have obtained positive proof that yours was the hand which sent both Matilda Clover and Lou Harris to their deaths. Like the other girls in Lambeth, you got them into trouble and then did away with them. Perhaps you did not mean to kill them, only procure an abortion. But there was enough strychnine in the medicine you gave them to kill a horse.
>
> My object in writing is to ask if you will retain me at

once as your counsellor and legal adviser. If you employ me at once, I will save you from all exposure and shame. But if you wait till arrested, I cannot act for you, as no lawyer can save you once the authorities get hold of the two letters which are at present in my hands.

H.M. Bayne (Barrister)

Swain stared at the clean distempered wall of the little room.

'This is mad,' he said simply. 'Quite mad. What blackmailer would threaten his victim with evidence that wouldn't get past the duty-sergeant on the desk of a town police station? Why make up names when there's a real girl lying dead in the Lambeth mortuary? Why on earth demand two thousand pounds from young Lady Russell, when she'd be more likely to pay that to get her husband hanged? And whoever heard of a blackmailer demanding that his victim should employ him as an attorney? As soon as he put in an appearance, he'd be nabbed. And he must know it. Not just for blackmail but probably for the murder of Nellie Donworth as well.'

'By the way,' said Lumley, bearer of yet more bad news, 'it seems neither Mr Smith nor Lord Russell could have done it. Mr Smith was on the platform at Exeter Hall last night, addressing a meeting on behalf of distressed trades. He was there before Nellie Donworth met her man and he was still in company with the Bishop of London when she died.'

'And Lord Russell?'

Lumley pulled a face, disparagingly.

'A rotten husband, p'r'aps, but he never killed Nellie Donworth. His nibs has been yachting off Alicante the past week. One or two cabin-boys might have a grievance. That's all.'

Swain sat in silence for a moment, trying to make sense of what evidence he had. The facts had the sticky inextricability of a madman's fly-trap. However he arranged them, they made no sense at all.

'Why?' he said, vexed to the limit of patience. 'Why write to Nellie Donworth in her own name, then murder her, and then try to blackmail two other men over the killing of two young women who aren't even dead? Who probably never existed except as names!'

'Shift the blame?' Lumley suggested. 'Implicate Lord Russell and Mr Smith in the warning note, which we'd find. We'd have to question them. They might pay up to avoid having two other murders alleged against them.'

Swain shook his head.

'Not without knowing the murders had happened. I take it Mr Smith has no objection to putting a notice in his window inviting Bayne to call?'

'No objection whatever,' Lumley said, 'only I wouldn't count on hearing anything more.'

Swain seemed to brighten up at this.

'We'll hear, Mr Lumley. You may depend on that. I daresay our man gets as much pleasure from his letters as he does from killing his victims. I just hope his next communication is a letter and not another girl screaming in tetanic convulsions.'

He sat in silence again, dreaming of the sunlit tranquillity of Edith Ryland's drawing room and the afternoon comforts which now lay tantalisingly beyond his reach.

'All right, Mr Lumley,' he said at last, 'let's make a start.'

4

'Taste that,' said Dr Stevenson. 'Go on. Taste it.'

He held the glass slide in Swain's direction. A tubby figure with a finely trimmed spade beard, the great pathologist was known in his profession, with affectionate disrespect, as 'The Ruler of the Queen's Navee'.

Swain hesitated.

'Taste it?'

'Go on, man! Go on!' Stevenson shook the slide at him impatiently. 'Taste it, but don't hog the lot.'

The bottle-green tint of the skylight above the autopsy table added a lurid quality to the electric radiance of the lamps, the tiled and whitewashed room having been built without windows. Nellie Donworth's body had been removed from the cold hygienic metal of the table before Swain's arrival, for which he was grateful. In the air there lingered the spirituous reek of formaldehyde. Once and once only had the inspector attended a post-mortem. The cutting of flesh he had imagined to be a gentle and almost silent act. What he had heard was more like the rending of tent canvas.

Swain touched his fingertip to the wetness on the glass slide.

'Tip of your tongue,' said Stevenson impatiently. 'Just a dab. No more.'

Cautiously Swain obeyed. He tasted at once a bitter and burning moisture. Stevenson nodded, approving the inspector's grimace.

'That's her liver,' he said confidently, 'or rather the evaporated contents of same. Enough strychnine to kill a herd of elephants.'

Swain spat into his handkerchief. On the shelves lining the far wall was a row of large, squat glass jars, one of them sheathed in white mackintosh. On the cord which bound it was an unbroken wax seal with the imprint of the Home Office upon it. A label in bold script identified it as 'Brain of Ellen Donworth'. The other jars contained what looked to Swain like cold meat on the day following the roast. The labels proclaimed the contents to be the stomach, liver, and kidneys of Nellie Donworth. The stomach, upon which Dr Stevenson had not yet begun, was tied with string at either end so that its contents would be retained.

'You see?' said Stevenson insistently. 'He had to put it in her drink or mix it with something to disguise the taste. Either that or persuade her to take it in a capsule. No one swallows strychnine for the fun of the thing.'

Swain tried to ignore the bitter residue which kept the nerves of his tongue crawling.

'How long would it take to work?'

Stevenson shrugged.

'Taken on its own by mouth, which no one would do, about ten minutes. Mixed with food or drink, it might be longer. About half an hour. The same would apply if it was

63

taken in a gelatine capsule which requires about fifteen minutes to dissolve in the stomach. There again, strychnine as a powder would work faster than if it was in tablet form.'

'So the man who gave it to her, even if he left her at once, hadn't been gone from the York Hotel more than about a quarter of an hour?'

'Probably not.' Stevenson put the slide back in its tray.

'Lumley might have seen him!'

'If he'd had any cause to be looking, Mr Swain. Which he didn't.'

He beckoned the inspector across to a bench upon which the glass beakers and distillation flasks were set out with several specimen tubes and a Bunsen burner. Holding up to the light a tube of the same clear liquid as on the slide, he continued to talk as if in praise of the dead girl in the next room.

'We still know too little about strychnine, Mr Swain, and less still about aconitine. Palmer destroyed half a dozen people at Rugeley in 1856 and all the men of science combined could find no trace in the bodies. Would a jury convict nowadays without greater certainty?'

'I doubt it.' Swain watched him mix sulphuric acid and manganese dioxide in a beaker, swilling the contents round gently.

'No,' Stevenson said. 'Fortunately for you, this young woman is easy to work with. Her kidneys stripped beautifully in dissection. You know, Mr Swain, we shall have our answer without so much as a glance at the rest of the viscera, though glanced at they must be.'

Putting down the beaker, he tipped into it the solution from the tube. Gently the mixture assumed a shade of the most delicate and beautiful violet. The inspector watched, fascinated by the liquid and luminous tint.

'An artist would give a fortune to be able to employ such a colour on canvas, Mr Swain. So subtle and yet so brilliant.' Stevenson put the tube into the rack and held the beaker to the light again. 'That is strychnine, Mr Swain. From her liver. Strychnine without question and in very, very large quantity.'

'Is that incontrovertible? In court? Could there be any dispute on the part of the defence that this was the decisive test for finding strychnine in the body?'

Stevenson put down the beaker and looked up at him.

'Dispute, Mr Swain? Surely not. The symptoms of poison by aconitine have a certain resemblance, in that the patient suffers tetanic convulsions just before death. But aconitine has a numbing taste while strychnine is bitter. You know from your little experience just now to which category this belongs.'

'Would your conclusions about colour testing be challenged?'

Stevenson frowned.

'I doubt it, Mr Swain. I have had some part in almost every death by suspicious poisoning since the trial of Dr Lamson ten years ago. Very few murders but one or two suicides.'

'Suicides?' Swain grimaced again with incredulity at such a method of self-destruction. 'By strychnine?'

'One or two.'

Swain asked the question to which all his other enquiries had been leading.

'Was there anyone, by suicide or foul play, who had the name of Matilda Clover or Louisa Harris?'

Stevenson looked at him for a moment, then shook his head.

'No, Mr Swain. No one of either name. Indeed, there has only been one woman in all my experience. And she a suicide, poor soul. Why do you ask?'

'Curiosity,' said Swain enigmatically. 'Unfinished business.'

As Dr Stevenson began work upon the jar containing Nellie Donworth's stomach, the inspector excused himself and went out into the autumn sunshine. After the cool days which had passed, there was an unexpected warmth in the air and a hint of Indian summer. A mild breeze ruffled the river surface beyond the Albert Embankment whose granite blocks formed a broad promenade for the inhabitants of Lambeth. Opposite St Thomas's Hospital, where Stevenson had carried out his post-mortem experiments, the Houses of Parliament rose against the blue midday sky like the pinnacled fairy palace of enchantment.

Swain walked under the embankment lamps and crossed by Westminster Bridge, making for Parliament Street and New Scotland Yard. The penny steamers, banners of smoke trailing from their tall funnels, queued at the pier with passengers from Greenwich and Rotherhithe. Their paddles turned idly and sent a swell of green river-water slapping against the dark weed-grown wall upon which rose the lawns and paths of the House of Commons terrace.

With the taste of strychnine still bitter on his tongue, Swain walked up Parliament Street towards Whitehall and then turned into the familiar precinct of New Scotland Yard where the banded stone of red and white marked Norman Shaw's new building for the headquarters of the Metropolitan Police.

Sergeant Lumley was waiting for him in the corridor.

'We spent all morning trying to find you, Mr Swain,' the sergeant said, quiet in his reproach.

'Post-mortem on Nellie Donworth, Mr Lumley.' Swain opened the door of his room and Lumley followed him in uninvited. 'And if anyone should care to be pedantic in the matter, I am not due on call for almost half an hour yet.'

'All right,' said Lumley, mollified but without respect, 'only this come for you.'

Swain took the envelope. It bore upon its cover the laboured copper-plate script with which he was now familiar. This time, however, it was addressed to him personally.

'After all,' Lumley said, exercising his sense of grievance more vigorously now that Swain had seen the cause of it, 'I wasn't to know, was I? I mean, for all I could tell, this might have been important.'

'Sit down,' said Swain quietly, 'and shut up.'

He slit open the envelope carefully along the top and drew out the sheet of paper inside it.

Sir,
    I am writing to say that if you or your satellites fail to bring the murderer of Ellen Donworth, *alias* Linnell, to

66

account, I am willing to give you such assistance as will bring the murderer to justice, provided the Government is willing to pay me £30,000 for my services. No pay if not successful.

A. O'Brien (Detective)

Swain let out a gasp of exasperation. The envelope bore a London postmark and was timed the evening before. While Lumley waited, the inspector stared at the glimmer of sun on the river wavelets, glimpsed between the roofs of Parliament Street in the mild day. Presently he gave another sigh.

'Just pray, Mr Lumley, that a copy of this letter has not been sent to the newspapers.'

5

The dusty sunlight of a mild autumn afternoon cast a long shadow of the man in the tall silk hat. He stood on the threadbare grass of the London common, black and still as a steeple against the red sky of the dying day.

Even in the approach of dusk the air was warm and acrid, tasting of soot like a railway terminus. From Wandsworth to Clapham, across the open land, the branches of the trees drooped and the last flowers wilted. Only the groups of women, the wives of shopkeepers and senior clerks returning from their promenade, caught the colours of summer in their silk dresses and parasols.

The man sat patiently on the green wrought-iron seat by the trees. His gloves were folded in one hand and his stick was laid across his knees. In his dark clothes and hat he was indistinguishable from thousands of men of his age and class.

Perhaps it was his air of patience which might have marked him out from the others. He had the look of one who watches with expectation — even excitement — for something to happen. Was he waiting until the last of the promenaders had left the common? If so, he smiled upon them all with extreme tolerance. An amateur photographer, with earnest face and belted tweeds, had erected his tripod and was now placing upon it a wooden box-camera with brass fittings. It was late in the afternoon for such a study but the man had positioned his wife and two children in a patch of sunlight just beyond the trees. As he ducked his head under the black cloth, the children in their sailor suits stood immobile and obedient during the long exposure.

With a look of indulgent good-humour, the man in the dark clothes allowed his gaze to move cautiously beyond the path where the last of the promenaders and the uniformed nursemaids dwindled to ghosts in the first vaporous mist of evening which gathered along the edge of the common. In half an hour the white globes of the street-lamps would form a chain of brilliance on the wide avenue whose portico'd houses overlooked the open grass.

Motionless as an effigy, the man in the tall silk hat watched the groups of girls and children gathered at the Lower Pond fifty yards away. Nothing in his expression showed his furious impatience for the photographer's family to be gone, leaving him lord of the prey. But the camera was now packed in its box of polished wood and the children in the sailor suits were turning away.

With a casualness which belied the growing excitement in his brain, the stranger walked in measured steps across the worn grass towards the pond's edge. There were five of them in all, three children of eight or nine and two girls of twice that age who had charge of them.

It was plain to see what had happened. They had been paddling in the pond, the children with their trouser-legs rolled or their dresses tucked up, the two girls with their hems held cautiously from the water. Now, as they prepared to leave, the little boy's Holland-barque had escaped from him, the light breeze in its sails of waxed paper carrying it to the centre of the pond. One of the two older girls, with the look of a pretty fair-haired housemaid, had waded into the pond until the water rose above her bare knees and touched the white cotton of the drawers low on her thighs. She stood in the gathering dusk, a charming study in dismay as the stranger thought. The fair hair, worn straight and fringed in the manner of a barmaid or waitress, formed the setting for a kittenish beauty of blue eyes and high-boned coquetry. The plain yellow dress was tucked into the waist of her drawers and the man in his dark clothes smiled at the sight of lower limbs revealed like a dancer's.

'Don't go further, Jane!' called her companion. 'It's not safe! Oh, don't!'

The stranger smiled again, hearing in her voice that the second girl feared more for herself than for Jane. He came closer and the one who had spoken looked at him in mute appeal. Hope and uncertainty mingled in her eyes. There was a sinister air to his tall hat and dark clothes in the twilight, the pond now remote from home and safety. But yet he smiled, as if to reassure them.

'Here,' he said gently, and held out to her the black silver-topped stick which he had been carrying.

The girl drew back from it a little.

'Oh, no,' she said, flustered, 'I couldn't. Really, I couldn't.'

The little boy began to cry quietly.

'Very well,' the man said, 'Jane shall take it.'

They drew further away from him, as if alarmed that he should know her name. Still smiling, he went to the edge of the water and held the stick out to the girl who stood knee-deep in the pond.

'Here,' he said, 'take it and hook the little fellow's boat in for him.'

Jane, in her disarray of skirt and drawers, blushed as she came and took the stick by the end extended to her. Not for a moment did the man's smile falter as he made a blunt appraisal of the bare legs below the knee and the narrow grace of her thighs which the movement of the white cotton suggested.

Quickly as she could, she turned and pushed through the water until it covered her knees again. Then by stretching to her limit, she was able to touch the rigging of the toy boat and draw it to her.

'Pretty child,' the man said softly, watching the movement of her legs and hips, 'pretty thing!'

With the little boat safe, Jane turned and waded to the pond's edge. The white pearls of the street-lamps outlined the

69

high road through the thin mist. Hastily setting her dress to rights, she stood before the man, returned his stick and thanked him. He looked more closely at the heart-shaped face and the fair fringe. Jane seemed almost as if she might drop a curtsey. Instead she forced a quick smile. The man put out his hand and touched the side of her face lightly. Jane checked her instinct to draw back, as if accustomed to the idea that a debt might be discharged by allowing her social superiors such familiarity.

'Pretty child!' he said softly. 'Pretty smiler!'

From his pocket he took a paper bag, holding it out to her. Jane drew back a step and the man laughed.

'Come now!' he said, chiding her playfully. 'See here!'

He opened the paper bag to her, revealing a bright jewelled Babylon of boiled sweets. In the last grey daylight they seemed to glow with blood-red, emerald-green, and sherbet-yellow. With a quick movement, he appeared to take one himself and pop it in his mouth. Without asking her again, he pulled out another and put it in her hand while she hesitated. His tongue shifted contentedly against his teeth, sucking gently.

'You see?' he said. 'You don't know what you're missing.'

The other girl and the children had drawn back a little. If Jane chose to make a bargain of some kind with a silk-hatted swell, it was not for them to spoil her chances. She stood with the boiled sweet hard and sticky in her palm.

'Pretty smiler!' the man said. 'Give me a smile for a sweet.'

Jane hesitated and the others drew further away. In the exchange between them, it seemed that Jane had conceded to the man some unspecified entitlements. Slowly she put the sweet in her mouth.

'Show me!' he said, teasing her.

Jane opened her mouth and showed a wet green gem on her quivering tongue. The man laughed and took a step forward, as if to close the gap between them. Moving further into the dusk, her companions began to walk away.

He touched her face again.

'Pretty thing!' he whispered, a new intensity colouring his words. 'Pretty slut!'

She flinched a little at the last word but still she hesitated to follow the others. The man's hand touched her face and the back of his finger was drawn down her neck as if he relished the fine silken texture of her young skin. When he put his hand to her face again, Jane rubbed against it like a pet animal, eager not to let good fortune escape her and yet too inexperienced to know how best to secure it.

She stood meekly while his hand touched the front of her dress where the silk was thin enough over her breasts for him to feel their shape.

'Are you a good girl, my pretty child?' he asked, eager and yet still taunting her. 'Ah, no! I think you are a good girl who would like to be bad. . . . Yes, I think so. Why, I can feel the wickedness through your clothes!'

Distant lamplight shivered on the surface of the dark pond where she had waded after the toy barque so short a time before. The girl understood all that was being said to her and the things to which it related. But she understood it only in theory and from conversation. That it should be like this in reality was something she had never expected.

'Pretty slut!' Now his hands were at her waist and the breath in his throat was louder, as if he might be angry with her. 'Ah, my pretty little slut. My pretty whore!'

The word came like a blow from the darkness. Whatever humour or affection there might have been in the earlier chiding was gone now. To be called a slut was not unfamiliar in certain household scoldings but the other word meant something else. It promised a certain use and an ordeal by the contempt of the man who used her. It was this, not the hands which travelled round her hips, that fired her fear and anger at last.

'That's enough!' she cried, backing from him. Already his outline seemed more ghostly in the dark.

'Come here!' Jane thought his shout was like her father's anger, nothing more. 'Come here, you bitch!'

But now she had turned and was running across the threadbare grass, following the others towards the street-lamps of the high road. As she stumbled in the grass, she spat the green globe of the boiled sweet into her hand and flung it from her, hearing it plop into the dark pond. The man made no attempt to pursue her.

In a few minutes she saw the others ahead and caught them, breathless and dishevelled. By now they were close to the high road, the echo of hooves in the mist accompanied by the clink of harness, the rumble of wheels from hansom cabs and growlers.

The other girl dropped back with her so that their whispers should not reach the children.

'Was it all right, Janey? What was it he wanted?'

'Nothing,' she said miserably, 'it was nothing.'

And then she bowed her head as she walked, too proud even in her humiliation to let them see the lamplight on her tears.

6

'You're not a varsity man, are you Mr Swain? Not a varsity man at all?'

Walter de Grey Birch sat at his desk with his back to the tall window which looked out on to the British Museum's courtyard.

'No,' said Swain reassuringly from his chair, 'not in the least.'

Mr Birch, with his bald and bulging dome of intelligence, had as much human appeal as a cold boiled egg in spectacles. Except, Swain thought, that in his case the egg was wide end uppermost.

'No,' said Mr Birch the palaeographer, investing the single syllable with a hint of distaste, 'not in the least.'

He looked at the four letters from Bayne, Murray and O'Brien laid out on the desk before him. Presently the rimless glasses caught the light again as he looked up once more at his visitor.

'*Timeo Danaos et dona ferentes*, Mr Swain,' he said with a continued pleasure in taunting the policeman's lack of education, 'I fear the Greeks even when they bring gifts. You will not, Mr Swain, see the relevance of that, I imagine.'

'Not really, sir,' said Swain politely, 'no.'

Mr Birch sighed at the impossibility of explaining problems so erudite to a man of so few accomplishments.

'A matter of scripts and hands, Mr Swain. Let me elucidate the matter as plainly as I can for you.'

'Thank you,' Swain said without the least trace of irony, 'I should be glad of a simple account.'

'I imagine you do not know much of script and calligraphy, Mr Swain?'

Swain assumed a mournful look of self-confessed ignorance.

'Very little, sir. I did, of course, admire your last paper to the Malone Society. Who could not? You described the interpolation of Secretary Hand into Humanistic Script during the Tudor and Stuart periods so lucidly that even I could understand your argument. The use of uncial "d" is evidently much later than any of us supposed.'

'What business of yours—'

'None, sir,' said Swain quickly. 'Major legal documents appear in Latin until 1727. To decipher Latin *and* the Court Hand of the Stuarts would be quite beyond me.'

The features on the egg-face were blank as a defensive wall.

'*Not* a varsity man, Mr Swain?'

'Oh no, sir. My father was a country schoolmaster in Dorset, near Shaftesbury. I was his only child, you see. He had a good deal of time to devote to my reading.'

Swain spoke as if making an apology.

'And did he encourage you to read the Humanistic Script of the Tudors, Mr Swain?'

The sarcasm seemed to pass over the inspector's head like a clumsily aimed rifle volley.

'No, sir. You did that.'

'Absurd, Mr Swain. We have never met before.'

The inspector leant forward, the wise equine face looking long at Mr Birch with an innocence which seemed more menacing than anger.

'When you were appointed to advise in this case, Mr Birch,

you became one of my people. As surely as if you were a suspect. Your abilities and your reputation became interesting to me. It would probably surprise you, Mr Birch, to discover what I know about you. It might cause you the slightest blush.'

Indignation and unease succeeded one another in the blue eyes behind the rimless spectacles. Then the cold mask of pedantry came down like a vizor.

'Well, Mr Swain, let us leave it there. Many people would regard a policeman as a clodhopper incapable of telling one end of a book from the other. I do not support that prejudice.'

'I'm so glad,' said Swain earnestly. 'Old Superintendent Toplady had the same kind of prejudice. He thought that a man who spent his life with poetry books and learning could not be a man at all. A Mary-Ann, he called such a person.'

'A Mary—'

Comprehension blossomed in Mr Birch's brain. He began to go red, from the nape of his neck upwards.

'Like you, Mr Birch,' Swain said casually, 'I prefer to make my own judgements. And now, if you please, we will have your opinion on these four letters and the man who wrote them.'

Mr Birch sat silent for so long, looking past Swain's shoulder, that the inspector feared he had gone too far. Perhaps the famous palaeographer was too shocked by a touch on a sensitive nerve or possibly too insulted to reply. At last he turned to Swain and began to talk in a tone as distant and precise as that of a lecturer in Euclidean geometry.

'Four letters have been presented to me for examination. Three, signed by Murray or Bayne, are written to Donworth, Lady Russell, and Mr Frederick Smith. The fourth, signed by A. O'Brien, is addressed to Scotland Yard. They are written in a similar script and at a random glance seem to be the work of one hand. Not so. The first author wrote the Murray letter to Ellen Donworth and the letter from O'Brien offering to help the police. A second author wrote the blackmail letter to Lady Russell. From the script, I deduce that both writers are men. The blackmail letter to Mr Frederick Smith is written by a woman, the third correspondent.'

74

It was now Swain's turn to be lost for words.

'That's impossible,' he said quietly. 'There can only be one.'

Mr Birch sighed and a glimmer of triumph lit the cold eyes briefly.

'Mr Swain, I have made a microscopic examination of these pages. They look alike, superficially. Perhaps those who wrote them conspired together to make them look alike.'

Swain shook his head emphatically.

'The criminal lunatic who murders poor women in such a manner is a solitary,' he said quietly, clinging to a hope of well-tried truth. 'They don't go round in gangs. Psychopaths are solitary.'

Mr Birch smiled. The inspector's discomfiture and his own unchallengeable expertise brought him visible pleasure. It would teach Mr Swain not to match himself against men more expert.

'I do *not* know whether they may go round in gangs or not, Mr Swain. I *do* know what a microscopic analysis of the letters reveals and I shall make my report to Sir Melville Macnaughten accordingly.'

Swain waited to hear the worst.

'The letter warning Ellen Donworth and the letter from O'Brien offering to help the police are written by the same hand and, indeed, by the same nib. It has the mark of a Waverley pen-nib with a slight defect at one edge. This causes a characteristic unevenness in the down strokes when that edge might be uppermost. There are also a few tiny particles of a hard red substance sticking to the paper. I suspect a spot of sealing wax had adhered to the nib.'

'And the two blackmail letters?'

Mr Birch frowned at his visitor.

'Not the same hand, Mr Swain. Not even the same hand as one another. They are, of course, in the same italic style but that is commonly used in copybook writing. The letter to Lady Russell is in a man's hand. But unlike the earlier two, the alphabetic characters are formed by double strokes. When the other writer forms a 't' or an 'h', he makes a downward stroke. He lifts his pen and adds the rest of the character. The

75

letter to Lady Russell is quite different. The vertical stroke of each character begins at the bottom, the pen travels up and then down along the mark already made.'

'He could have done that deliberately.'

'No, Mr Swain. It was his natural manner of writing. I will tell you something else about Lady Russell's correspondent. He was probably Spanish or Portuguese. The details of the characters as he writes them have two minor ornaments of script from the Iberian peninsula.'

'This is ridiculous!' said Swain helplessly.

'No, Mr Swain. It is a good deal less ridiculous than your initial and inadequate examination of the documents which led you to suppose that only one criminal was involved. I come now to the fourth letter written to Mr Frederick Smith. A great curiosity. The direction of the pen and the slight cursive quality of the script are characteristically feminine. I will spare you the trouble of considering whether one man might have written in all these styles, including the woman's. In forgeries of that sort there are always unnatural stops, starts, and pauses, as the forger follows his model. I find no indication of such imperfections here.'

'I don't believe in gangs of psychopaths,' Swain said quietly.

'Two crimes, then, Mr Swain. The letters to Miss Donworth and to yourself were written by one man who may or may not be the murderer. The other two, to Lady Russell and Mr Smith, have nothing to do with the murderer. They are the work of a second group of criminals, intent merely on blackmail in the wake of the murder. They don't mention Donworth. Only Clover and Harris.'

'Then how did they know so much about the murder, and know it so quickly?'

Mr Birch shrugged.

'Unfortunately, Mr Swain, that is one problem you will have to encounter without any assistance on my part. My compliments to Sir Melville Macnaughten – and I bid you good day.'

Outside in the courtyard of the museum, Sergeant Lumley said reprovingly, 'I don't see what use there was getting him into a wax.'

'He deserved to be waxed,' said Swain furiously, 'embalmed in wax if possible. An Englishman, a Spaniard, and a woman! Did you ever hear the like of it?'

They walked together towards the tall ironwork of the main gate and railings.

'Supposing I was you,' Lumley said cautiously, 'I wouldn't say too much about Mr Birch. Disrespectful things, that is. He's got a lot on his side. Guildhall and the Bank of England have him on retainer for examining counterfeit bank drafts and letters of credit. He may be sour as vinegar and mean as a stoat, but he's got a lot of reputation on his side. When it comes to handwriting.'

'I daresay,' Swain strode on unimpressed, 'but what it comes to here, Mr Lumley, is murder. And I'll be damned if I waste the time of the division questioning women and Spaniards when there's a silk-hatted maniac called Fred on the loose.'

Something of the anger roused by his meeting with Mr Birch still flickered in Swain's heart as he turned his key in the latch of Edith Ryland's front door. Among his superiors he now sensed a belief that the murder of Ellen Donworth might be an isolated killing, not the prelude to a series of horrors like the Whitechapel slaughter two years before. The attempts to blackmail Lady Russell and Frederick Smith were the work of opportunists, so ignorant of the true facts that they had even got the name of the victim wrong. The death of Nellie Donworth would be thoroughly investigated and the murderer, if possible, brought to trial. Yet the suggestion that a wave of blood was about to break over Lambeth was strongly to be deprecated. So said Sir Melville Macnaughten.

The two rooms which Swain occupied on the top floor of the house were at the end of a little corridor leading from the narrow attic stairs. They would have been quarters for the maidservants if Edith Ryland had had any servants. Their doors were at right angles and both windows overlooked the narrow garden at the rear of the house with its rectangle of lawn, its lichened apple tree and brick boundary walls.

By an agreement never referred to in so many words, the

attic level and its two rooms were his own exclusive territory. The arrangement ensured his well-marked privacy and a degree of separation that gave respectability to a bachelor under the same roof as a widow and her daughter. For his part, Swain never locked his doors. To do so, he believed, would be an act of discourtesy to a woman in her own home. He was, in that sense, one of the family.

He was about to put his hand on the door-knob of the room which served as his parlour when he heard a movement beyond it. It was the light casual sound of limbs being drawn up or garments carefully arranged. In the shadowy light of the little corridor he remembered the scene in his bedroom one year before. Rachel waiting for him, lying beneath the counterpane in her petticoats. With quickening apprehension he pushed open the door.

She was sitting in her brown dress on the rug before the black-leaded fireplace, her legs drawn under her and her back resting against the chair. It was the casual and compliant attitude, suggestive of a fond animal, which she often adopted in her mother's drawing room. Though the evening was dark, only the tall steady flames of the gas fire lit the room. From the warmth which greeted him, Swain guessed that she must have been sitting there for the past two hours while the world outside faded in the twilight.

Without speaking, conveying displeasure by silence, Swain crossed the room to the white mantel of the central light and put a match to the gas.

Rachel brushed a troublesome hair from her forehead with the edge of her hand, looking up at him.

'You needn't have done that,' she said coolly. 'It was nice to be sitting in the firelight. People look different by it, more interesting.'

Swain took off his coat and put it down.

'Did your mother send you up here?'

Rachel's face was a study in pity for his denseness. Swain noticed, as if seeing her for the first time in this guise, that she seemed suddenly to have lost the fullness of adolescence. The points of the cheekbones were more prominent and her chin more finely shaped. Even her eyes had some quick nervous-

78

ness of movement, replacing the stolid curiosity of the child.

'Of course she didn't.' Rachel dismissed the suggestion patiently. 'I came here to wait for you. Because I wanted to see you.'

'We should talk elsewhere,' Swain said firmly, hanging up his coat, 'in the drawing room with your mother. . . .'

The girl got to her feet, coming up behind him and putting a hand high on his arm.

'Don't be silly,' she said quietly, 'I came here to talk to you alone. In any case, she's not in the drawing room. It's Wednesday. She's gone to Streatham to propose on my behalf to poor Cousin Henry.'

He turned round, aware too late that he had betrayed his alarm at the thought of such an arrangement being true. Rachel looked at him solemnly for a moment longer and then smiled.

'Poor Cousin Henry,' she said.

Swain relented a little.

'All the same,' he said, 'you ought to be downstairs and I must stay up here.'

Rachel turned the reddened-bronze bob of her hair away, as if she might begin to weep. Yet the quiet voice in which she answered him was firm and level.

'I only wanted to talk to you,' she said simply, 'to be with you. You used not to mind. It used not to make you angry.'

Swain sighed and, conscious of the indiscretion, put his own cold hand over the warmth of hers.

'You used to be a child,' he said gently, 'now you are a woman. A young woman, I daresay, but old enough to be wife to Cousin Henry or any other man.'

The exasperation of the day, Mr Birch's visions of Spanish and female psychopaths, the ready acceptance of the absurdity by Sir Melville Macnaughten, made him incapable of the understanding he owed her. With something like a sense of guilt Swain took the girl by the arm and began to lead her towards the door. Abruptly, Rachel shook herself free and faced him, such anger in her green eyes that he thought she was about to stamp her foot. All her affection was withdrawn from him in the humiliation of being rejected.

'You fool!' she said, insulting him directly for the first time in six years. 'You don't understand, do you?'

Swain stared at her, marvelling at the spirit and rebellion which he had provoked.

'The man who killed the girl in Lambeth!' Rachel watched his face closely. 'The man you can't find. That's what I wanted to talk to you about.'

Swain's irritation was immediately and unexpectedly replaced by a sense of despair. Whatever his anger at her conduct, the realisation that she intended nothing towards him filled him with melancholy.

'I see,' he said quietly, 'I'm sorry then.'

But Rachel, having been scorned, now turned upon him in her triumph.

'What else should I want to talk to you about?' she said. 'What else is there?'

'Nothing.' Swain felt the sadness harden in his breast. 'Nothing whatsoever.'

'The man you can't find,' Rachel announced abruptly. 'He's been found.'

'Where?'

Her anger faltered at the sharpness of his reply.

'On the common. On Sunday. Jane Hope found him.'

'Sit down,' said Swain firmly, 'properly. In the chair. Begin at the beginning. Who found him and where is he now?'

Rachel shrugged and obeyed.

'Just as Janey was leaving the pond with her sister and the little ones, the man came up to them. He was tall, with a moustache, dark clothes, and a tall silk hat. It was getting dusk and they were the last to leave. He talked to Janey, touching her and calling her names.'

'Names?'

'Slut,' said Rachel with equanimity, 'and another that was worse than that. The others went off and the man made Janey take a sweet and put it in her mouth. He was so beastly to her, using names and touching her, that she got away and ran off after the others...'

'The sweet!' Swain snapped the question at her. 'What about the sweet?'

'She threw it away when she ran,' Rachel explained indifferently. 'Janey threw it in the pond.'

'And the man?'

'That's all,' Rachel said. 'You'll have to ask Janey the rest. That's all I know. She's sister to the maid at Streatham.'

'All right,' he said gently, 'all right.'

But Rachel stood up, her anger cold and measured.

'If I'd only waited here because I liked you and wanted to be with you – just to have someone to talk to even – you'd have scolded me and sent me off. Just because I heard about your beastly man on the common, it's all right!' To his dismay Swain saw the movements in her throat and the pricking of her tears. 'I think you're a brute. I'll never come to this room again as long as you live here!'

She walked with quick, nervous steps along the little corridor. Swain heard a door slam on the floor below and then the muffled but unmistakable gurglings of the girl's sobs.

That night Alfred Swain dreamt dreams he was to remember long afterwards. He woke once convinced of the reality of a female presence in the bed beside him, an ambiguous body in which the charms of Edith and Rachel Ryland were combined. When he slept again, it was to meet Dr Stevenson who talked of how the two women yielded easily under the post-mortem scalpel. Swain woke in the morning with a feeling of nausea and in a state of far greater exhaustion than when he had gone to bed.

As the horse-tram bore him towards Whitehall Place, he pondered a remark of Sergeant Lumley's made several years before. It did a man no good, in Lumley's view, to be a bachelor beyond thirty. Perhaps it was being a bachelor in a house with two women, Swain thought. Better to be billeted with a section, to hear the loud guffaws and talk of which man had had his greens last night and with which doxy. Healthier, perhaps.

He was still meditating on this when he entered the little room assigned as his office. On the desk was a directive from the Assistant Commissioner. Swain and Lumley were to devote their best energies to checking all men of Spanish extraction living in the Lambeth area and any woman associated with them who was both literate and of a criminal disposition. Fred, of the tall silk hat and moustaches, was to take second place.

'Damn them!' said Swain mildly. 'Damn and blast them all!'

7

The stranger in a tall silk hat turned the corner of Hercules Road. He walked very slowly past Orient Buildings with their heavy mock-Venetian façade in yellow brick and gritstone pillars, painted over to resemble marble. Outside the shabby apartment block, the girls who rented its rooms paraded on the pavement for hire. There was little traffic in the damp and narrow lane of Hercules Road itself. But beyond the corner lay the shops and smart terraces of Westminster Bridge Road, a main artery south of the river. A man in search of such pleasures as the young women offered had no need to risk robbery with assault in the Southwark mint. A few yards from Westminster Bridge Road stood the portico of Orient Buildings and the brightly dressed girls with their feathered hats.

Though the man walked slowly past them, his eyes appraising each pair of stockinged legs revealed by the raised dresses, he said nothing. At the sight of their prey escaping them, the girls began to jeer at him.

'Lost yer voice?' they shouted after him. 'All eyes and no balls! . . . Too mean to give us a tune on yer penny whistle! . . . I hopes the coalman does more for your missus than you do. . . Garn, get out of it. . .'

The man turned slowly and walked back. They watched him in silence, ready with their insults but eager to hear him as well. He stopped in front of the first girl and spoke in a clear quiet voice.

'Listen to me, you whore, and listen to me well. I have an eye for a face – and a long memory. Cross my path again, any of you, here or elsewhere, and I will give you in charge to the nearest policeman. The man who rids our streets of such filth as you deserves to be rewarded for it. The curse of hell upon the lot of you!'

The girl standing immediately in front of him drew back a little, as if afraid that he was going to strike at her. Her companions set up a sardonic hooting at the man to send him on his way. Yet the spirit of their earlier insults had been subdued. Their derision echoed a resentment of defeat.

Unhurried by their threats, he turned the corner and began to walk through the busy traffic towards the southern end of Westminster Bridge, half a mile away. The mild autumn day was dulled by smoke from the railway overhead which crossed the street on its way to Waterloo. With a din like stage thunder the expresses passed above him, drowning even the rumble of cabs and delivery vans which crowded the roadway itself.

Beyond the railway arches the street opened out into the bridge approach. With its public houses and music halls this was the heart of pleasure south of the river. To one side the entrance canopy of Astley's Amphitheatre extended over the pavement. The walls of the Canterbury and Gatti's Palace of Varieties were lost beneath promises of entertainment in blue and red lettering. Head Balancers and Comedy Acrobats competed for attention with the Black Fun of the minstrels and 'Under One Flag', a Divertissement in Two Tableaux.

Another shriek of a whistle and a down-draught of smoke marked the passing of the wagons overhead. When the vapour cleared, the man in the silk hat had crossed Addington Street and was walking towards the last buildings on the southern bank of the river, where the street rose under its curved gas-lamps at the beginning of Westminster Bridge. The shops to either hand had been converted from the ground floors of Georgian brick terraces, masked by soot and decay. The upper floors carried the darkened paintwork of boards advertising Flor Rothschild Cigars, Elliman's Embrocation, Menier's French Confectionery.

He paused at the largest of the shops, a tobacconist's which occupied a pair of adjacent ground floors. Egyptian Cigarettes in pictured boxes and Old England Snuff in painted porcelain jars upon the shelves gave the establishment an air of the most exceptional prosperity. Close to the bridge, it was an easy walk across the river from the Houses of Parliament, several of whose members were among its frequent customers.

The proprietor, an importer of Turkish and Egyptian tobacco, attracted such custom by staffing the shop with young women of a disposition which was flirtatious within the limits of respectability. Two of them were visible at that moment, one behind the counter and the other arranging a row of Flor Rothschild boxes and Sullivan cigars in the window. It was the girl at the window who held the stranger's attention.

He knew that her name was Sally Petts, which like other details of her background and her habits had been noted in his little book. She was a girl of sixteen or seventeen with her fair hair put up and curled at its edges in the manner of one of Sir Frederic Leighton's models or the young Ellen Terry in the paintings of G.F. Watts. Yet there was an irreverent quality in her slim prettiness and sceptical blue eyes which would have disqualified Sally from the attentions of those artists.

The stranger, however, found himself powerfully attracted and disturbed by her. He paused, watching her step up on to a chair to reach the top corner of the window with a feather duster. As she did so, the hem of the long dress rose a little to offer a glimpse of slim calves in black stockings. The silk of the material tightened on the curve of her hip.

It was the girl at the counter who noticed him first and seemed to blush on Sally's behalf. Her lips moved in a warning so emphatic that the stranger could read the words.

'That man's watching you again!'

Sally looked up, not at her companion but at the tall stranger in his dark clothes and silk hat. He returned the stare of her blue eyes before letting his gaze descend to the shape of her legs and then up to the narrow curve of her hip. There was no humour in his face, nothing of the wag or even of the lecher. The face was long and impassive with a thick but evenly clipped moustache. As he watched the girl, the ellipse of his eyes was cold and immobile as stone. Though he wore a tall hat, he gave the impression of a man whose head was high-domed and bald as if it had been shaved.

At the sight of him, the prettiness and animation left the girl's face, drawn and tense with a sudden fear. Instinct told her that this was a man who would look upon the death of others with a dispassionate content.

She scrambled down from the chair and ran to where the other girl stood behind the counter. But now the man was gone, walking away towards the river bridge through the mild autumn sunlight. It seemed that he was standing by the ornate doorway of Coade's Artificial Stone showroom, the last building on the near side of the street. Then the figures of the midday crowd concealed him from view.

Sally went back to the window and resumed her dusting, moving the chair a little and working along the ledge. Her companion withdrew to the back of the shop. It was ten minutes later when Sally looked up from her dusting and saw the man again, staring at her with the same humourless eyes and the callous grimace of the butcher or the executioner. His lips moved in a syllable of contempt, slowly enough for her to read them. This time she ran to the shop door, slammed it and slid the bolt across.

Alone in the shop, she called out to the other girl who had gone into the back room. There was no response. The man smiled at last, standing outside the bolted door, his eyes on the victim, sure of his prey.

Running into the back room, Sally found it empty and knew that she was entirely alone in the building. No sooner had she shut the rear door of the shop and bolted it than someone outside tried the handle. She knew it was the man in the tall silk hat who had walked down the alley behind the buildings. He was going to break in and murder her. Unlikely though it seemed in the middle of the day, she knew he was going to do it. Sally had seen his face and the calm cruelty of the steady eyes. She knew he would do it.

Terrified of being cornered by him in the back room, where no one would see what was done to her or hear her cries, Sally ran out into the shop again. He was there at the glass door, watching her, the line of his mouth betraying amusement and contempt at her efforts to evade him. The crowds of men in their dark suits and the business girls from the offices paraded past with no idea of the drama that was unfolding. They saw only a formally dressed man, who might have been a doctor or a solicitor, standing with his back to them as he waited for the door of the tobacconist's shop to open. None of them noticed the fear in the face of the pretty girl with her Ellen Terry ringlets as she sought refuge from the man.

It was a game to him, perhaps, taunting her by the terror which he woke in the girl's heart. Again his lips moved in the slow obscenity of sexual insults. Much as she dreaded him, it seemed that Sally Petts could not draw herself away, as if she dared not miss a single word of the silent mockery.

And still the lunchtime crowds moved over the river from the offices of Whitehall, down Westminster Bridge Road with its little shops and cafés. No one would notice. No one would save her. Never having confronted such a fear before, Sally felt panic like a physical pain in her breast and entrails. She began to scream for Milly, for Milly who had gone and could not hear her. Someone surely would see what was happening and come to save her. But no one saw and the sardonic smile of the man who waited his chance had almost become a sneer of triumph.

He stepped forward, took the handle of the door and pushed with growing force. The feeble bolt gave a little, its screws having needed attention for some time. Sally knew that he would burst it open in a moment more, follow her into the back room and there put an end to her in a manner she could imagine only as a vague and suggestive horror.

Leaning more heavily on the frame of the door, pressing the handle with renewed energy, his face seemed to darken with a spasm of anger. A muscle pulled in his cheek. The cold eyes glinted. When he formed the silent insults, his lips worked as if he might spit on the glass. Sally, her back to the counter and her hands supporting herself against it, began to tremble. She shouted wildly, as if someone in the crowd outside might hear her and see what was happening.

And so it appeared to be. To her astonishment, a pair of men who had been standing by the edge of the pavement turned with a balletic precision, took three steps forward and grabbed the stranger by either arm before he had any idea of being noticed.

'I'll trouble you for a moment of your time,' said Alfred Swain gently, holding the man's arm in a double-handed grip.

It was then that Milly, who had run across the bridge to New Scotland Yard, began to knock at the rear door of the shop. Sally slid down, her back to the counter as she crouched on the floor, and burst into tears. With Swain and Lumley holding either arm, the stranger's face relaxed in a quick smile of amiability, as if willing to forgive whatever misunderstanding might have arisen between them.

Later that afternoon, in a bare distempered room reserved for such interviews, Inspector Swain confronted Henry Slater across the wooden table. A uniformed constable stood with his back to the door in the manner of one who hears nothing said by either party.

'Again,' said Swain leaning forward patiently, the long intelligent face watching the suspect gently. 'Again, Mr Slater, if you please.'

Slater was not quite bald now that his hat had been removed. He possessed a narrow rim of curly hair above which his baldness rose. It transformed him at once from murderer to clown.

'I have nothing to apologise for,' he said quietly. 'Nothing to answer. In fact, nothing to say. Were I a vindictive man, which I am not, Inspector Swain, you would be called to answer for this.'

Swain sat back in his chair, crossed one leg over the other, and looked at Slater's bland innocence.

'A young woman was terrified half to death this morning, Mr Slater. By you. By your leering and your threats, by your obscenities and your attempts at violence. It is through your own conduct that you sit here now.'

There was a flicker in Slater's expression, a brief betrayal of anger.

'You take the word of a lazy little slut who closes her master's shop in order to spend an hour or two of idleness? You choose to believe a little fool who locks the door against his customers and then calls the police if they become angry with her?'

'You threatened her with violence,' Swain said, 'I was there.'

'Prove it, if you can!' Slater's mouth gaped in an ill-formed snarl. 'I threatened her with a recommendation to her master that she should be dismissed from his employment for her slatternly ways. And that, Mr Inspector Swain, is a threat I will carry out. She would call the police and make up a story, would she? Indeed! We shall see about that, Mr Inspector!'

'We shall,' said Swain quietly as the constable with his back to the door eased his shoulders a little and clasped his hands again behind him.

Mild sunlight patterned the floor of the room with a dappling of window glass.

Slater stood up.

'I have committed no crime. Prove one, if you dare. You have no right whatever to keep me here. I shall go.'

'Sit down,' said Swain gently.

'That little bitch! The verminous Miss Petts! I will have a writ on her for this. And I will answer you nothing for her!'

'Sit down, if you please.'

'I can have you for this, if I choose, Mr Inspector. False arrest. I am senior clerk at Cockerell and Boyd, a firm of the first repute. . . .'

'You were,' Swain acknowledged the truth of it, 'until you were dismissed last month. Mrs Dodd, with whom you have rooms in Kennington Park Road, confirmed that to my sergeant half an hour ago.'

'Be damned to you,' said Slater bitterly, 'I shall have no more of this. I will answer nothing for Miss Petts, but I will have satisfaction of the pair of you!'

He stood glowering above Alfred Swain.

'You must answer to me,' Swain said quietly. 'If you leave this room, I will have you taken in charge before you reach the end of the corridor. You will answer to me, Mr Slater. Not for Miss Petts but for the murder of Nellie Donworth.'

Slater sat down heavily without being told to do so.

'Mad!' he said. 'You are quite mad! The pack of you!'

But he spoke in the gasp of one who has had the breath knocked from him by a sudden blow.

'There is also the matter of a young woman indecently accosted and threatened on Clapham Common last week.'

'I was not upon the common last week.'

'Wait until you hear,' Swain said more sharply. 'Indecency, Mr Slater. Indecency is not quite beyond you, is it?'

'I have murdered no one. I have not been on the common since the summer. You will not, I promise you, embarrass me by this talk of indecency.'

Swain nodded.

'I should think not. Indecency would not embarrass you, Mr Slater. You and I both know what treasures of it lie in the drawers and cupboards of your rooms. Do we not?'

He had been keeping back this revelation and knew at once that the trap had been sprung to perfect effect. Slater's protest now assumed the form of a wail of indignation.

'By what right do you enter my premises—'

Swain interrupted him by a hand raised mildly.

'No, Mr Slater. The premises are Mrs Dodd's. She made not the least objection. Indeed, your failure to pay your lodging money for the past fortnight makes it improbable that *you* have right of entry there yourself.'

He got up and walked over to the door. The constable stood aside as Swain looked out into the corridor.

'Mr Lumley, if you please!'

As Swain went back to his chair across the table from Slater, Lumley came in carrying a leather-bound notebook and a small box.

'Over here, Mr Lumley, if you will be so good.'

Slater glared first at Swain and then at the sergeant.

'I'll say nothing!'

The inspector nodded.

'You might be wise in that, Mr Slater. First we will take the matter of the notebook. Thirty names and addresses of young women. Nothing strange in that perhaps for a man of libidinous tastes. But then, why should there be such details in each case, a note of their habits and movements, where they may be found or followed? And why, in each case, should there be such wicked expressions of desire for them as we find here? You will not, I suppose, deny that the writing is in your hand?'

'A man may write as he pleases in his own home and in his own book!'

'He *may*, Mr Slater, but is he well advised to write of such lewdness as we find here? Should he commit to paper visions of a young woman snared in his net?'

'Read your Bible, Mr Inspector! You will find a worse fate there preached for the state of whoredom!'

'But the name of Sally Petts does not occur in the Bible, Mr Slater, as it does in the hell-fire of your little book.'

'There is worse in the Bible than what I write!' Slater shouted back.

Swain sighed.

'Divine wrath is exercised a little differently in a more civilised age, Mr Slater. Harlotry bows before the Town Police Clauses Act and the legislation on contagious diseases.'

'Bring Sally Petts to court as a witness and I will prove her a whore in front of the entire world!' Slater shouted.

Swain leant forward with infinite patience.

'You may prove Nellie Donworth a whore – very easily, for that was her only profession. And yet if you murdered her, you shall hang by the neck as surely as if you had killed the purest woman in England.'

Sergeant Lumley, who had so far stood back from the encounter, now handed the inspector the little box.

'And there's these,' he said.

Swain opened the box, a red oblong of Florentine leather-work large enough to hold collars or envelopes. Inside there lay a pile of photographs, a few black and white, the rest in yellowed sepia, cracked at their edges by too frequent handling. Each glum little humiliation seemed to have been posed by men and women who looked inanimate as wax-works.

'A man has a right. . .' Slater began.

'He has,' Swain said thoughtfully, 'he has indeed. How-ever, a man does not have a right to commit murder. Nor does he have the right to abuse and terrify young women on

90

Clapham Common or in the Westminster Bridge Road.'

'Prove it!'

But Swain looked mildly at his suspect in the manner of one who wishes only to clear up a misunderstanding.

'I mean to do that, Mr Slater. I really do. And if the proof comes home to you in the death of Nellie Donworth—'

'It can't!' Slater had been loud before, now he was shrill.

'If it does, Mr Slater, then in a couple of months' time, at eight in the morning, you shall form part of a religious procession. Across a bare prison yard, Mr Slater, to the execution shed, with your hands strapped behind your back, neat and tidy. You shall be one of that unusual group of men and women, Mr Slater. Those who have heard the priest intone the opening verses of their own burial service – and who have been dead before the end of it.'

Sergeant Lumley frowned at the bare boards of the floor. Mr Swain had gone too far. Slater was terrified now. He was terrified that they would prove him guilty, even though he were innocent. No one would get another word out of the former chief accounting clerk of Cockerell and Boyd.

Half an hour later, Swain and Lumley were alone together.

'Charge him or let him go, Mr Swain,' Lumley said reproachfully, 'that's the law. Once you let him go, that's an end of murder. And what could you hold him for now?'

His feet on the table and his chair tilted at an angle which made its joints creak, Swain tapped a pencil against his teeth.

'Indecent assault,' he said whimsically. 'Threatening behaviour. Clapham Common.'

'And Sally Petts? At least we *saw* him after her.'

Swain looked at his sergeant in amazement.

'It's time you were better acquainted with your beat, Mr Lumley. Sally Petts's mother is Cissie York, the bloater with a pitch by the Waterloo flower-stall. Sally might be sold over and over as a child-virgin to the carriage trade in St John's Wood. I'll be damned, Mr Lumley, before I go into court with such a witness.'

'Murder, then?'

'Murder, Mr Lumley.'

'But you can't charge him. He won't stay.'

'He'll stay until the identification parade over the little matter on Clapham Common, Mr Lumley. He'll stay of his own accord. Otherwise, I've promised him a day in court with Miss Petts. He might go free. He'd *probably* go free. But not before the world had heard about his collection of pictures and the evil little dreams of his notebook. See?'

'Not ethical,' said Lumley, shaking his head.

'But still far the best thing, Mr Lumley. When it comes to watching a young woman die as Nellie Donworth did, I'll save my ethics for someone other than Slater.'

Lumley continued to grumble, as if grasping for truth.

'You can't take law into your own hands, Mr Swain. It won't do at all.'

Swain brightened up at this. He set his chair straight and looked up at the sergeant's plump, worried face.

'But then, Mr Lumley, we are the law. And whatever it is we have to do in order to prevent another girl dying as Nellie Donworth did, we shall do. All right?'

But Sergeant Lumley continued to look plump and worried. Even to please Inspector Swain, he could not bring himself to say that it was 'all right'.

8

'Take your time and think carefully before you say anything.' Swain guided the girl across to the door whose upper half was a glass partition covered by fine lawn. It gave a view of the room beyond without any of those on the far side being able to see Jane or the inspector.

'It was getting dark,' she said doubtfully. 'We'd have left the pond before. Only for Harry's little boat floating away like that.'

Swain took her gently by the arm and drew her to the glass.

'I know,' he said reassuringly, 'but you stood close to him, didn't you?'

'Yes.' Jane put her lightly clenched fist to her mouth uncertainly.

'If you can be sure – quite sure – that one of those men is the person who threatened you on the common, I want to know. But you must be sure. Because they stand there now, it does not mean that any one of them was that man.'

They looked through the glass. Along the far wall of the room, Slater and half a dozen officers of the division stood identically dressed in tall silk hats and dark coats. They looked to Swain like a chorus-line of Stage-Door Johnnies from a music-hall song-and-dance act. In arranging the line-up, he had been scrupulous, not putting Slater in the centre or at either end. The suspect stood, expressionless as the others, second from the left.

Jane looked up and down the line. Her eyes came to rest on Slater.

'That's him,' she said.

'No, it's not!' It was the second girl's voice. 'It's not him.'

Swain spun round, the anger of exasperation swelling in his heart. He had put Lumley under strict orders to keep the other girl in a separate room until Jane delivered her verdict. Now both the girl and the sergeant were watching him.

'Mr Lumley!' But Lumley's plump complacency withstood Swain's anger. 'One at a time! There can be no identification offered in court where there has been a chance of collusion between witnesses.'

Lumley opened his mouth but the second girl intervened again.

''Course it's not him,' she said scornfully. 'The one on the common never had that funny hair showing under his hat brim.'

Swain turned back to look. No one had prevented Slater from edging his hat up a little so that the clown's frizz of hair sprouted out under the brim. It seemed suddenly to be his most characteristic feature. The sinister death's head became a jester's totem. Janey now began to look doubtful.

'Well?' said the second girl impatiently. 'Is it like him?'

'P'r'aps not.'

'*Course* not. Was more like that other with the funny eyes.'

She pointed to Constable Fowler whose lips seemed formed in a slight silent whistling to while away the tedium of his duty.

'He *might*. . .' Then Jane stopped again.

'I'll say!' said the other girl disdainfully. 'Don't you know the one you picked? That's old Slater, the Bedroom Window man. 'f it had been him on the common, I'd soon a-seen!'

Swain decided that the time had come to end the farce of the identification parade. He turned to the two girls with fastidious courtesy.

'Thank you,' he said quietly, 'that will be all. We are both grateful to you for coming here and doing your duty.'

They scrutinised his face for irony or anger. But there was none. The mild horse-face was implacable as a mask in its polite dismissal of them.

'That's all?' There was no mistaking the disappointment as the moment of fame slipped from them.

'Thank you, yes. Be so good as to leave your names and addresses with the sergeant at the desk. The constable at the far door will show you the way. If there should be any further questions in the matter, you may be sure I shall let you know.'

As the two young women turned and walked away with a distinct air of dejection, Swain pitched into Sergeant Lumley.

'What the devil was all that about, Mr Lumley? Who in hell told you to bring a second witness in here while the first was making an identification? You do realise what you've done, I suppose. Do you?'

Lumley looked at him with weary indifference.

'Stopped you making an ass of yourself, Mr Swain.'

Such blatant insubordination made the inspector hesitate. He had an uneasy sense of having walked into a snare.

'There was an identification procedure under way—'

'No there wasn't,' Lumley said. 'I didn't come in here for anything to do with that. You're wanted upstairs. Sir Melville Macnaughten. In the Assistant Commissioner's office. And I'm to tell you that this identification lark is definitely over. Finished. Washed up.'

The snare tightened about him.

'Meaning what?'

'I wasn't told,' Lumley said defensively. 'You still want them standing in line like that, do you? Or shall I go and tell them to dismiss?'

'Get rid of them,' Swain said irritably, 'and put Slater back under lock and key. Watch him and listen to him.'

'If you say so. . .' Lumley began.

'I do!'

'Still, I shouldn't like to be wearing your backside by the time the Assistant Commissioner gets through with you.'

The confident tone of Lumley's impudence depressed Swain's spirits further still as he went up the stairs to the new offices on the upper floors of Norman Shaw's Scotland Yard building. At this level they were more like the drawing rooms of Portman Square or Regent's Park than the distempered offices and interview rooms of the lower floors.

Despite his foreboding, the confrontation with Sir Melville Macnaughten was not as bad as Sergeant Lumley had promised and, presumably, hoped. Swain was shown in by Superintendent Proctor, assistant to the Assistant Commissioner.

With the courtesy shown even to his subordinates, Sir Melville rose from his chair beyond the broad partners' desk which occupied the space before the sunlit window. Clipped grey hair and beard, trim suiting and upright stance suggested the military hero called from the colours to fight a secret battle against London crime.

'Do sit down, Mr Swain. For a moment.'

Swain took the chair indicated and the two men faced each other across the red leather terrain of the desk with its brass lamps and the opaque white china of their shades. Sir Melville returned to the papers he had been reading while Swain stared out at the view through the wide window. Beyond the new imperial grandeur of the Northumberland Avenue hotels the brown river glittered in afternoon light, barges and penny steamers moving upstream against the ebb tide.

At length Sir Melville drew breath deeply and looked up.

'This must stop, Mr Swain.' He laid aside the last sheet of paper.

'Sir.' Swain managed to invest the syllable with an equal weight of enquiry and assent.

Sir Melville looked at him for a moment longer without explaining.

'The Lambeth poisoning, Mr Swain. I shall be obliged to you for following the directions given to you in the manner of investigation. Random arrests of suspects will get us nowhere.'

'Slater wasn't random, sir. He was ripe for plucking.'

Sir Melville sighed again and shook his head.

'He's not the Lambeth poisoner, Mr Swain.'

'I didn't arrest him for poisoning, sir, but for making a public nuisance of himself in the Westminster Bridge Road.'

'Was that why you put him on an identification parade, Mr Swain?'

'He might have been the man who threatened that girl on the common, sir.'

'And he might not, Mr Swain. From now on you will please follow the lines of investigation. Mr Slater is not evidence in the murder. The anonymous letters *are*. They were written by a woman and at least one man with Spanish calligraphy. Of that we can be certain.'

'And Slater? How can we be certain he's not involved?'

'Mr Slater,' said Sir Melville emphatically, 'has a claim to have been elsewhere on the evening that Ellen Donworth was poisoned. He was there from the time before she could have been given poison until an hour or so after she died.'

'I'd think twice before taking his word or that of anyone associated with him,' Swain said moodily.

'And Superintendent Lockyer of P Division?'

Swain said nothing. He knew that some monstrous stroke of ill fortune was about to fall upon him.

'Superintendent Lockyer.' Sir Melville repeated the name in a sympathetic tone. 'He had Mr Slater in his cells at Peckham lock-up all that time. A lady dressing for dinner – and hence undressing after her day's work – reported a man watching bedroom windows. A highly respectable road off Denmark Hill. Mr Slater was apprehended. He refused at first to identify himself. The lady declined to become involved. At last Mr Slater gave his name and address. He was released with a caution. A caution is the most that Lockyer could do under the circumstances. It was early in the morning by then. Mr Slater could not possibly have had anything to do with Ellen

Donworth's death.'

Swain closed his eyes, then opened them slowly as if he hoped that Sir Melville, the office, and the whole malevolent world around him might have disappeared. From time to time a man might have bad luck. Yet a malign thunderbolt of such wicked accuracy was more than he deserved.

Sir Melville stood up and turned to the window, his hands clasped behind his back. He spoke, still facing the glass and the view of the Thames beyond.

'So you see, Mr Swain, it really will not do. Follow the handwriting. It is the only certain path before us.'

'Spaniards and women?' Incredulity amounting almost to distaste coloured the inspector's tone. Sir Melville turned again.

'In two days, Mr Swain, the new issue of *Tit-Bits* will be on sale. On Saturday, there will be the *Police Budget* and half a dozen other picture papers and trash. Those who edit them have been good enough to tell me that at least two of their weeklies will carry stories on the death of Miss Donworth. They propose to tell the nation that the Lambeth poisoner has made fools of the police and got clean away. The final paragraph in *Tit-Bits* informs its readers that there is a senior officer at Scotland Yard who is so stupid that even his own colleagues are beginning to notice. You see, Mr Swain, our masters of the popular press begin to lose patience with us. Believe me, the others will follow.'

'He'll be caught, sir.' Swain stood up, facing Sir Melville across the desk. The Assistant Commissioner shook his head.

'Not if you see a psychopath in every nuisance of Slater's kind. And not if you wait for the murderer of Miss Donworth to strike again. He may not do it again. If he does, he will leave you little evidence of value. I doubt, Mr Swain, that you would recognise him even if you saw him. Am I the Lambeth murderer, Mr Swain?'

'Sir?'

'The psychopath, Mr Swain. The man with the lust for murder and the taste for crowing over his victims. That man, Mr Swain, is a criminal of superior intelligence. Cleverer than you or I, perhaps. His greatest cleverness is in appearing to be a normal and even charming member of society. An agreeable young man or an older man of the most perfect manners. I might be he, Mr Swain. So might you. Not Mr Slater, who goes peeping at bedroom windows.'

'No, sir,' said Swain respectfully. 'And Mr Slater?'

Sir Melville sighed.

'You will release him, Mr Swain. You will apologise for taking up his time and for the misunderstanding. Then you will release him. Let him know that he is likely to be watched. Believe me, he is not your man.'

Swain's mouth moved in the slightest tremor of distaste and disapproval.

'And his notebook, sir? And the photographs?'

'Keep them,' said Sir Melville brightly. 'He will hardly bring a court action for their return. Let him know that we have him in mind. I doubt that he will bother Sally Petts again.'

'And the matter of the common, sir?'

'Had best be dropped, Mr Swain. There is no proof. You found no store of poisoned sweets in Slater's room. We do not know if the sweet given to the girl on the common was deadly or not. Only when she had sucked to its centre would the poison have been released. Follow the evidence, Mr Swain. The blackmail notes.'

'There's been nothing for a couple of weeks, sir. Nothing more to work upon.'

'Except women and Spaniards,' Sir Melville said, indicating that the interview was now at an end.

'Yes, sir.'

Swain turned and went towards the door. He was halfway there when the Assistant Commissioner said, 'Mr Swain! You are a reading man, are you not?'

'I hope I may be, sir.'

'Let me commend to your attention a book by Dr Ellis published a year or two ago. It is called *The Criminal*. There you will find an account of the man you seek. The psychopath. It may persuade you to take the advice I have offered. He could be you or I, Mr Swain, the man who murdered Ellen Donworth. He could be Lord Russell or Mr Smith, for all you could tell by his manner and appearance. He appears to be a killer of a new kind, Mr Swain, an aberration of the present age.'

With that, Sir Melville sat down at the broad desk again and returned to the perusal of his papers.

9

The haggard glare of early gaslight shone in a series of foggy haloes through the light mist of the December afternoon. Swain walked quickly through the area of quiet canals and handsome cream-painted terraces which ran along the streets north of Paddington station. Children, muffled up against the chill dampness, bowled their hoops intently on the long pavements. Nursemaids and the young mothers of Maida Vale or Warwick Avenue in fur-trimmed coats walked slowly behind their scampering children.

Swain was heading for Paddington Green and the secluded row of St Mary's Terrace. He stopped at number nine, went up the steps and rang the bell. The door was answered by a man of thirty whose face had a gravity and distinction more proper to old age. The hair was dark brown, the beard and moustache were reddish gold with a silken and well-kept look. It was a face which women might have adored, in its quiet and courteous wisdom. Why then, Swain wondered, did it make him feel uneasy?

The eyes. Their gaze was steady and not unkind. Yet there was a hint in them, as it seemed to the inspector, of a troubled soul. Having expected that the door might be answered by a maid, Swain was momentarily taken aback. Then he said, 'Dr Ellis?'

The man with the troubled eyes opened the door wider.

'Mr Swain. I am alone at the moment, as you see. I prefer to be so when I am working or when I have visitors on professional matters.'

'Your practice—' Swain stepped into the hall but Ellis interrupted him.

'—I am not in "practice", Mr Swain. A locum occasionally, but not in practice. My time is spent writing and following up certain case histories.'

'Of criminals?' Swain asked politely.

Ellis pushed open the door of his room, its walls lined with bookcases, shelves filled by uniform runs of bindings in olive green and dark blue. At one end there was a collection of paperbound works bearing the imprints of French and German publishers.

'Not criminals, Mr Swain. Please sit down. Tea, I cannot offer you at the moment. No, Mr Swain, I am writing a book on the nationalisation of health, the provision of care for all.'

'Sir Melville Macnaughten . . .'

Ellis sat down and smiled for the first time.

'Sir Melville Macnaughten and I have a mutual friend, hence our acquaintanceship. My opinion was sought in the matter of the Whitechapel murders – the crimes of Jack the Ripper. I fear I was of little practical assistance. I am not even certain that I shall be of help to you. Sir Melville was not very specific in his request to me.'

Swain glanced round the room with its dark paintwork and polished mahogany, the velvet drapery of its green curtains. To have such a study as this, lined with a wealth of learning, remained an unrealised dream of his adolescence and youth.

'If you can,' he said, 'I should like you to describe to me the man I am looking for.'

'Assuming that some or all of the notes are the work of the murderer?'

Swain inclined his head in acknowledgement.

'I shall never find him, Dr Ellis, by arresting every man in London who makes himself a nuisance to women. I must know the sort of man I am looking for. Is he a psychopath? Was the murder of Ellen Donworth a single aberration, or would he kill again?'

Ellis looked up, as if surprised at Swain's innocence.

'This man will kill again if he gets the chance, Mr Swain, you may depend upon it.'

'Without fear or remorse?'

Ellis seemed about to smile and then thought better of it.

'Mr Swain, the character of the psychopath in this instance is very simple. He does not live by your moral laws nor by mine. What is evil to you is desirable to him. You will find that he is a man of intelligence, perhaps of fine intellect. Yet this is combined with a hatred of the world around him and all its moral values.'

'You might say that of some social reformers,' Swain said.

'You might, Mr Swain. But they are motivated by benevolence and rejoice in it. Theirs is a healthy hatred. The psychopath is solitary, vindictive, or egotistical. He lives a life that is parallel to normality but quite unlike it.'

Swain's finger traced a pattern on the leather arm of his chair.

'How is he recognisable among a mass of ordinary men and women?'

'He isn't, as a rule,' Ellis said calmly. 'He is likely to be self-confident and self-righteous. His cleverness is a hair's breadth away from the statesman, the great actor, the famous preacher. Great wits are sure to madness near allied, Mr Swain. On the other hand, the psychopath is not dull-witted or stupid. Your Mr Slater is not he. Nor are those other men who make a nuisance of themselves in that way.'

Swain touched his fingertips together.

'Then how, among men of intelligence and apparent respectability, shall I recognise him?'

'You won't,' said Ellis simply. 'The man who killed Ellen Donworth or wrote those letters can slip on a mask of amiability and moral decency as easily as you or I can put on a shirt or a hat. For that reason, you must expect to find a man who lives two lives. One is likely to be that of the gregarious, responsible citizen. The other is the solitary existence of the moral alchemist in his laboratory of evil. You see?'

Swain nodded.

'Then how can he be caught?'

Ellis folded his hands and the troubled eyes met Swain's with a look of pity.

'I doubt whether he will be caught, Mr Swain. In almost every way his conduct will be unpredictable —'

'— How many women must die before . . .'

But Ellis soothed the outburst with a gesture.

'Wait, Mr Swain. The murders may stop without the man being caught. It happens sometimes that the psychopath is like

101

a dreamer in his evil phases and then wakes as a normal moral being. The Whitechapel murders, the killings of the Ripper, are a case in point. They ended because Druitt in a fit of self-loathing took his own life.'

'And if evil is his waking life?' Swain asked.

'Then you will know soon enough, Mr Swain. Other young women must die as Ellen Donworth did.'

'How many must there be before he reaches his final victim?'

Ellis paused, as if formulating his words with great care.

'The final victim, the one he will prize above all others, is not a woman, Mr Swain. You are that final victim.'

Swain stared at him, the long mild face blank at the casual suggestion.

'Explain that, if you please.'

Ellis shrugged.

'You do not believe – do you, Mr Swain? – that the psychopath is merely a man with a too-strong sexual urge? If that were all, he might satisfy it with such women as Ellen Donworth and never shed a drop of blood. No, Mr Swain. It is power, rather than sex, which drives him. I doubt whether sexual intercourse with these young women would hold the least attraction for him. To have power over them is the lust which intoxicates him. And what greater power is there than that of life and death? What finer and more exquisite pleasure than to doom to death the girl of his choice by the torments of tetanic convulsions? To you or me, Mr Swain, the sight of such a death is both pitiful and repugnant. To the man you seek, it is the supreme excitement.'

Swain concealed his disgust behind the gentle, intelligent mask.

'And I, Dr Ellis? You think I stand in danger of a dose of his strychnine?'

Ellis assumed a polite smile, obligatory and humourless.

'No, Mr Swain. I suspect he has reserved you for a finer fate. The pleasure of power is the pleasure of supremacy – of being the master. As though the killing of the victim were not enough, the psychopath must display his prowess to the world. In our world, Mr Swain, that takes the form of making

102

fools of the police and the authorities. For, after all, in his own moral universe the psychopath is the supreme authority. In the war of each against all, he is to triumph publicly. Power, Mr Swain. Power and triumph. The death of women and the mockery of men. Of such men as yourself. Now, perhaps, you understand?'

'No,' said Swain glumly, 'I don't and can't. It's an alien creed.'

'The very word, Mr Swain. Alien. Clinically, a state of alienation.'

'To want power with such exultation.'

Now it was Ellis himself who showed the animation of triumph.

'And you, Mr Swain? Is there not power of some kind which you covet? Think about it. Power over a woman to make her love you? Power of decision and command in your profession? Such things are very common, Mr Swain, and often benevolent.'

Since the death of Nellie Donworth, Swain had from time to time tried to imagine the feelings of the murderer. Once or twice there had come unbidden to his mind a thought of Rachel Ryland or Edith reduced to such a pitiful extreme as the dying girl in the shabby Duke Street bedroom. Compassion and revulsion were all that he had felt. Now there was talk of power. Power over Edith Ryland? He was not even sure what it would mean. Power over Rachel? True, there were moments of exasperation when he might have wished for it. But its aphrodisiac qualities were lost upon him.

'Benevolent,' he said thoughtfully, sitting in Dr Ellis's leather armchair. 'I can't see it. I don't think my thoughts in terms of power over people.'

'Your actions,' said Ellis gently, 'actions as well as thoughts. And power over yourself. The sense of power that may come from steady work, from the achievement of goals. A disease, perhaps, Mr Swain, but one that is universal.

In the lamplit room with the glow falling on the rich bindings and polished furniture, Swain was possessed by gloom. Ellis had told him all that there was to tell, but it was not what he had wanted to know. He felt like a sick man who had opened a confidential medical report and read there of his own approaching death. It almost seemed that he would have done better never to ask his questions.

In the twilit street, beyond the uncurtained window, a thin Christmas snow had begun to fall. As they parted at the doorway, Dr Ellis allowed his eyes to wander uneasily over Swain's face, as if seeking the symptoms of a spiritual sickness.

'I hope I may have been of assistance,' Ellis said.

'I'm grateful for your time.' Swain held out his hand. 'It was good of you to spare it.'

He could not bring himself to acknowledge the other man's help, knowing that Ellis's explanations had left him just where he was before receiving them.

By this time of the afternoon, the streets with their white scattering of snow were filled by men in heavy coats and women with their fur collars turned up. There was something indefinably sensual, Swain thought, about the dark fur resting against the delicate cheek of the women he passed. That it could inspire such hatred or vindictiveness in the man who killed Nellie Donworth was something beyond his comprehension. He knew that passions of the kind existed and he strove to understand them. Lost in thoughts of this, he went down into Warwick Avenue and stood braced against the cold while he waited for the horse-bus which would take him to Trafalgar Square.

At seven o'clock he stepped off the bus at Morley's Hotel and began to walk down Northumberland Avenue. The pseudo-classical grandeur of its new buildings in snow and lamplight gave the thoroughfare a look of Paris in the days of the Second Empire. Swain breathed the sharp winter air and put psychopaths from his mind.

At that moment he noticed the crowd which had gathered outside the glass doors of the Metropole Hotel. There was a quite unusual amount of activity, portmanteaus and hat-boxes on the pavement, a line of hansom cabs stretching almost to the Embankment.

Other men and women, not included among the departing guests, had pressed round a notice which someone had fly-posted on the wall by the hotel doors. Swain could just make out the bold black type which headed the bill.

TO THE GUESTS OF THE METROPOLE HOTEL
ELLEN DONWORTH'S DEATH

Copies of the notice were being handed about the crowd and several, which had been discarded, were blowing about the damp pavement. Swain snatched one up and read it.

> Ladies and Gentlemen,
> I hereby notify you that the person who poisoned Ellen Donworth on the 13th of October last is today in the employ of the kitchen of the Metropole Hotel. I beg you to believe that your lives are in peril as long as you remain in this hotel.
> Yours respectfully,
> W.H. Murray,
> Det. Superintendent,
> New Scotland Yard.

Pushing his way through the crowd, Swain reached the broad wooden bar of the reception counter. He recognised Mr Symonds, the assistant manager.

'Mr Symonds!' Swain brandished the damp and foot-muddied bill. 'What the devil is this?'

Symonds's face was a study in anger and despair.

'That, Mr Swain,' he said, 'is for you to find out.'

'There's no one called Murray at Scotland Yard. Superintendent or otherwise.'

Symonds bit his lip.

'For that matter, Mr Swain, there's no poisoner in the hotel kitchen. There are eight people working there. I've checked them all. They were working here on the night of 13 October from four in the afternoon until eleven. Saturday is a busy turn. None of them had time to go poisoning girls in Lambeth.'

'Then who had this printed?'

'I don't *know*, Mr Swain!' Symonds patted the desk in his agitation. 'I do not *know*.'

By now the lobby was crowded. The guests were leaving with restraint and dignity. But they were leaving none the less, in couples and family groups. The lobby with its pillars faced by mirror-glass, its chandeliers and grained walnut panelling, was crowded by the men and women with their luggage. The blue-uniformed porters of the Metropole in their gold-braided caps struggled to keep order. Swain looked on the scene in despair. True or not, the thought of the Lambeth poisoner stirring strychnine into the consommé was enough to get the English bourgeoisie moving.

He turned to Symonds again.

'There's no printer's name on the bill. That makes it illegal for a start.'

Symonds looked at him hopelessly.

'Mr Swain, he'd hardly slander Scotland Yard and put his name to it! Would he?'

'He might have had it done abroad,' said Swain, looking at the printed notice again. 'It might even have been done by sight. A printer who didn't understand English and had no idea what he was setting up in type. Paid to do it by someone who must have had a grudge against the Metropole Hotel.'

He glanced at Symonds with a premonition of the assistant manager's reply.

'No, Mr Swain. Someone who had a grudge against Scotland Yard. Much more likely.'

A suitcase slipped from a pile and clattered to the floor just behind Swain as he stood at the counter. The jabber of departing guests and the shouts of porters made a pande-monium of the marble-paved lobby. The mirror-glass on the pillars and the framed panels of it upon the walls reflected and amplified the heaving and surging of the crowd.

'Leave this to me,' Swain said abruptly to Symonds, 'I'll get to the bottom of it!'

He walked through Whitehall Place, towards the red and white striped brickwork of lately built headquarters for the Metropolitan Police. Striding down the corridor to his office, past the sergeants' room, he shouted for Lumley. When Lumley appeared he was holding an unopened envelope.

'This come for you,' he said apprehensively, 'afternoon

post. Sent from Charing Cross office yesterday evening.'

'Don't bother,' said Swain bitterly, holding up the damp and muddied notice from the Metropole. 'I've got one already.'

But he took the envelope, laid it carefully on his desk and slit it open down one side. As he expected, there was only a single sheet of paper inside.

Swain was so certain it was a copy of the Metropole Hotel notice that his first reaction on seeing the message was one of incomprehension. It was printed in crude capitals, as his name and address on the envelope had been.

HELLO! HELLO!

DING! DONG! BELL!
MATILDA'S GONE TO HELL!
WHO DID HER IN?
BETTER ASK NELLIE DONWORTH!

GOODBYE!

'Mr Lumley!' Swain threw open the door and found the sergeant standing, plump and meditative, in the corridor. 'First thing tomorrow, I want questions asked down every street off the Waterloo Road and Westminster Bridge Road – and Lambeth Road for good measure. I want anyone who knows Matilda Clover. Anyone who *is* Matilda Clover. Anyone who's *heard* of Matilda Clover. And I'll want every case of a suspicious death within the Metropolitan area on my desk, if you please.'

Sergeant Lumley hung his head a little, resentful and yet embarrassed.

'The Assistant Commissioner had one of those messages, Mr Swain. There's not to be any time spent on Matilda Clover. It could be a name just invented. In that case, we'd have the whole division out looking every time this man made up a new name. He could tie us in knots. Perhaps Nellie Donworth used the name sometimes. She'd got half a dozen different ones. Sir Melville says we can't risk a wild-goose chase with a real girl dead. You must admit, Mr Swain, he's got reason on his side.'

'Reason?'

Alfred Swain rarely lost his temper and felt acutely foolish on the occasions when he did so. But this afternoon had produced a bewildering answer from Dr Havelock Ellis, a public taunting at the Metropole Hotel, a private sneer in the letter addressed to him, and now a reprimand from Sir Melville delivered by Sergeant Lumley.

'Yes,' said Lumley, 'reason. Sense. It's sense, isn't it?'

'I doubt it,' said Swain, his eyes glittering with rage, 'I very much doubt it. Mark my words, Mr Lumley. Before this is over, someone is going to be very sorry for what has happened this afternoon. Very sorry indeed!'

'For what, Mr Swain?'

But in his ill-temper, Swain could not trust himself to dispel the ambiguity. He was almost trembling with anger and vexation as he went back into his room and shut the door upon the world.

3
A Nasty Business

10

Sharp Christmas weather was followed almost at once by signs of an abnormally early spring, as if winter had come and gone in a few weeks. On a January evening Alfred Swain kept his promise to Rachel Ryland and her mother of a visit to the 'ballet' at the Canterbury Music Hall in Westminster Bridge Road. It was in part to make amends for his treatment of the girl and in part a reward for her information about the encounter on Clapham Common. Edith Ryland had hesitated at first, seeing no need to accompany her daughter and lodger as a chaperone. Then, to Swain's relief, she accepted the invitation.

The old pillared interior of the Canterbury had been remodelled so that it resembled a domed oriental palace, gold-painted stucco mouldings adorning the boxes and gallery. When the house lights were reduced to glimmering shards of glass along the walls, there was a new warmth and conviviality to the wide auditorium.

Swain sat with his two guests, politely attentive near the rear of the stalls. On the stage, the 'Fish-Ballet' was performed behind a thin gauze curtain by ladies in silver fleshings which fitted tight as their own skins. The smart little hats covered by scales and the skittish little fins which hung from the back of their waists merely added to the suggestiveness of their costumes. With waists narrow and haunches fully rounded, the girls skipped and pranced beyond the aqueous shimmer of gauze in the brilliance of limelight. Each bosom filled out with deep breaths of exertion, the thinly clad thighs shimmered perceptibly with the impact of the jumping, and their hips curved rhythmically and as visibly as if they had been naked.

Inspector Swain, susceptible to their desirability, wondered how it was that so much could be offered without a blush under the pretext of 'ballet'.

While his eyes followed the swooping and twirling of the six mermaids on the stage, he heard behind him the chatter and laughter of the Long Bar which overlooked the street. The rattle of glasses was accompanied by a tantalising smell of oysters served with brown bread and butter at a shilling a plate.

The Long Bar was a world apart from the vast and gilded auditorium. It was the meeting place of clerks masquerading as top-hatted swells and the more discreetly painted girls of the neighbourhood who offered themselves for hire in demure bonnets and cloaks. These Lambeth girls and their admirers made their bargains over oysters with hock or champagne at the round marble tables on wrought-iron stands. Then the couples would return to the run-down apartments of Orient Buildings or some other tenement in the little streets which ran off the Lambeth Road.

The trade of the Long Bar never spilt over into the auditorium, crowded with family parties and the industrious tradesmen of the district.

As the fish-ballet ended, the main curtain came down to a storm of applause, leaving the apron stage clear, while the scene was changed, for the comic singer with his ragged paint-spattered clothes and his broad paintbrush.

> Slap-dab, slap-dab,
> Up and down the brickwork,
> Slap-dab all day long . . .

Swain touched Rachel's arm and as the two women looked at him in the golden dusk of the auditorium he formed the word 'Sherbet!' in exaggerated dumb-show. Pushing his way past the other seats he walked out slowly to the Long Bar and stepped into the brilliant contrast of chandeliers shining on white pillars and mirror-glass. The room was crowded by men standing with their girls, men guffawing together in self-conscious jollity, the couples sitting at the tables and the girls discreetly for hire who loitered close to the bar itself.

None of them approached Swain. Perhaps they saw him for what he was. In any case he belonged to the family world of

112

the ballet and the comic song. None of the girls in the Long Bar would risk poaching on such territory and causing a scene.

Swain pushed his way politely through the crowd to the bar with its mahogany panels and rows of coloured bottles under a dado of white stucco, darkened by tobacco smoke like a brown tooth. In the babble of voices behind him he picked out Irish and even French among the familiar Lambeth. He watched the blonde and bunned girl at the bar put three glasses of sherbet and a gin with warm water on the little tray. Then, turning round, he made his way carefully across to the side of the room. A woman of sixty with a lively voice and dead eyes stood on her own, watching the others. Her ginger hair was thin from being repeatedly coloured and frizzed. As the light fell on her from one side Swain saw the pallor of her bald scalp through the thin puffed-out hair. The paint on her face combined with this to give her the look of a circus clown. He stood in front of her and indicated the gin and warm water on the tray.

'Take it, Polly Peach,' he said gently, 'it's for you.'

She looked at him, only her mouth moving in a quick fat-lipped smile.

'Long time since you treated me, Mr Swain.'

'Long time since I wanted anything from you, Polly.'

The dead eyes watched him and the paint on her lips cracked a little as she grinned. Polly Peach took the warm glass.

'It'd be a pleasure, Mr Swain. Any time.'

Swain tried not to shudder at her innuendo.

'How's life treating you, Poll?'

'Handsome, Mr Swain.' There was an edge to her brag which betrayed the self-confident lie. 'There's a lot of girls here got reason to thank me.'

'Is there really?'

She sipped the warm gin, pulled a face of surprised approval and then thrust herself close to him. Swain stood his ground.

'When they're finished here, they all come to me. The dancers and that. A girl may be past it for the ballet, still she can turn a bob or two my way. I've had Sara the Kicker and

113

Wiry Beth, both in the Canterbury ballet till last summer. If ever you was in need, Mr Swain ... A girl of that kind that's bran' new to the business ... Untouched ... You know. I don't say you *are*, Mr Swain, but if ever you *was* ...'

'I'll bear it in mind, Polly.'

'I like to help out, Mr Swain, you know that. I must make money same as you or anyone else. Still I like to give a helping hand.'

'I'm sure I don't know how we should manage without you, Miss Peach.'

'Go on, Mr Swain! You're laughing at me. Ain't you?'

She snuggled closer in order to give him a light, familiar nudge.

'I want introductions, Polly. To two girls. I shan't promise to make you rich but you won't be the poorer if I find them.'

Polly Peach drew back and her lips formed a sour pout.

'Once a jack, always a jack,' she said gloomily. 'I can't be a party to having girls run in, Mr Swain. You know that. Even if I wanted to. I'd only be on the wrong end of a strap or a hand – worse still an Italian blade – from Flash Fred or one of the men.'

Swain sighed.

'Listen, Poll. There's nothing against these two. Nothing. I shan't so much as feel a collar. But if I don't find them and they should go the same way as Nellie Donworth ...'

He left the rest unspoken. Polly Peach let the gin grow cold in her plump paw. The name of the dead girl stirred the dull eyes at last with slow apprehension.

'I don't know, Mr Swain. I don't *know*! You only seen the nice side of Fred Linnell and his sort. He blacked my eye once, almost for nothing. Easy as saying good morning.'

'Matilda Clover,' Swain said, 'and Louisa Harris.'

'Again?'

'Matilda Clover and Louisa Harris. Lou Harris.'

Polly Peach drew a deep breath and relaxed.

'That's easy, Mr Swain. Never heard of either.'

'And if they worked this manor, you would hear of them, Polly, wouldn't you?'

'I'd hear of them, Mr Swain.'

'Then don't mess me about, Miss Peach. Especially not when you've been treated to gin and water. I want to meet those two girls.'

As her anxiety increased, the old bawd's voice got quieter.

'Leave it out, Mr Swain! Please! I wouldn't cross you just for that. If I knew the names, wouldn't I say so? God's honour, I never heard of either. Not in any house here nor in Southwark. Nor anywhere else. Not now, not anywhen.'

Swain thought for a moment, then he assumed the tone of a reasonable man offering a fair bargain.

'I tell you what, Polly Peach. If you're telling me the truth, there's an end of it. However, if I should find these two have ever so much as trod an inch of this parish, it will be another matter. Mr Lumley and Constable Dawkins shall take root outside the doors of your houses and we'll find men for Flash Fred Linnell too. They'll have a friendly word with any gentleman that thinks of going in with one of the girls. See? And I shall be obliged to let Flash Freddie know the cause of all the aggravation he's suffering. I don't even like to think of what he might do to you, Polly. Really I don't.'

She was angry now, as well as frightened.

'You're cruel, Mr Swain . . .'

'I'm known for it, Miss Peach.'

'And I never heard of them! Either of them! If I do, I'll tell you straight away. I'll even ask round the village for you. I could put it to Flash Fred himself – subtle, like.'

'Subtle.' Swain looked thoughtfully at the bawd, the powder dry as brick-dust on her face, except where it was streaked by perspiration. 'Yes, Miss Peach, I should try being subtle if I was you. I'll be asking Flash Fred too. Only perhaps I shan't be quite as subtle. Put it this way. If I find that you're doing as told and acting helpful in the matter, then you and your shabby little trade will be none of my business. But if I should discover otherwise, then you and Freddie Linnell can look forward to more grief than half a dozen funerals. All right?'

He watched the resentment sparkle and die. Polly Peach nodded and the inspector turned away. As he reached the door with his tray of sherbet, he glanced back at her. The eyes

115

were dead as stone again but, as the evening trade picked up, her mouth cracked open in a welcoming smile.

The comic singer had gone through his repertoire, had been encored and now brought the audience roaring into the chorus.

> Slap-dab-slap with the whitewash brush,
> Talk about a fancy ball!
> I put more whitewash on my old girl
> Than I did upon the garden wall!

Swain handed the glasses of sherbet to the two women.

In the din of the chorus, Rachel had to put her lips so close that they touched his ear and the softness of her bobbed red hair touched his cheek.

'What kept you?' she shouted.

He turned his head to reply.

'Nothing to speak of!'

Without intending to, he allowed his lips to prolong their contact with the girl's ear in the ambiguous touch which was hardly distinguishable from a kiss. But when he glanced sidelong at her, Rachel was staring at the military ballet of 'soldier girls' on the stage, as if she had noticed nothing whatever.

11

On the following morning it was Swain's turn to be on weekend call as duty inspector. Taking his copy of Tait's *Recent Advances in Physical Science* from the drawer of his little desk, he glanced briefly towards the roofs of Northumberland Avenue and the Embankment. A thin drizzle had just stopped and the pale sunlight of the early year shone on bare branches which glittered like the tinsel of the ballet with fresh droplets.

He opened the book and began to read. After half an hour there was a knock at the door. It was Lumley.

116

'There's post, Mr Swain,' he said holding out an envelope.

Swain looked at it and saw the carefully printed capitals in which the last scornful message had been written.

'Wait,' he said to Lumley. Then while the sergeant watched uneasily, Swain slit open the envelope and drew out a slip of paper. Like the message received on the day of the Metropole Hotel hoax, it took the form of a nursery rhyme.

> EMMA AND ALICE WENT ON THE SPREE,
> DRINKING GIN AND PORTER,
> EACH LAY DOWN WITHOUT HER GOWN
> FOR A MERRY LITTLE SLAUGHTER.

Swain stood up, his lips tight and face suddenly white with the anger of shock.

'I want every report, Mr Lumley, every report of murder and unnatural or suspicious death in the counties and boroughs for the past six weeks. Since the last note. I want wires to every police station, each division, to see if there's been a report since yesterday. Anything that has Emma or Alice associated with it. And any death, whatever the name, which might involve our man.'

Alone again, Swain stared from the little window. The sun had gone and the trees were dark as the props of an unlit stage. Emma and Alice. The names were common enough to belong to thousands of girls in the London area. Like Matilda Clover or Lou Harris they might very easily be the names under which the girls worked and not those they were baptised with.

Swain turned suddenly from the window and went out into the corridor. He found Lumley uncorking the speaking tube which linked the department to the criminal records office in the basement.

'Another thing, Mr Lumley. I want details of any prostitute known to the police who has the name of Emma or Alice.'

'That's half the pavement artists in town!' Lumley said helplessly.

'And I want to know which of them is dead!'

The sergeant turned a plump, begrudging face.

'Play fair, Mr S. They'll only have one man on duty down the records office today. He'll never have time . . .'

117

'Just get on with it, will you?'

As soon as he saw the reproach in Lumley's small dark eyes, Swain felt ashamed of himself. His show of ill-temper was not characteristic of him. He was like an actor imitating the manner of his more boorish colleagues.

'Just do it, Mr Lumley,' he said quietly, 'please.'

The answer came far more quickly than he had expected. For six weeks past, the extent of the search, there had been no suspicious or unnatural death involving either an Alice or an Emma. Of prostitutes known to the police in the Metropolitan district, eighty-six bore the name Emma and one hundred and three were called Alice.

Swain took his pen and began making notes on a sheet of paper, as if he had been doing simple arithmetic.

'It's different this time, Mr Lumley,' he said, scratching at the official stationery.

'Oh, yes?' The sergeant's jaws moved in plump, ruminating scepticism. 'How's that, then?'

Swain looked up, astonished that Lumley could not see it.

'They're still alive. Nellie Donworth was dead when he wrote his blackmail notes – and when he wrote to us. Emma and Alice are still alive. They *must* be. We've no record to tell us the contrary.'

'Not easy to warn 'em on a Saturday,' Lumley said. 'Eighty-six of one, and a hundred and three of the other. And the section being only on call.'

'It's not possible.' Swain folded the paper and put it in his pocket. 'We wouldn't know where to find them. Ten to one they've changed addresses, even if only to stay one step ahead of us. For all we know they're using different names as well.'

'Doesn't leave much.'

Swain stood up and straightened his tie.

'I'm going to ask for every man the commissioner's office can let us have. I'll assume that he's most likely to kill a prostitute in the Lambeth district again. For the next few days, I shall ask for uniformed patrols that will either prevent murder or catch him if he tries it.'

They were in the corridor.

'And after a few days?' Lumley asked.

'It won't matter.' Swain dusted down his jacket with his hands and pulled at his cuffs. 'By the time he wrote this note, the preparations were made. He's on his way, Mr Lumley. On his way to commit murder now. By every law of logic he *must* be. . . .'

12

That Saturday evening, in the early lamplight, Swain assembled the officers of his patrol at the southern end of Lambeth Bridge. In a single span the graceful ironwork suspension with its ornamental lights linked the Albert Embankment and the Victoria Tower Gardens adjoining the Houses of Parliament, the gothic towers and terraces in weekend darkness.

Swain stood where the main road on his own side divided from Lambeth Palace Road, running between St Thomas's Hospital and the leaded mediaeval windows of the Archbishop's residence. With Lumley in plain clothes, there were two uniformed sergeants and twelve constables. Sir Melville Macnaughten, summoned from lunch at an Alton Towers house-party with Lord Shrewsbury, had given his authorisation by wire. Three sergeants and twelve constables was a smaller patrol than Swain would have liked, but larger than he had expected.

'Pay attention, please,' he said, like a teacher with his class. As they shuffled into silence the clock on the square tower of St Mary's Church struck seven.

He had told them the reason for the patrol beforehand. Now only the details needed to be rehearsed.

'Patrol singly,' Swain said, standing on a slight rise in the pavement to address them. 'We're too short-handed to double up. The patrol area is a triangle, bounded by the river on the north and by Lambeth Road and Blackfriars Road on either side until they converge at the southern end in St George's Circus. I want three men in each of those two roads, three more in Waterloo Road and Westminster Bridge Road which lie more or less parallel between them. Concentrate on those four arteries from the river bridges down to their meeting at St George's Circus. Each man will patrol down every side street he comes to until it joins the next main artery. Then he will patrol back down the side street to his main beat. Each man should complete one beat every hour. By patrolling singly, there will be a police officer at any given point at intervals of about twenty minutes. Sergeant Booth will keep a general surveillance on the passenger entrance of Waterloo Station. Sergeant Bradley will cover the Albert Embankment promenade.'

There was a muffled hoot of derision at the easier beats which the two sergeants had drawn.

'Any questions?'

'Yes.' Swain recognised the tall ginger-haired figure of Constable Moat. 'How long does this beat go on for, Mr Swain?'

'Probably until the small hours of the morning,' Swain said firmly, 'possibly all night. Unless something happens before that.'

'What's the arrangements for breaks, Mr Swain? Is there to be tea or anything?'

'I shouldn't think so.' Swain felt an unworthy satisfaction in dismissing the protest. 'I'll see what can be done.'

The patrol began to shift and murmur. Alfred Swain was at his best when working alone or with Lumley. He was not, by nature, a commander of men.

'Shut up and listen!' The shifting and murmuring stopped. 'You've been told what to look for. Every one of you has a whistle and a rattle. If you get into trouble in the normal manner and need help, spring the rattle. Don't use the whistle. If you find evidence of the man we're looking for, then use the whistle. Short blasts repeated. One long blast to cancel the signal. Don't get it wrong or you'll mess up the patrol and the whole exercise. Has everyone got that?'

It seemed that they had. Swain allowed Lumley to despatch patrols, three men at a time, to their destinations. They were under orders to look for assaults, in any form, upon the street women of Lambeth and Southwark. Where the hand of

120

'A. O'Brien' or 'H.M. Bayne' or 'W.H. Murray' appeared, they were to raise the alarm at once and try to prevent the escape of any man who resembled 'Fred'.

'He won't get far if he uses the same poison,' Swain had told them in the parade room that afternoon. 'Strychnine begins to work very fast. The pain begins within a few minutes. You might catch him almost as soon as it's done, if the victim cries out straight away.'

To warn every Emma or Alice in the business had proved impossible. All the same, the patrolling constables were under orders to alert the street girls wherever possible. Any man offering them something 'special' to eat or drink as an aphrodisiac was to be kept dangling while the girl tried to get a message by one of her companions to an officer of the patrol.

'If there's anything else we could a-done,' Lumley said confidently, 'I'd like to know what it is.'

The two men walked through the inadequate lamplight of Lambeth Palace Road towards Westminster Bridge.

'Don't be a fool,' said Swain softly, 'we've done almost nothing. All the advantages are with him, whoever he is. While we're waiting for him to poison an Emma and an Alice in Lambeth, he might have slit the throats of two girls of the same name in Whitechapel or Camden Town. Even if he comes this way and we catch him, they'll be dead first.'

As it happened, Swain retained a private hope that this might be prevented, if only by frightening off 'A. O'Brien' by the sight of uniformed police patrols. That, however, would merely postpone and not prevent the horror which was promised.

At the far end of Lambeth Palace Road, by the last of the Georgian terraces, they came out at Westminster Bridge Road. The little shops were still open for the Saturday night trade, though the traffic in the early evening was no more than a few hansom cabs and horse-buses. A stillness over the neat rows of the terraces was broken only by the thunder and the fiery cloud of express trains crossing the iron bridges on their approach to Waterloo.

By contrast with the shrill clamour of the street markets in the Waterloo Road, it seemed that Westminster Bridge Road was a haven of calm. At its northern end, by the iron bridges, the commercial buildings of the stone works and the drainpipe manufacturer, the Lion brewery and the Lambeth water supply, were unlit and silent. Swain heard the echo of his own heels on the pavement.

'Listen,' he said to Lumley quietly, 'just walk and listen.'

They walked and listened the length of Westminster Bridge Road. Like the patron of a Hoxton melodrama, Swain was waiting for the inevitable blast of the whistle or the wild anguish of a scream. His heart seemed to leap to his throat at a demonic shriek behind him, but it was only the warning of the last express from Waterloo to Portsmouth, clearing the line ahead.

The tranquillity of St George's Circus, the new Catholic cathedral and the old pillared elegance of the Bedlam lunatic asylum with its lawns and railings belonged to a different order of existence. With the anger of one who has been made a fool of and does not know where to fix his revenge, Swain turned and began to walk back up the length of Westminster Bridge Road.

''Course,' said Sergeant Lumley, trying to offer consolation, 'it might not happen. It doesn't *have* to.'

'Shut up and listen.'

'It might *not*, Mr Swain.'

'Shut *up*!'

They walked slowly onwards, Lumley now a plump and reproachful presence beside his commander. A whistle blasted the quiet darkness as they turned into the clamorous side street of the Lower Marsh. This time it was blown by human breath but there was no repetition. To Swain's exasperation, the stillness of the evening was carrying the sounds of Waterloo station into the streets, including the guard's whistle as the trains pulled out.

The Lower Marsh was an intersection of two-storey tumbledown buildings, with archways leading to small and foul-smelling courtyards. Children played noisily, sailing paper boats in open drains, the day's washing swaying and flapping on the lines stretched high above. Most of the whitewashed houses were patched by damp, the walls bulging

122

here and there as if doomed by a diseased and monstrous growth. A few young women, in gowns with muddied hems and bonnets whose feathers had been freshly coloured, stood in the lighted doorways. At a little distance from each, her keeper in moleskin breeches and jacket leant against the house wall, sucking at a clay pipe or watching the passers-by.

Swain saw one of his uniformed constables coming towards them. The man saluted.

'Nothing to report?'

'Nothing yet, sir. Quieter than usual for Saturday. Sight of all these uniforms, I suppose.'

'No suspects?'

'I counted forty-three tall gentlemen in silk hats and with moustaches,' the constable said. 'Didn't ask 'em if they was called Fred. They might all have been.'

'All right,' said Swain irritably, 'carry on.'

The constable saluted and walked away towards Westminster Bridge Road. At Waterloo Station, Sergeant Booth had nothing to report but much to request.

'With respect, Mr Swain, we can't ask 'em to keep patrolling until after midnight without a break. If one isn't arranged, they'll take it anyway. Somewhere out of sight. Much better we should know what's what.'

Swain took out his watch. It was half-past eight and the full din of the street market now filled the Waterloo Road as it had done on the night of Nellie Donworth's murder.

'Very well, Mr Booth. Starting at half-past nine, take one man in three off duty for half an hour, in rotation. If we're still patrolling at midnight, give them another break. Refreshment to be had from the coffee stall only. All right?'

'Sir!' said Sergeant Booth gratefully.

Swain gave his attention to the Waterloo Road. Among the stalls, the proprietor of the Punch and Judy show in Trinity Square had set up an entertainment of a quite different kind. The lamps flared on a board above the entrance to the booth, advertising 'Parisiana – Entrance One Shilling'. Outside a girl in a short black corset, boots and helmet, adorned by tassels, plumes and peacock-feather tail, stood shivering and glum to advertise the erotic delights of the peep-show. Swain looked at the men waiting to hand their shillings to the man at the makeshift pay-box. He counted those with tall silk hats and moustaches. After sixteen, he gave up counting and turned to Sergeant Lumley.

'See that Sergeant Bradley gets the details of refreshment breaks for the men, Mr Lumley. Quick as you can. Then meet me back here. This very spot.'

Before Lumley could reply, a whistle-blast burst from the darkness somewhere in the immediate neighbourhood. Swain and Lumley paused, expecting an innocent explanation or the longer sound to indicate a false alarm.

But the blast came again, short and shrill, repeated and repeated with raucous urgency. It was like the desperate pumping of blood in a dying body, the harsh imploring breath.

'Over there, Mr Lumley!'

Swain dodged between the traffic of the Waterloo Road, seeing the astonished faces of the stall-holders and their customers. Lumley and Booth followed him. There was a uniformed constable crossing higher up, near Waterloo Bridge, and another coming up from St George's Circus.

'Stamford Street!' Swain yelled the words with all the breath he could spare and plunged into the noise and crowds of the narrower street which joined the Waterloo and the Blackfriars Roads.

There were five of them now: Swain, Lumley, Booth and the two uniformed constables. Ahead of them about halfway down the length of Stamford Street was a long block of houses, the better class of the Southwark brothels, with wrought-iron balcony-ledges at the first floor and iron railings to enclose their basement areas. Drab and solid in appearance, they still retained a hint of regency aspirations in their fanlights and doorways. Outside one of these doorways, Swain saw the helmeted figure of the constable with the whistle.

For the first time since the horror of Nellie Donworth's murder, he knew that the killer was within his grasp. If the strychnine had only just begun to work, it was impossible that the man who administered it could have got clear of the house

124

and the long street before Swain and the others sealed it off.

'Mr Lumley!' Almost winded, he turned and bawled at the sergeant just behind him. 'Into the lane! Round the back! Stop anyone getting out that way! I think we've got him!'

He came up, gasping, to the constable with the whistle.

'You can stop blowing that thing now. We've got enough men to be going on with. Now. Sharp! What's happened?'

'Two girls in convulsions, sir,' said the uniformed man quietly. 'Real bad. Started at the identical time.'

'How long ago?'

'Not ten minutes, sir. I was right by when I was called in.'

'He *must* still be here!' Swain turned to the next man, 'Fast as you can. Lambeth police station. Every man they've got in L Division. Seal off Stamford Street and approaches. Let no one out. Probably a man with a tall silk hat and moustache. But it could be *anyone*. Commandeer the first hansom you see.'

He watched the constable break into a run down the length of Stamford Street, the pavement echoing to his boots.

'Mr Booth! One constable on either end of Stamford Street. No one goes past. He can't have got by us as we were coming in and if he went the Blackfriars way we'd probably have seen him ahead of us. Send your other man to watch the river bank. Mr Lumley's round the back of the house, watching the lane. We can hold our man if he's here. When the Lambeth officers get here, I'll have every inch searched.'

It amazed even Swain to think that, against all the odds, he had run to earth the man whom the gutter press was beginning to call 'The Ripper's Apprentice'. The door of the house was open but he slammed the knocker hard as he went in.

Polly Peach appeared at the foot of the stairs, her dry-powdered face assuming an easy grief. Swain stopped, having forgotten in the confusion that this, too, was one of Flash Fred Linnell's houses.

'Mr Swain!' For a moment he thought the old bawd was going to embrace him and weep on his shoulder.

'Where is he!'

The walls rang with his shout.

'Who, Mr Swain?'

'The man who was with your two girls!'

''E never was, Mr Swain. Not here. He never was here with 'em. They won't die, Mr Swain, will they? They won't ...'

'Mess me about, Polly Peach, and I will see you done for accessory to murder. You'll hang as surely as the man who mixes the poison.'

Shaking with anger himself, he felt the old woman tremble in her fear. Polly Peach began to weep, the tears washing their paths through the paint and powder.

'They was took bad about twenty minutes after they come home, Mr Swain. Honest! He was to have followed them. He give 'em a sov to pledge it. On'y he never come, Mr Swain. God's honour that's the truth!'

'How long had they left him?'

Polly Peach gave a little preliminary whimper to show her sincerity.

''Bout half an hour, Mr Swain. They met him in the promenade of the Oxford, made their arrangements, and then come back here first in a 'ansom.'

For the first time, Swain felt the gulf of uncertainty open beneath him.

'That's almost an *hour*! Half an hour to get back here and then twenty minutes before the convulsions!'

When Polly Peach replied there was the first trace of anger in her squealing sincerity.

'It's *true*, Mr Swain. 's what they said. They couldn't have come back much quicker. They've suffered harm from what he gave them there. I can't tell you what.'

'Strychnine operates in a few minutes,' Swain said savagely. 'Even on a full stomach it doesn't take an hour – nor half an hour.'

'I don't *know*, Mr Swain. They said he gave 'em pills. Tall man in a silk hat and moustache.'

'Pills?'

'Long oval things, Mr Swain.'

At last Alfred Swain understood. He had lost the battle, and representing the forces of law and order, he had been made a laughing-stock. The entire Lambeth constabulary was about to arrive and witness the extent of his humiliation.

'Capsules,' he said simply, 'capsules, Polly Peach.'

'Mr Swain?'

'The pills, Polly Peach. Hollow inside. You fill them with medicine, close them up and swallow them. It saves unpleasant tastes. By the time the capsule dissolved and let the poison out it might take half an hour to work on a full stomach.'

'Oh, Mr Swain!'

Her lower lip quivered and he thought, flinching from her, that the old bawd was about to cling to him for consolation in her bereavement. From the rooms above, Swain heard human cries of a kind which made his spine tingle with cold. He turned to the open street door and called Sergeant Booth.

'Quick as you can, Mr Booth! A doctor from St Thomas's or anywhere else. We think it's strychnine. He'll need chloroform or morphia. And the sooner he can get a growler here to move them into hospital, the better.'

Booth turned and set off down the street towards Lambeth police office and the nearest telegraph. Swain turned to the constable who had been nearby when the cries began.

'Anything,' he said, 'anything at all that was said about the man who did this to them! They must have said something to you.'

The young man looked self-conscious.

'Not really, sir . . .'

'Think!' said Swain ungratefully.

'They wasn't in much of a state to . . .'

'Anything at all!'

'He had a silk hat, black clothes, and he was called Fred.'

'What else?'

The young man blushed a little.

'Bald head and moustache, one of 'em said, sir.'

'Yes?'

'The other said he had dark hair and was clean-shaven . . . The poor creatures was hardly in a state to remember much. . .'

Swain stared at the young constable, controlling his bitter frustration with difficulty. His mind was possessed by the single thought that he had failed the two girls who now lay in their death agonies in the upper rooms of the shabby Stamford Street house. He felt that he owed them his presence now, as if to make amends for what had happened. At the same time he dreaded the scene which would be enacted in the next hour or so.

Conscience and indecision plagued him for a moment as he stood on the ill-lit pavement. Having made up his mind to go back into the house, he felt an unworthy sense of relief as a voice shouted from the darkness. It came from the direction of Waterloo.

'We got 'im, Mr Swain! I think we got 'im!'

Swain turned to the young constable, whose blush of self-consciousness had faded to a sick pallor.

'No one is to enter or leave this house, except a police officer or a doctor. No one. Anyone not in uniform is to show identification. All right?'

'Sir,' said the young man sharply.

Swain turned into the faint drizzle and the darkness, prepared to meet the Lambeth poisoner at last.

Just short of the Waterloo Road with the harsh white gaslight of its stalls and booths, a group of twenty or thirty men and women had pressed excitedly round a pavement quarrel. Swain pushed his way through and saw a figure in dark clothes and silk hat removed, standing between Lumley and a constable. It was Henry Slater, the Bedroom Window Watcher.

'He was doing a bunk along the back lane,' Lumley said confidently. 'Someone after him as well. Managed to catch him before he got into the Waterloo Road, however.'

Slater, hatless and down at heel, glared at Lumley but said nothing. The inspector's expectation faded and then rekindled. *If* there was more than one killer . . . This time it *could* be Slater . . .

'Lock 'im up, the dirty brute!' said a man at the front of the crowd. ''E got no right to be doing that to girls . . .'

'Mr Truscott,' said Lumley, as if making a formal introduction of the man to Swain, 'Billy Truscott of the Punch and Judy, and the Parisiana peep-show booth in the road there.'

'Tableau,' said the man pedantically, ''s a proper tableau.'

128

'Mr Truscott was chasing the suspect. Seems Mr Slater been hanging round and acting funny with the girls in this area tonight . . .'

Before Swain could interrupt, Truscott's indignation got the better of him again.

'My Lucy. Lucy that does the posing. I'll not have her treated so. I'd break 'is bloody 'ead for 'im, supposing I was give the chance!'

'What exactly has he done?'

It was almost too good to be true that Slater should be his man after all. Yet surely it was not impossible.

'Done?' Truscott's anger abated a little and he became plaintively reasonable. 'There's a way of looking at a girl – and there's another way. A man that pays his shilling is entitled to sit and look his fill. I don't care for long-stoppers but I never turn 'em out. This nasty specimen was something different. Supposing you'd seen how he looked at her all that time, you wouldn't need to ask!'

'I have a very good idea of how he looked at her,' said Swain drily. 'Mr Slater and I are old acquaintances.'

'And saying those filthy things to her when he got up from the front bench to leave. *Awful* things! You'd a-gone after 'im, Mr Swain. I can tell you that!'

'And that was why. . .'

'Two hours, looking at her as if she was dirt. My Lucy!'

'Two *hours*?'

'All that time. From the minute we opened. Looking at her like that! My Lucy!'

A self-pitying catch was audible in Truscott's voice.

'Was he alone? Was there anyone with him? A girl of any kind? Did he speak to any girl?'

Truscott looked at Swain with suspicion and distaste.

'A girl? You think any girl would want to keep company with an animal like him? Course there wasn't! He sat on the first bench on his own . . . Just as if he'd got a smell about him . . .'

'For two hours?'

'I said, didn't I?'

Swain looked at Lumley.

'Let go of him.'

''Ere!' Truscott's voice was shrill with outrage. 'What about my Lucy?'

It was Slater who spoke at last, dusting his hat which seemed to have rolled on the pavement but looking Swain steadily in the eye.

'I could have a grievance against you, Mr Swain. Very easily. And you'd know about it, if I had. All about it. I promise you that. There's lots of people would say I had every right to feel a grievance. Lots of 'em.'

He put the hat on his head.

'What about . . .' Truscott began. Swain talked him down.

'The only reason, Mr Slater, that I shan't charge you now is that two young women are dying in agony, in one of these houses, from strychnine poisoning. They're my concern. I'll attend to you when I have the leisure.'

Slater's eyes, staring at Swain's, had the cold blind look of wet pebbles.

'There again, Mr Swain,' he said softly, 'it's not given to us all to die easy. Is it? You might find that for yourself, one of these days.'

The quirk of a smile was just visible on the man's lips. Swain resisted the tempting luxury of annihilating it by a punch in the mouth.

'See there's no violence, Mr Lumley. Let him go. He's not the one we want.'

Without waiting to see the sequel, he turned back down Stamford Street. He was surprised to see a growler from Lambeth police office outside the house and a girl being lifted into it. She gave a forlorn cry as the men moved her gently on to its floor.

'What's this?' he said irritably to the young constable.

'Inspector Bennett, sir. Lambeth Division. Decided this was the quickest way to get her to a doctor. There was no one could come here straight away.'

'And the other girl? Are they taking her?'

The constable lowered his eyes.

'No, sir. She's gone, sir. Passed away while they were bringing this one out of the room. I'd say it was the best thing

130

for her, if you could have heard her. They'll take her presently. Poor little thing.'

Swain went in through the open door and found Polly Peach standing at the foot of the stairs with a face like a tragic mime.

'It wasn't my fault, Mr Swain! What could *I* a-done? I never so much as *saw* 'im'! How was *I* to know?'

'Leave it out, Polly,' he said wearily. 'All I want from you is to know where they came from. The two girls.'

Her tears stopped in an instant and she was eager to help.

'New girls, Mr Swain. Up from Brighton, a few weeks ago. First time in London. Worked down at Muttons before.'

Even in the moment of their deaths, she touted them as if for the benefit of a jaded client. It was more than Swain could endure.

'All right, Polly Peach. I'll be back for the details. Tomorrow.'

She peered at him curiously.

'Mr Swain! You never asked their *names*!'

'I know their names, Polly. They were Emma and Alice.'

Uneasy admiration for this professional skill brightened the old woman's eyes.

'That's right, Mr Swain. Alice Marsh and Emma Shrivell. How d'you twig that, then? Who was it told you?'

'I don't know, Polly,' he said quietly. 'But if I have to arrest every swell that smiles at a rip in Lambeth, I will bloody well find out.'

'If there's anything, Mr Swain . . .'

He paused in the open doorway and turned towards her.

'One thing, Polly. Mr Henry Slater. Bedroom Window Slater. Don't let him in here. And warn all your girls to keep clear of him. He's getting nastier by the minute.'

Without waiting for her reply, he closed the door behind him and went down the steps.

Swain walked through the damp night towards the Waterloo Road, grappling with the elements of tragedy and satanic farce which made up the 'case' of the Lambeth murders. Anger and resolution possessed him on behalf of those who had died. Yet he could not rid his mind of the terrified cries of the girl who lived in agony. The encapsulation of the strychnine had been intended to ensure that she should not be permitted what Slater called 'an easy death'. It was to be the next day before Emma Shrivell died after six more hours of atrocious suffering.

13

'There's two,' Sergeant Lumley said, 'come while you was having your rest-day. Both of 'em a bit nasty but one specially so.'

He laid two sheets of paper on Swain's desk.

'I'll take the nasty one first,' the inspector said.

Lumley pushed towards him the smaller of the papers, crudely printed in capitals with an ordinary pen.

> DID YOU ENJOY THE
> LITTLE JOLLY IN
> STAMFORD STREET?
>
> WASN'T IT FUN?

To his surprise, Swain felt nothing of the fury or revulsion which he expected. A cold and rational sense of resolve possessed him now.

The other letter was more elaborately penned. He recognised it as being identical in style to one which Walter de Grey Birch had identified as being written in a woman's hand.

'Sent on to us,' Lumley explained, 'by the Honourable Frederick Smith and received at his offices in the Strand yesterday morning. It must have been written the day after the murder.'

Swain looked at it.

> Sir,
> On Saturday last two girls living at 118 Stamford Street, Waterloo Road, were poisoned by strychnine. The names of the girls were Alice Marsh and Emma

Shrivell, both ruined by you. One letter incriminating you, found in Nellie Donworth's rooms – one letter *you* wrote – is still in my possession along with enough other evidence to hang you a dozen times over. Judge for yourself what hope you have of escape if the law officers ever get hold of these papers.

If you employ me at once, I can still save you. If you wait till arrested before retaining me, I cannot act for you. No lawyer can save you once the authorities get hold of these papers.

I repeat that if you wish to retain me, you must just write a few words on paper, saying: *Mr. Fred Smith wishes to see Mr. Bayne, the barrister, at once.* Paste this on one of your shop windows at 186 Strand next Tuesday morning. When I see it, I will drop in and have a private interview with you. I can save you if you retain me in time, but not otherwise.

Yours truly,

H. Bayne

Swain looked at the letter, turning it over in his hands.

'Mr Smith pasted a notice last time,' Lumley said. 'Never a sniff of anyone.'

'A woman's writing?'

'Mr Birch would swear it in court.'

'A girl Mr Smith crossed somehow? Nothing to do with the murder? Just wanting to make trouble for him – splash a little mud so that a few blobs may stick?'

Lumley pulled a face.

'There *was* a letter in Nellie Donworth's room and it mentioned Mr Smith. How could the blackmailer know that without being a party?'

'Talk,' said Swain thoughtfully. 'Even policemen talk when they shouldn't. Details of a murder get round the village in a few hours. What I don't understand is the madness of it all. How could a blackmailer expect to get away with it? A demand for money, yes. But acting as a barrister for his dupe? It's absurd.'

'So's poisoning young women,' said Lumley unsympathetically, 'insane.'

Swain shook his head.

'Not insane, Mr Lumley. If he's insane, he can't be hung. I want him hung. Put somewhere where he can't harm anyone again. In lime beside the prison wall.'

At that moment there was a tap at the door and a uniformed constable delivered a sealed envelope. Swain broke it open.

'Dr Stevenson, Guy's Hospital,' he said presently. 'There was enough strychnine in those poor girls to kill half of Lambeth. They'd been fed tinned salmon and bottled beer which slowed down the onset of the spasms. And there were gelatine traces in the stomach. He gave it to them in capsules. It delayed the start and made sure that they died more slowly. Alice Marsh took eight hours to die – and the man who did it is out there somewhere, laughing.'

Lumley said nothing. Presently Swain looked up.

'Your rest-day on Thursday, Mr Lumley?'

'Yes,' said Lumley uneasily, 'why?'

'Good.' Swain collected the papers and put them in a drawer. 'You'll have time to come with me.'

'Where to, Mr Swain?'

'To a funeral,' said Swain confidentially. 'It's just possible that the man who finds all this so funny won't be able to resist the chance of a last laugh at his victims. If he does, then it shall be his last laugh until they top him. See?'

Lumley conceded the point, though putting up a show of resistance.

'I'm not due another rest-day for two weeks, Mr Swain.'

'Then you couldn't spend this one in a better fashion, Mr Lumley,' said the inspector, smiling for the first time that morning.

14

On the day of the double funeral, a mist more appropriate to autumn than to spring hung upon trees and railings. Like a physical malaise it oppressed the suburban avenues of

Dulwich and Streatham, ending in a vast silence which made Wimbledon Common the edge of the world. Among the tombs and cypress trees of Tooting cemetery the droplets plopped and dripped from every branch on to lawns and paths. The cortège of the paupers' funeral, the coffins cheaply boarded and draped in black, approached the two freshly dug graves. All pretence at ritual and ceremony ended at the wrought-iron gates. The municipal hearse with its double burden was moving at a businesslike pace and the stragglers on foot were almost running to keep up with it.

'Seems to me,' Lumley said, 'if I murdered someone, last thing I'd do is go to the funeral.'

He shivered and did a little jig in the concealment of the trees to encourage his circulation. Swain grunted and looked gloomy.

'Look at 'em,' he said bitterly, 'Polly Peach and her courtiers!'

From the foggy perspective of the cemetery gates emerged a strange procession. Polly Peach, at the head of it but supported by two of her house-bullies, each having the shoulders of a coal-heaver, was still obliged to waddle after the hearse as fast as her fat little feet would move. The plumes which were lacking on the two funeral horses appeared black and quivering on Polly's hat. She was sobbing a constant refrain.

'What shall I do without my little darlings! What shall I do!'

A few girls in simple black dresses followed the old bawd. Most of them looked to Swain no older than fourteen or fifteen. It was likely that they had been hired in the neighbourhood to swell out attendance at the burial of two girls who were almost strangers in Lambeth at the time of their deaths. The rear of the procession was brought up by two boys of seventeen or eighteen in black suits and tall hats hired from one of the Mourning Warehouses in the West End. The clothes already appeared crumpled and there was mud down one trouser-leg. Swain guessed that the proceedings had begun with a 'funeral breakfast' in the bar of the Mason's Arms, close to the yard where mourning coaches were parked. By now the two boys were walking arm-in-arm,

135

veering unsteadily from one side of the cemetery path to the other.

'I don't see Fred with his moustache and silk hat in this lot,' said Sergeant Lumley, the reproach now plainer in his voice. Though he had not spoken much about the loss of his rest-day, it seemed that the memory of it was never far from him.

'Wait,' said Swain patiently, 'just wait and watch.'

The hearse had now stopped by the open graves, steam rising from the horses' breath and adding to the miasma. As the last of the mourners arranged themselves, the bell of the mortuary chapel began to toll and a clergyman came hurrying from its door, as if such briskness kept out the raw chill of the morning. Polly Peach tottered towards the edge of the first grave and then fell back against the support of her two impassive bullies.

'Good God, what a hole!' she said loudly, putting aside her grief in simple fear of mortality.

Sergeant Lumley scowled.

'He's not here, Mr Swain! See for yourself.'

'Shut up,' said Swain quietly. 'Show a little respect.'

They watched from a distance as the two coffins of cheap pine were heaved out of the hearse and lowered with minimum ceremony.

'For we brought nothing into the world . . .' the priest's voice moved easily through the familiar cadences, 'and it is certain that we take nothing out of it.'

'That's true,' said Lumley, 'and those two poor little whores never had much in between either.'

'Shut up,' said Swain patiently. Then he caught his breath. 'Will you look at that!'

Two wreaths had been handed down from the hearse, as nearly identical to one another as was possible. Into the bed of moss, the wreath-makers had woven pale orchids and red roses, each bloom having the waxy perfection of the hot-house.

'That cost someone all right,' said Sergeant Lumley appreciatively.

Swain waited for the clergyman to finish. Then he walked

casually forward to Polly Peach.

'That was nice, Polly. Very nice. Expensive too.'

He looked down at the raddled old face, brick-dust powder trapped in lines and pouches. The eyes were brimming, their paint a little smudged on the lashes.

'Mr Swain?' For all her grief, the voice was sharp and alert as a market huckster's.

'The wreaths, Polly Peach. A nice thought on your part.'

'Not me, Mr Swain. I ain't one for wreaths. Not on such a slight acquaintance as I had with them two little. . .'

'Darlings, Miss Peach?'

'Something of that, Mr Swain. Still, you know and I know, they was fools to themselves and the rest of us. They brought a lot of trouble to Stamford Street.'

'Business slack, is it, Polly?'

Lumley straightened up from his examination of the engraved card attached to each wreath.

' "Wasn't it fun?" ' The sergeant walked up to the other two. 'That's what it says on each of them wreaths. "Wasn't it fun?" And it's signed Wattie.'

Polly Peach took an unsteady step backwards, her two bullies moving forward defensively.

'Now don't start, Mr Swain!' she squawked. 'Don't start on me! I never seen them wreaths till the mourning-coach came and they was already on the coffin. I never heard of Wattie.'

'Walter,' said Swain patiently, 'Wattie is a diminutive of Walter.'

'I still never heard . . .' The old bawd was well-nigh screaming at him.

'Don't do that, Miss Peach,' Swain said reprovingly, 'not here.'

'Wouldn't I tell you, if I knew?'

'I doubt it.' Swain stooped to inspect the cards for himself. 'And I don't suppose I should believe you if you did. You'll get me going again, Miss Peach. That's what you'll do. That idea of mine. Having a uniformed officer outside the door of both your houses, questioning every man that goes in. I don't suppose many would. Not after being required to give their names and addresses.'

'Bastard jack!' The bullies were holding her back now rather than supporting her. Polly Peach's face seemed to twitch with fury as she struggled to break free and brawl with her tormentor over the newly dug graves. The rest of the mourners looked on expectantly.

'You've yourself to blame, Miss Peach,' said the inspector coolly. 'I asked you to put the word about for Matilda Clover. Nothing. I've made similar requests for Lou Harris. Nothing. I don't owe you anything, Polly Peach. Nothing whatsoever.'

'Bastard!' shrieked the old woman.

Swain turned to the bullies.

'Take her back to the mourning-coach and put her in. You, Strapping Luke, I know where to find. Likewise, Billy Odd-Job. The rest of you, stand fast until I've spoken to each. Anyone who goes missing before I get to them will be fetched back in rough fashion.'

The surpliced clergyman who had watched the fracas, dumb with outrage, stepped forward over the cold debris of earth.

'And I?' A trail of moisture showed in the quiver of his lower lip as he faced Swain. 'Am I to remain here?'

'No,' said Swain bleakly, 'I fancy we shall manage this well enough without you.'

He watched the robed figure turn and walk away, the cool breeze whipping and snapping at his clerical bands.

The exercise of interrogating the mourners was futile, as Lumley had predicted from the start. None of them was Wattie or Walter. They had never heard of him. Nor did they respond to the names of Matilda Clover and Lou Harris.

The cab which had brought the two policemen started out again into the traffic which flowed towards Kennington and Westminster Bridge. Opposite the wrought-iron railings and lodges of the cemetery, the mourning-coach stood empty by the kerb, where the road ran past the public bar of The Volunteer. From within, as lunchtime approached, came the sounds of Polly Peach and her party lamenting the deaths of the two young women in a luxury of easy grief.

In what remained of his investigation into 'Wattie', Swain found only frustration and fury. Afflek and Dawes, the Lambeth undertakers, remembered the delivery of the two

138

wreaths to the mourning-coach yard. They had been carried in by a porter under the instructions of an elderly woman.

'A shabby old woman,' Lumley said, reporting the news to Swain.

The inspector looked up from his desk where he was compiling his report on the progress of the investigation for the eyes of Sir Melville Macnaughten.

'An old *woman*?'

'A shabby old woman,' said the sergeant insistently. 'The sort that could be hired by a man to run his errand and never see him before nor afterwards.'

'The mourning-house – did they recognise her?'

'There wasn't anything about her to recognise.' Lumley spoke as if Swain should have known better than to suppose otherwise. 'An old woman in a shabby coat and hat that might have fitted ten thousand of her sort.'

Swain got up and closed the folder upon the report he had been working at.

'And that's the end of Wattie,' he said sourly. 'You and I, Mr Lumley, stand just about where we did on the night Nellie Donworth died.'

Lumley watched him carefully.

'Where's that, sir?'

'Nowhere,' said Swain wearily, 'nowhere at all. Wattie could be any man in London – even a woman. The few people who've seen Fred can't agree as to his height, his face, even whether he has hair or not. Matilda Clover and Lou Harris can't be found alive and there's no entry for them in any of the registers of deaths for the past ten years. All our murdering friend has to do is to make up more names of non-existent girls he claims to have murdered – and off we go on the chase again. Dammit, Mr Lumley, he could make us deploy the entire Criminal Investigation Department. We can't follow up all these clues, even if we want to.'

'There's evidence, though,' said Lumley encouragingly.

Swain appeared to ignore him and began to pull his coat on. Then he turned to the sergeant.

'Oh, yes, Mr Lumley. There's evidence all right. Volumes of malicious claptrap supposed to be written by women and

139

Spaniards. Lunatic letters from the killer offering to solve his crimes for us if we pay him. Wait till the press gets hold of those.'

'There's only been one letter like that, Mr Swain,' said the sergeant reasonably.

Swain turned back to his desk.

'*Two*, Mr Lumley.'

The inspector opened the drawer into which he had put his folder and drew out a sheet of paper.

'No one has seen this, Mr Lumley. Only the coroner and Sir Melville. You may just as well see it now as after the report goes in.'

Lumley took the sheet of paper and read it.

To the Foreman of the Coroner's Jury, Town-Hall, Lambeth

Sir, I beg to inform you that one of my operators has positive proof that a medical man of St. Thomas's Hospital is responsible for the deaths of Alice Marsh and Emma Shrivell, he having poisoned these girls with strychnine. That proof you can have on paying my bill for services to George Clarke, Detective, 20 Cockspur Street, Charing Cross, to whom I will give the proof on his paying my bill.

Yours respectfully,
W.H. Murray

'George Clarke?' Lumley handed the paper back. 'George *Clarke*?'

Swain replaced the letter and locked the drawer.

'There was a George Clarke, an inspector in this division. And he lived in Cockspur Street. He was allowed to retire from the force more than twelve years ago, after being cleared at the Central Criminal Court of charges of corruption and perverting the course of justice. He tried to find a place as landlord of a public house. The brewers wouldn't have him. He died five years ago or more.'

'This is the maddest thing of the lot,' Lumley said.

Swain nodded.

'Except that this time he doesn't call himself H.M. Bayne, Barrister, and even as W.H. Murray he's not a Scotland Yard officer. He was when he had the Metropole Hotel warning printed.'

'So of course you're going to Cockspur Street,' Lumley said, as if about to accompany Swain there.

Swain looked up at him, surprised but unmoved in his decision.

'No, Mr Lumley. I'm going where I should have gone a long time ago. Home. I've had so much of this case that I can taste it and choke on it. I'm due a rest-day and I'm taking it. There's nothing like a rest and a book for taking a man out of himself.'

Lumley was about to say something on the subject of his own day of rest, spent at the funeral of Alice Marsh and Emma Shrivell. He looked at Swain, at the distant expression on the long, intelligent face, and decided to cut his losses.

15

Alfred Swain relaxed with a full stomach and a warmth of well-being. The gas murmured in the hearth of his little room and the flame in the mantel made ghosts upon the wall. Open in his hands as he lay back in the easy chair was the dog-eared copy of Tait's *Recent Advances in Physical Science*. It was time to settle accounts with the elusive nature of the planet Mercury. Beside him on the table, reserved for later on, as if it were a child's treat, was a newly acquired copy of Swinburne's *Atalanta in Calydon*. Swain had peeped already and liked what he saw.

> And soft as lips that laugh and hide
> The laughing leaves of the trees divide,
> And screen from seeing and leave in sight
> The god pursuing, the maiden hid.

The game of love, played in all its pagan joy, was to follow the exercise of the intellect upon physical science. Swain envied no man that evening. Not for months had he felt so content in the anticipation of such enjoyment. After a moment or two the method of calculating the orbit of Mercury was fixed in his mind and he was prepared to confront the discrepancy between this and the observed orbit.

From the other chair, Rachel said, 'I suppose a man ought to read as much as he may.'

Swain grunted and tried to shut out the sound of her voice. Rachel shook the bronze-tinted bob of her hair into place, came across and picked up *Atalanta in Calydon*.

'Is this one nice? Should I like it?'

'I've no idea,' Swain said, 'I haven't read it. If you want to, take it down to the drawing room and read it for yourself. Or you could read aloud to your mama. . . .'

The last desperate suggestion seemed an answer to the problem of Rachel. She went back, swaying her hips in an exaggerated fashion, and sat down in the chair again, crossing her legs.

'You were much nicer in the music hall,' she said, a look of breathless expectancy in the pale face with its neat chin, 'when it was dark. When you kissed me. . .'

It was the first time she had referred to the ambiguous brush of his lips on her ear and Swain heard her with a sense of a doom long anticipated.

'You did,' she said gently, 'I know. I wondered after that what I should call you. I mean, Mr Swain or, perhaps, Alfred. I never thought of you as Alfred when I was little. . . .'

'Mr,' said Swain helplessly, seeing the planet Mercury dance tantalisingly beyond perception.

'Mr Alfred Swain.' Rachel got up. *Atalanta in Calydon* lay on the carpet. She sat down by it and reclined with her shoulders propped upon Swain's knees.

'Tell me, Mr Alfred Swain. . .'

'You should be downstairs,' he said uneasily. 'You owe it to your mama. . . .'

He put a hand on her shoulder, as if to send her away. But Rachel took the hand in hers and began to count its fingers, over and over. Swain knew that every rule of good sense and decorum required him to snatch his hand away. He failed to do so.

As she held his hand to her, he could feel through the brown dress the slight but firm swell of her breast. There was warmth too, the warmth of a body that he had treated all the time as a child or a statue.

'Tell me, Mr Alfred Swain,' she murmured, 'do policemen offer rewards for information received?'

His feeling of unease deepened suddenly.

'Not as rule,' he said. 'Why?'

'But information that would solve a murder?'

'Probably. Yes. It would depend.'

Unable to sustain Tait's *Recent Advances in Physical Science* with one hand, he let the volume slide to the carpet. Rachel took his second hand.

'A reward that didn't cost much,' she said. 'Hardly anything. That would be all right, wouldn't it?'

'I don't know.' Swain retrieved his right hand and closed the book beside him. 'If you have such information, anything like that at all, it is your duty to tell the police. Rewards don't come into it.'

'I only know what *you* ought to know by now,' she said, gazing at the tall glowing towers of the gas fire.

'What do you know?'

Rachel turned back her head until it rested on his knees and they saw one another's faces upside down.

'Where Matilda Clover is.'

It was impossible, Swain thought. It was her game, or a trick.

'Where?'

Rachel looked at the fire again.

'She's dead, poor thing. Four months or more.'

'How can you tell that?'

Rachel gave a little frown, almost hidden from him.

'I went and looked. In the registers of deaths at Somerset House. Anyone can do it. I wanted to show you what I could do. What I *would* do for you. For you, Mr Alfred Swain.'

'That's impossible.' Swain felt relief again. 'Ridiculous. Those registers were checked by an officer of the Criminal

143

Investigation Department as soon as the name was mentioned. Don't you know it's one of the first things anybody would do? And when the girl was mentioned in a second letter, the registers were checked again.'

'What name did they check?' Rachel asked innocently.

'Matilda Clover. And Louisa Harris as well.'

'As in four-leaved clover?'

'Yes.' Swain's self-assurance faltered. From the girl's quiet triumph he guessed that the same vindictive fate still haunted the enquiry.

Rachel kissed the hand she was now holding again.

'Exactly.' She kissed the hand again. 'What a pity that policemen never go to a school like Miss Broughton's.'

'What the devil has that got. . .'

'Because they might learn a little German there.'

'*German*!'

But Swain already knew, with a sick certainty, what was coming next.

'That's right,' she said.

'Klover!' He looked at the upturned face. 'Klover with a k?'

'Yes,' said Rachel encouragingly, 'born in England but perhaps her father was German. Twenty-seven years old. Someone who only *heard* the name might write it down the wrong way. All the same I shouldn't bother about her if I were you.'

'Oh?' he said glumly. 'Why?'

'Because she wasn't murdered.' Rachel settled comfortably back against his knees again.

'And does Miss Broughton's academy for young ladies also give lessons in forensic medicine?'

'There's no need to be spiteful!' Rachel smacked the hand, lightly but primly. 'It's all written down there. She died of delirium tremens. Alcoholic poisoning. Drink.'

'Get up,' said Swain gently, 'come on!'

He helped the girl to her feet. Rachel got up obediently but then stood inconveniently in his path, hands lightly on his shoulders.

'What happens now?'

Swain extricated his brain from problems of physical

144

science once and for all. The planet Mercury danced away through mists of incomprehension.

'The Assistant Commissioner,' he said impatiently. 'The Home Office. Exhumation orders.'

'Suppose she's in Germany? Suppose they burnt her down at Woking?'

Swain paused, knowing that such was the twist of events which the malign spirit watching over his investigation was likely to endorse.

'We'll see.'

He tried to push her from him.

'The reward,' said Rachel gently. Her face looked up at him. Without waiting for Swain's response she pushed against him and his arms felt her body extraordinarily light and frail, more than when she had been a vigorous tomboy of thirteen or so. She demanded the kiss and Swain, dreading the repercussions, treated her as an equal in desire.

Rachel, who had been standing on her toes, set her heels to the ground again.

'I love you, Mr Alfred Swain,' she said gently.

'You can't,' he said, more unnerved by this than by the kiss, 'you only think you do. I'm twice your age.'

With her arms round him, hugging tight, she let out a long sigh.

'We're both grown-up,' she said. 'That's all that matters. I've loved you since I was a little girl. But this is different. Never anyone else. You used to say you loved me when I was little. You said I could marry you when I was grown-up.'

'Just a game,' he said desperately, defending a last attachment to the freedom of his single existence. 'A game for children.'

'And did you stop loving me?'

Now or never, there was only one answer, however much he might regret it in the days to come.

'No,' he said, hugging her back, 'how could I?'

'That's settled then,' Rachel said, kissing him quickly and running downstairs.

Swain had a terrible premonition that the girl was about to report the entire incident to her mother in an outburst of joy.

He went down in his overcoat and found Edith Ryland standing by the coloured glass of the hall door.

'I must go to Whitehall Place,' he said quickly, 'I know it's late but I'll be as fast as I can. There are one or two messages to be left.'

Mrs Ryland smiled gently and nodded.

'You won't be back till breakfast, Mr Swain, if I know you.'

'I'll try.'

He had opened the glass door and was turning the handle of the street door when he heard her voice again.

'Mr Swain!'

He turned and saw that a more troubled look had replaced the uncertain smile.

'Mr Swain,' she said, 'Rachel mustn't bother you. Not with all you have to do. It's good of you to be so kind to her. More like a father than any man could be. But if she's a bother, when you need to work or be quiet, you must send her packing downstairs.'

'Yes, Mrs Ryland.' He opened the door and felt the cold draught of the February night. 'Of course. She's no bother but she ought to spend her time with you. . . .'

The smile returned to Edith Ryland's face, gentle and grateful. Swain closed the door behind him and stepped from the entanglements of private life into those of public duty.

16

Matilda Clover, as she continued to be in Swain's notes, had not been buried in Germany or burnt at the new Woking crematorium. For the past twenty years the boroughs of central London, whose graveyards were overburdened by shallowly buried corpses and reeking with putrefaction, had transported their dead to the new and airy cemeteries of the suburbs. Like Alice Marsh and Emma Shrivell, Matilda Clover had been buried among the lawns and gothic monuments of Tooting.

Two days after Rachel's revelation, Swain and Lumley returned to the scene of Polly Peach's funeral outing. This time they were accompanied by Dr Stevenson, two grave-diggers, three uniformed constables, a clerk from the Lambeth coroner's office and a Home Office secretary with the exhumation order.

'They divide 'em,' said Mr Despard the coroner's officer, speaking confidentially to Swain and indicating with a sweep of his arm the expanse of elaborate monuments and humble mounds. 'Over there is privates, the ground bought in perpetuity. Crosses and obelisks, weeping Niobes and little angels. The architecture of the modern age, Mr Swain. Over *there* now is what we call commonses. That's paupers and common graves. Often more than one to each. They get twelve years' rest. Then they have to give place to others. The men work at night by firelight, digging them up and putting the remains of coffin or corpse on great fires. The neighbour-hood doesn't care for it, of course, fires in the cemetery by dark and knowing that they're corpse-burning. All the same, Mr Swain, it has to be. Doesn't it? If they don't buy the land, then they don't have the right to stay. Twelve years they get. Long enough for most. Not much left of 'em by then.'

'Really?' said Swain politely and distanced himself a little from Mr Despard and his enthusiasm for the laws of burial. It was almost nine o'clock and the light frost of the February night had yielded to thin sunlight. Where the green canvas screens were erected round the grave, the frozen grass had broken out in fresh dew. Matilda Clover had been buried no more than twenty yards from the railings along Tooting Common. Already the sightseers, drawn by the spectacle of the screened enclosure, were standing with their faces at the wrought-iron bars. Women in cloaks and bonnets watched with a grimace of revulsion, yet watched all the same. Boys in caps and shorts formed eager little groups and discussed the goings-on in shrill voices. A few girls waited uneasily and men with short clay pipes puffed patiently, as if waiting for the curtain to rise on a melodrama at the Hoxton Britannia.

Swain stood at the head of the grave, where the ground had been marked out by white tape, according to the instructions

147

on the cemetery keeper's plan.

'Right,' he said sharply, 'let's get on with it.'

The two grave-diggers stepped forward, spades slicing and slapping at the wet earth. When the turf was laid aside they worked with slow laborious skill, turning up a pile of muddy clay which grew beside the excavation. Dr Stevenson drew a silver flask from his pocket and held it towards Swain. The inspector shook his head, watching Stevenson undo the chained cup which formed a top to the flask and pour himself a measure of brandy.

At last the spades hit hollow wood.

'Carefully,' Stevenson said, 'very carefully, if you please.'

They uncovered the wooden shell, dark with damp as if it had been buried a hundred years rather than a few months. The men slid their ropes under it and hoisted the coffin slowly to the grass. Then the two diggers and three constables lifted it cautiously on to the handcart for its journey to the cemetery chapel. The sightseers began to run along the railings, eager for whatever horror the spectacle might afford.

In the chapel, the coffin was laid on an anteroom table. Dr Stevenson nodded and the constables began to unscrew the lid.

'Stand back, if you will,' Stevenson said, tying on his gauze surgical mask.

The two constables lifted the lid clear and Stevenson looked down into the coffin. Then he looked up again and his voice was clear through the gauze mask.

'What the devil is the meaning of this?' he asked irritably.

Swain took a mask from the box and stepped forward, holding the gauze across his mouth and nose. Inside the coffin lay a corpse, preserved immaculately as a waxwork. It was the figure of a dapper little man in his sixties, dressed as if for a wedding in a grey suit with a flower in his buttonhole. Though the flower had wilted, the corpse itself had the look of a wedding guest taking a light nap after too heavy a meal.

Swain stood back and removed his mask.

'Close the lid,' he said to the two constables. 'And where in hell is the cemetery keeper?'

The malign fate which watched over his investigation

seemed present in the very air he breathed, precipitating him down the madcap slope of events which made up the case of the Lambeth poisonings.

The keeper, register in hand, arrived a few minutes later. He looked at the numbered plate on the coffin lid and checked it against his entries.

'That ain't Matilda Clover,' he said.

'I know it's not her.' Swain kept his voice low and courteous with difficulty. 'Where is she?'

The cemetery keeper ignored the question.

'This gentleman shouldn't have been buried there.'

'*Where is she?*'

'In some other plot.' The cemetery keeper assumed a look of affronted dignity. 'Must be.'

'Which other plot? There must be hundreds of commonses.'

'No telling that, Mr Swain. All the same, this one hadn't any business to be where he was. No business whatsoever, sir.'

'There must be hundreds of plots...'

'Sixteen hundred, more or less, Mr Swain.'

'We can't dig them *all* up!'

The keeper consulted his register.

'No, sir. I don't suppose you can, come to that. Still, it's as well to have this one out from where he had no place to be.'

Swain fought against the sheer luxury of losing his temper.

'Suppose we dig at the plot where this one is supposed to be buried. Where would that be?'

The keeper consulted the register again. Mr Despard of the Lambeth coroner's office sidled reassuringly up to the inspector.

'It's not a constant thing, Mr Swain, but bodies do get put in the wrong plot. Not much talked about in public, for the distress it must cause. Best let such things lie quiet.'

'Just how often does it happen?'

'It's the mourning-houses,' said Mr Despard soothingly. 'They don't give quite the care to the dead that they do to the living.'

Swain's anger had given way to stark incredulity.

149

'Do you tell me, Mr Despard, that people all over England are attending the funerals of total strangers in the belief that the bodies are those of their own people? Tending graves? Putting flowers for those they never knew from Adam?'

'Does it matter, Mr Swain? Dust and ashes! Does it matter?'

'I should think it did, Mr Despard. There might be a riot if people knew the truth! Yes, Mr Lumley?'

'They're ready to dig the plot where this gentleman *should* have been, Mr Swain. Perhaps it was a simple mistake. Just two of them swapped over. Best try the simple answer first.'

'All right,' said Swain bitterly, 'I suppose it's as good a chance as any. Tell them to put this one back.'

Mr Despard was at his elbow.

'A point of procedure, Mr Swain. If another grave is to be opened will it not require a new order from the Home Secretary? The present order covers only the sepulture already dug.'

Swain looked at the eager young clerk in dismay.

'By the time we've finished, Mr Despard, we might have to dig up a hundred graves. If there's going to be a separate order each time, we shan't find Matilda Clover this side of next Christmas.'

'But there's rules, Mr Swain!'

'Look!' Swain took the little man indulgently by the arm. 'There's a murderer out there who's killed three people we know of. He claims to have killed two others. Goodness knows how many more he's put to death. I'm not waiting until next Christmas, Mr Despard. Not till Easter, if it comes to that.'

Mr Despard's brow formed lines of concern.

'I couldn't be a party to a breach, Mr Swain. Not to a breach of *burial* regulations.'

'Then turn your back, Mr Despard,' said Swain firmly, 'and look the other way.'

By noon they had exhumed a portly man, a tradesman in appearance, and two elderly women. Of Matilda Clover there was no sign. The crowd at the railings grew in size and in the intensity of its interest. There were now piles of earth beside four open graves.

'Talk sense, Mr Swain!' said Lumley urgently. 'We can't just go on and on!'

Small boys at the railings began to chant, 'Burke-and-Hare! Body-snatchers! Burke-and-Hare!'

'Get rid of them!' said Swain furiously to the keeper.

'Can't do that, Mr Swain. That's common land there. Can't move them from common land.'

Two more diggers replaced those who had been toiling since early morning. By dusk they had opened five more graves, three more old women, a man with a dog, and a child.

'You can't, Mr Swain,' said Lumley reasonably, 'you can't just go on and on. . . .'

The crowd at the railings was growing hostile.

'Body-snatchers!' shouted an old market-wife. 'You leave 'em be! That's our people that's buried there.'

The cemetery keeper appeared again.

'You can't do it, Mr Swain,' he said quietly. 'There's bad feeling beginning to grow. Three families that's got their folk buried here has gone to the Rector of St Luke's to have a stop put. You'll have *him* on our necks in a minute.'

'Get some fires lit,' said Swain irritably, 'big enough to light the area. If the diggers won't go on, I'll have constables working here tonight.'

An hour later, the Rector of St Luke's appeared.

'This is a disgrace,' he said to Swain in a stage-whisper, 'a scandal! An abomination! I shall report the matter to the Assistant Commissioner myself.'

'As you please,' said Swain savagely. 'I've seen three young women put to death. Two more are alleged to have been killed. If I can't find the man, there's more that must die in agony by the same method. They scream and vomit in their anguish, Mr Beales, like nothing you ever saw. Report that to whom you choose.'

The Rector withdrew to formulate his complaint.

'I'll be at home if you need me,' Stevenson said. 'There's no more I can do unless you find her.'

When they were alone together, Lumley said, 'Suppose she's not here at all? What if she was sent to the wrong cemetery? What then?'

'I don't know,' said Swain grimly. 'Wherever she is, I want to know what she died of.'

The night was cold enough to disperse even the most patient voyeurs at the icy railings. By dawn, two teams of diggers had opened twenty-six graves without finding a coffin whose number matched that for Matilda Clover in the register.

'There's going to be a God-Almighty row over this,' Lumley said to the last of the uniformed men still on duty. 'Talk about the General Resurrection. Will you look at the state of this cemetery!'

The uniformed man scuffed his feet for warmth.

'Could be worse, Sarge. They could have had to dig the private graves instead of the commonses. You'd be knee-deep in summonses for trespass by now.'

Lumley scowled. The spades of the diggers struck frozen turf above the twenty-seventh grave with a metallic reverberation.

'Half the bloody country's probably buried in the wrong place,' the sergeant said. 'That's why there won't be a fuss, perhaps. No one wants to let on.'

Presently there was a shout.

'We've got her, Mr Lumley! I think we've got her!'

It was Alfred Swain standing by the last of the open graves.

The coffin which was drawn up on the diggers' ropes appeared newer than the rest and boasted brass handles. There was even a plate, as well as a number. It identified the corpse as being that of Matilda Clover and her age at death as twenty-seven.

'Thank God for that,' said Lumley in a tone of unaccustomed piety.

While the handcart was brought, Swain went to wire for Dr Stevenson.

Sergeant Lumley was standing on duty outside the cemetery chapel, his breath condensing in clouds of steam, when the inspector returned.

'This'll do you a bit of good, Mr Swain, all things considered.'

The sergeant spoke with the plump self-confidence of one who had never ceased to believe in the wisdom of his colleague's persistence.

'Perhaps,' said Swain sceptically.

'Oh, it will,' Lumley said. 'From now on, you'll be whiter than the whitewash on Sir Melville Macnaughten's wall. And that other bit was smart too. Very fancy.'

Swain removed his hat and peeled off his gloves in the chapel vestibule.

'Which other bit, Mr Lumley?'

'That spelling of her name.' Lumley edged closer. 'How did you twig that, then?'

Swain drew a deep breath of damp graveyard air.

'You know how it is, Mr Lumley,' he said disingenuously. 'One gets a sense of these things after a while.'

'I'll say,' Lumley said approvingly. 'Smart as new paint, that was.'

17

'*Walter* Harper?' Swain looked at Stevenson across the metal dissecting-table. Behind the great pathologist's head was a shelf of jars, apparently containing potted meat in broth, but labelled 'Brain of Matilda Clover', 'Intestines of Matilda Clover', and 'Stomach of Matilda Clover'.

'Walter Harper signed her death certificate.' Dr Stevenson took down one of the jars – 'Liver of Matilda Clover' – and for a full moment of nausea Swain thought it was to be opened without more ado.

'A young medical man from St Thomas's,' Stevenson said, patting the jar affectionately. 'Inexperienced. Poor Matilda. She was aged prematurely and far gone in drink. One of the workhorses of harlotry. She roomed in Orient Buildings, on Hercules Road.'

'Young Harper,' said Swain eagerly. 'He was—'

'Wrong, Mr Swain. He was wrong. But the mistake was one that an experienced doctor might have made. The young woman was sodden with drink. Convulsions resembling delirium tremens. She even sought a cure for her habits a few weeks earlier. Anyone might have drawn the wrong conclusion.'

'If it was a mistake,' Swain said darkly.

'Come on, Swain.' Stevenson eased the lid of the autopsy jar a little. 'Most medical men in this country wouldn't know a case of strychnine poisoning if it was labelled for them. Because they never *do* see it. Poor Matilda must have had twice the lethal dose in her guts. But any man from St Thomas's might have called it alcoholic poisoning. There isn't time to open up every drunken young street-girl who dies in a stupor.'

Swain looked at the jar in the pathologist's hands.

'For God's sake don't open that while I'm here. I've had my fill of graves and their inhabitants for the present. Tell me about Walter Harper. What's he like?'

'Red in the face just now,' Stevenson said. 'If your stomach turns that easily, why not get them to put you back on frauds and embezzlement.'

'I mean to. What's his moral character? Do you know?'

Stevenson shrugged.

'A bit fast, like most of his age and type. Good-natured. A lot of young men who spend their days up to their elbows in other people's surgical wounds might tend to go wild at night. Like soldiers home from war.'

'You mean he goes whoring?'

Stevenson looked wistfully at the jar.

'He might. When a young man goes on the spree in a place like Lambeth, he doesn't find himself accosted by vestal virgins.'

'*Walter* Harper?'

'Walter.'

'Right,' said Swain, 'thanks very much.'

He was almost at the door when Dr Stevenson spoke again.

'Find out who wrote those letters telling you that Matilda Clover and Lou Harris had been poisoned. There's your murderer, surely.'

'Yes,' said Swain sardonically, 'thank you very much. To date, those letters appear to have been written by two women and three men, one of them a Spaniard. Not to mention a lunatic barrister and a blackmailing madman with his own printing press who keeps offering to solve the crimes he's committed if only I'll pay large sums of money to a dead man at a non-existent address. There's room for anyone in that little company, including a man called Walter.'

Dr Stevenson shrugged again.

'As you please, Mr Swain. But your correspondents, however mad they may be, are the ones who knew the girl had been poisoned.'

'I begin to think,' said Swain gloomily, 'that I must have been the only person in Lambeth who *didn't* know what had happened to her.'

He closed the door behind him and stepped out gratefully into the cold February sunlight.

Noon began to strike from the clocks of St John's and the other churches in the neighbourhood of Waterloo as Swain threaded his way through the traffic of cabs and horse-buses towards the pilastered façade of the York Hotel. For the moment, his meeting with young Dr Harper was to be postponed.

Polly Peach was sitting at a corner table with her two bullies. Dressed in pink and with ribbons on her bonnet, the old woman resembled a large ceremonial kite. Only the waxed and powdered mask of her face identified her bulk, above the waist, as human. Turning his back on the long mahogany bar with its glow of bottles, Swain edged through the chatter and the smoke until he stood before her.

'A word with you, Miss Peach,' he said coldly. 'Alone, if you please.'

The bullies hesitated, looking from Swain to their mistress and back. Polly Peach patted their hands, curved her lips in a practised smile, and ushered them away. Swain sat down opposite her.

'How's young Mr Harper, Polly Peach?'

The paint on her lips cracked a little as she made a moue and furrowed her brow in pretending a vain attempt at recollection. She relaxed and shook her head helplessly.

'You'll start me off again, Polly,' said Swain gently, 'you really will. You'll start me thinking about my duty to protect

155

you by having a uniformed man on the door of each of your two houses. Saluting the customers and taking names and addresses. Just for the safety of you and your girls while this nasty business lasts.'

Hatred glimmered for only an instant in her dark little eyes, quickly followed by a blank stare.

'Mr Harper?'

'Mr Harper, Polly. A young medical gentleman. Apt to be on the spree with other young medical gentlemen, as a rule.'

'Oh!' She gave a spirited little laugh at the foolishness of her memory. '*That* Mr Harper!'

Swain's heart jumped. For the first time since the investigation began, he was going to be lucky.

'*That* Mr Harper, Polly. Mr *Walter* Harper, Polly. As in *Wattie*. The wreaths in the cemetery, Polly Peach. "*Wasn't it fun?*" And signed *Wattie*.'

In his triumph he had gone too far and it was no consolation to see how near the truth he had been. Like a door slammed shut, Polly Peach's face assumed its hostile mask.

'Heard of him, Mr S. Never saw him.'

She was frightened, of course. He had overdone it. But Swain caught the desperate lie in the tone of her voice.

'There!' he said. 'You've done it now, Polly Peach. You've started me off again. . . .'

'Listen!' Polly Peach's old voice cracked as she leant across the table to him, flecks of saliva flying with her words. 'You can put a dozen of your bastard jacks on every one of my doors. And still I can't tell you what I don't know.'

By now there were a dozen men, glasses in hand, watching this encounter from a distance and smiling.

'All right,' said Swain reasonably, 'I tell you what, Polly Peach. Flash Fred Linnell. You owe him quite a bit, don't you? The Governor. Every house down Stamford Street and up the alleys owes its bit to Flash Freddie. Not to mention a sovereign or two to Sammy Strap. The trouble is, Poll, that Flash Fred Linnell seems due for turning over. If I was too busy investigating the present matter, I shouldn't give it another thought. But, supposing I had time on my hands, I'd have to give Flash Freddie a pull. Expected of me.'

'You young bastard,' she said softly.

'Oh no, Polly Peach. I'll give credit where it's due. To you. I don't suppose Flash Freddie would go down for long. Six months perhaps. Sammy Strap might go for longer. Grievous bodily harm and so forth. But Flash Fred must be in a wax even over six months. And I'll give credit, Polly. I shan't hide the favours you've done us and the little rewards that's been paid you for tipping the nod to the law where Linnell is concerned. Mind you, Polly, I shouldn't care to be wearing your skin when Fred gets out of jail. Still, what's that compared to a good clean conscience?'

The old woman's mouth assumed a ragged snarl.

'A shiddle-cum-shite kiss-my-arse bastard jack!'

'Don't, if you please, Polly Peach,' said Swain gently. 'It won't help you.'

'You think Flash Fred'd believe your nastiness? Do you?'

'But I shouldn't be the one to tell him, Miss Peach. He'd hear the tale from others. Those he'd believe without a second thought. Now, why ask for trouble, Polly, when you needn't have it? Naturally, Flash Freddie would want the skin off you if the worst should happen and that might grow back quite nicely. But men like Sammy Strap don't like to leave off without hearing a bone or two crack. Wouldn't mend easy at your age and with your weight too. Worse than that, you'd never work a house again. Young Fred Linnell would see to that. The parish union, perhaps, or picking wet crust out of the gutter-wash.'

She was frightened again. But now it was fear of being hurt, brutally, and the misery of picking food from the cobbles and gutters. Polly Peach and Alfred Swain were familiar with the same scenes. Old women huddled on the pavements at night, gnawing on orange peel gathered after the market stalls were cleared away.

'I don't want you in trouble, Polly,' said Swain gently, 'I don't want anything that can hurt Linnell. Just tell me about Walter Harper. If there's no harm in him, there's an end of it. If there is, then the sooner he's tidied away, the sooner you and your girls can go back to business, safe and snug.'

It was gentleness and reason which moved the old woman

157

after all. When she gave way to him, her capitulation was total, like the breaking of a dam by its waters.

'I never knew harm of him, Mr Swain. God's my judge.'

'He is, Miss Peach. Was Mr Harper ever at the house in Stamford Street?'

'Only with his friends!' She was now as desperate to please him as she had been defiant before. 'Larky young fellows. There was no harm. . .'

'Did he ever see the girls elsewhere? Alone? Promenade bars or cigar divans?'

'He might. I dunno, Mr Swain. How could I? And as God is my judge. . .'

'Not again, Miss Peach, if you please!'

'I *never* knew his name was Walter. Never. Young Mr Harper. That's all.'

Swain nodded.

'Called himself Fred, did he?'

'Not that I know of.'

ave seen n you don't know, Miss Peach. Do you? What he did when he met the girls alone?'

'P'r'aps I don't.'

'Silk hat and moustache?'

'They all have those!'

'Did he call himself "Fred"?'

She thought for a moment.

'Not in the house. No. On the other hand, a young swell that picks up a girl in a promenade bar isn't likely to give his actual name. Is he?'

'Was he at the house after Alice Marsh and Emma Shrivell came there?'

'Not that I know of.' Polly Peach was defensive again now. 'I got two houses to watch, Mr Swain. I can't, in reason, swear to all that goes on in each of them all the time. There's anything up to a dozen girls using both of them.'

Swain sat back in his chair.

'All right, Polly. You've got no more to fear from me. Unless I hear you've been talking to young Mr Harper about our conversation.'

'I wouldn't, Mr Swain. I don't owe him that! On'y don't

say a word to Flash Freddie, will you?'

The sight of Polly Peach simpering sent an instinctive shudder down Swain's back.

'Not a word, Polly Peach. Not a single word. Unless I should find you've been playing me up. That, of course, would be another matter entirely.'

'But I haven't, Mr Swain! I haven't! As God is—'

'Then you've nothing to worry over, Miss P.'

He got to his feet, longing for the open air now quite as fervently as he had done an hour before in the stench of spirits and formaldehyde which filled Dr Stevenson's chamber of anatomical horrors.

Sergeant Lumley was waiting for him on his return.

'You're wanted upstairs at three o'clock, Mr Swain. Sir Melville in person.'

'Why?' Swain took off his coat. 'Or is it a secret?'

It occurred to him that the sergeant's plump face had an air of quite exceptional smugness.

'It's the diggings, I expect,' Lumley said.

'The graves that were opened at Tooting?'

'Not them.' Lumley licked his lips.

'Then what?'

'There's eight applications for exhumation of bodies come to Sir Melville this morning, for consideration by the Home Secretary later.'

'*Eight*? Who the devil from?'

'Relatives of young ladies that died of alcoholic poisoning,' Lumley said. 'Seems their daughters and sisters were models of temperance and sobriety but must have been poisoned by strychnine. Only the scoundrels that signed the death certificates put alcohol down as the cause. The families all want the characters of those dead girls set to rights by having 'em dug up and examined.'

'The world is mad!' said Swain helplessly.

'Still, Mr Swain, that young fellow Harper put down drink instead of strychnine for young Matilda Clover. Didn't he? It's the news of that that's started off the others. And he did do it. Didn't he?'

'Yes he did, by God!' said Swain furiously, withdrawing to his room and closing the door with a superfluous slam.

159

18

'It won't do.' Sir Melville Macnaughten, trimly bearded as a frigate-captain scanning distant horizons, gazed across the sunlit river reach to the brewery and stone-works on the south bank. 'It won't do at all, Mr Swain.'

Swain's long intelligent face studied the back of his commander's head.

'There are three things, sir. Mr Walter Harper. Lou Harris. And the anonymous letters. Of the three, I fancy Mr Harper just now.'

'The notes are in five different hands,' Sir Melville said. 'Three men – one probably Spanish – and two women. One of the women, by the way, crosses the down-stroke of the numeral seven in a continental manner. Mr Birch has seen Mr Harper's report to the coroner. He assures me that Mr Harper did not write any of the notes.'

'He could still have killed Matilda Clover with strychnine and put it down as delirium tremens. Not only giving her the poison but able to watch her die as well.'

'One more thing.' Sir Melville turned from the window. 'There hasn't been another letter. Four days since Miss Clover was exhumed. The inquest convened. But this time, no letter.'

'Perhaps we've got too close, sir.'

'Harper?'

'He might be the poisoner, sir, with the five blackmailers riding on his back. He does the killing, they find out somehow and try to extort money from men like Earl Russell or Mr Smith.'

'Only the murderer could have known Matilda Clover died of strychnine. That was in the first note to Lady Russell.'

But Swain had thought of this.

'Two possibilities, sir. Walter Harper poisoned her and the others. Most murderers like to brag. Perhaps, if he's friendly

160

with one of Polly Peach's girls, he might have said something in drink. If that girl knew of someone who had a talent for extortion, she might let on. . . .'

'And the other?'

'Harper was part of the blackmail, not a murderer. He falsified the death certificate, knowing who had killed her. And then his friends began to ask their price.'

'And Lord Russell and Mr Smith?'

'Perhaps they had nothing to do with Donworth. But one of them *could* have been Matilda Clover's customer, after all. Wouldn't they pay to avoid scandal, let alone suspicion of murder?'

'But they didn't,' Sir Melville said sharply, 'they came to us.'

'Bluffing it out.' Swain measured his fingertips against each other. 'Often the best way with blackmail.'

The Assistant Commissioner turned back to the river view and was silent for a long time. The case clock on the wall ticked the seconds away with its elegant brass rhythm. Swain prompted him.

'There won't be any more notes, sir. That's my bet. Which means we should never know the answer. Murders like this sometimes stop because the man revolts at his crime and kills himself. Sometimes he just stops because he's had enough. Or else the hounds are too close to him. Or he emigrates to the colonies. A hundred reasons. If we wait for him to give himself away we'll never know who killed those four girls.'

'Letters in five hands from blackmailers. Messages in printed capitals from the murderer. Is that the suggestion?'

Swain nodded. 'And there will be no more of them.'

Sir Melville Macnaughten blew out his cheeks at the difficulty of it all.

'Mr Harper, then.'

'He must be close to the centre of all this, sir, even if he's not the man.'

'And Lou Harris? The other girl in the letters?'

'No death certificate since 1890, sir. We've tried like spellings of the name. Also Hardy, Harty, Harry, Harvey, and even Hargreaves, in case it was misheard. There's nothing.'

161

Sir Melville sat down, took his pen and pulled a blank sheet of paper towards him.

'What do you want to do, Mr Swain?'

'Private-clothes duty, sir. Mr Harper lodges in Lambeth Palace Road, just opposite the hospital. Popular with students and doctors, that area is. I could get a room in that house quite easily. Miss Sleaper's.'

'Under what pretext?'

'Schoolmaster turning to medicine to go as a missionary. Some do start late. My father always wanted to, but never did.'

'How can you be a schoolmaster?'

'By talking and acting as my father did,' said Swain gently, 'I know enough books to do that. As for medicine, it won't be expected I should know much to begin with. In a week or two it'll be over – one way or another.'

Sir Melville made a note and shook his head.

'The public doesn't like secret agents, Mr Swain. Policemen in disguise. And most of all, juries don't like them.'

'They'll like it even less when the first *respectable* young ladies start screaming in their death agonies from strychnine,' Swain said facetiously.

'All the same. . .' The pen made a second note.

'Sir!' Swain made his last attempt. 'The wreaths at the double funeral. "Wasn't it fun?" Wattie! He *knew* the girls! Polly Peach good as admitted it. If he sent the wreaths he's very likely our man. If someone who knew of his dealings with the girls sent them as a joke, that still puts Mr Harper at the centre of all this. I'm so close now, I feel I could reach out and touch the man we want.'

'But not arrest him?'

'Not till I know who he is.' Swain paused. 'There's a time in every case like this. You stand on one side of a gulf that's narrow but deep. You can see what's on the other side, almost touch it. But you can't quite jump the gap. Not quite.'

Sir Melville took off the pince-nez he used while writing and tapped the narrow gold of the frame on his thumb.

'There are other ways, Mr Swain. Chemists keep a poisons register. They can be checked. Lists of purchasers could be

162

drawn up and verified.'

'Sir.' Swain spoke as if to a fractious child. 'Chemists sell poisons to registered medical practitioners. They ask the name and address of the customer and look him up in the Medical Register. If the details are correct, he buys the poison. They don't ask for identification. Even if they did, he could forge something. If you or I knew the name and address of a doctor in a country district who wouldn't be known here, we could go to Priest's in Parliament Street this minute and buy enough strychnine or aconitine to do away with every man in this building.'

'Can you be sure?'

'I've tried it, sir,' said Swain gloomily, 'at two shops. I told them why, after they'd checked the register.'

'All right.' Sir Melville added another line of writing and signed the paper. 'Two weeks, Mr Swain. At the end of two weeks the surveillance ends. After that we must face the world and tell it the truth. Whatever the truth may be. Draw lodging allowance and expenditure on the usual scale. Clothes allowance? No. That doesn't apply under a month.'

'Very good, sir,' said Swain meekly.

He took the envelope in which Sir Melville had sealed his instructions to the commissary officer for Swain's private-clothes duty. Then the Assistant Commissioner looked up.

'Before you next masquerade as a medical man in order to test the provisions of the Poisons Act at chemists' shops, see that you have my authorisation.'

'Sir,' said Swain respectfully.

'Subterfuge, Mr Swain!' Sir Melville's tone indicated that the discussion was now to close. 'It does no good to our reputations. No good whatsoever, Mr Swain.'

4
Private Clothes

19

It was the cat, Swain supposed, which typified the household of Miss Annie Sleaper at 103 Lambeth Palace Road. Yellow-eyed and tiger-striped, it lay in the parlour chair, morose and gazing upon the lodgers with calculating envy. The curious regularity of its tabby markings gave it the look of a stage conjurer's creature or the familiar of a fairground clairvoyant.

Annie Sleaper herself fulfilled none of Swain's expectations. She was less the gentle maiden-lady of sixty, keeping house for her paying guests, than a femme fatale gone to seed. The bold line of her nose and chin, elegant and daring forty years before, had now assumed a cruder dominance over thin painted cheeks and narrow lips. Swain thought of her always as requiring a silk cabbalistic headscarf and a crystal ball.

The sunlit parlour was a curious mixture of chintz and mahogany, ferns in china pots and framed prints of harem bathing scenes by Alma-Tadema and Sir Frederic Leighton, breathing a limply voluptuous air into the stuffy velvet-draped room. Annie Sleaper combined propriety and suggestion in equal parts. She was decorous in all her dealings with Swain. Yet it would not have surprised him altogether had she stepped from among the potted ferns in a yashmak, jewelled bodice, and gauze pantaloons.

One of her four rooms upstairs had been vacant. Swain, the new soi-disant medical student, had rented it without difficulty and without explanation. The window of his room looked directly across the road to the medical school of St Thomas's Hospital with its Italianate bell-tower. From the landing behind, he could see part of Archbishop's Park and the cluster of mediaeval buildings with gate-house and square tower making up Lambeth Palace.

None of the other three 'medicals' lodging with Miss Sleaper was a young man. Walter Harper, despite his reputation, was a congenial and even a facetious companion in his middle thirties. To the letters after his name, he was now adding experience of work in the famous hospital. Quite tall, with flat dark hair and red face, he wore the mask of healthy sociability.

His opposite, both in temperament and in sitting across the table from him at breakfast and dinner, was Bone. At first Swain had been disconcerted to hear that Bone was doing in reality what he only pretended to do for the purposes of surveillance. Disillusioned by life as a senior clerk in his uncle's firm, Bone was reading medicine with evangelical ambitions.

'Money is the great obstacle,' he remarked to Swain in their first exchange of confidences, 'the great curse to such an undertaking.'

Swain had prepared this part of his story with care.

'I was lucky,' he said, 'I inherited from my parents. Being without brothers or sisters, you see. And you? How do you manage, Mr Bone?'

'They sponsor me,' said Bone vaguely. 'The Countess of Huntingdon's Fund. On the understanding that my skills are put at the service of their mission. You might do worse than approach them, if ever you need to.'

'Yes,' said Swain meekly, 'thank you. I'll remember that.'

Humourless and overbearing, Bone looked like his name: white, thin, and hard. The blond hair, lightly oiled, deepened the pallor of his taut face. Being called 'Bone' earned him the most unsubtle ragging by younger medical students, all the more exquisite to his tormentors for his unsmiling piety. They would question him about his medical mission in great earnest, suddenly addressing him by suggestive and preposterous variations on his surname. But in his solemnity, Bone failed even to see the possibility that a rational man could find amusement in such a name. At the least departure from flat and literal conversation, when no humour was intended, Bone would none the less channel the talk to moral earnestness by injunctions like: 'Joking apart, however. . .' or 'But let's be serious, though. . .'

Swain, not much given to facetiousness himself, found

Bone's company oppressive.

The third lodger was an American visitor, Thomas Neill, who had already qualified in Canada at McGill and was now attending a special course of lectures at St Thomas's, funded by his own medical school. He had the long pale face of the laconic humorist and the tall dome of intelligence. A cast in one of his eyes was the only blemish on this pattern of the droll or raconteur.

At dinner, Annie Sleaper took the head of the table while the little maid Natasha, her blond chignon bobbing like a docked tail, hurried round with plates and tureens. Miss Sleaper's pose was one of affected knowingness at the ways of her 'young men', who were, by common consent, devils with pretty women and never to be trusted. Swain could believe it of Walter Harper. That anyone should think it of Bone was beyond even the scope of conjecture.

Dr Neill, as the eldest, took the other end of the table with a wry and good-natured sense of his responsibilities. He brought with him phrases of absolute novelty to Swain. As the plates were set, Neill would take the bread in one hand, the knife in his other, and ask of each, 'May I slaughter the loaf for you?'

He was always first to take his place, five or ten minutes before the others, as if eager to begin the little chores which Miss Sleaper assigned him. Yet he ate slowly and fastidiously, by contrast with Harper who consumed his food as if he feared it might be snatched from him. Swain watched the table-manners of his suspects and potential suspects, entranced at the thoughts their conduct provoked and the deductions which might be drawn.

So far as Miss Sleaper allowed herself any flirtation with her lodgers, it was Dr Neill who received her attentions. When his name was spoken in association with that of any woman, Miss Sleaper would look up with a thin, wicked smile.

'We'll have to keep an eye on Dr Neill,' she would say. 'Oh, yes. We know all about Dr Neill, don't we?'

And Neill would open his hands and arms with a despairing shrug of mystified innocence.

At the same time, it was a facetious mythology of 103

Lambeth Palace Road that Dr Neill and Annie Sleaper nourished a consuming passion for one another. This was the basis for much banter between them and an occasional aside by Walter Harper. Mr Bone, pale and firm, ate as if he heard nothing of such things. There was a moment, however, when Swain wondered if the humorous fiction cloaked a reality. Sounds in the night, which might have been the creaking of hinges or the sighing of boards under a footfall led, in his imagination, from one bedroom to the other.

Of his three fellow lodgers, Neill was the most good-natured in his behaviour, showing a characteristic American blend of sentiment and wry humour. Harper was loud and jovial but, perhaps, selfish and even cruel in his enjoyments. What of Bone? Was there anything in him to cause suspicion? Swain watched him as they ate. Bone worked at his food, there was no other word for it. He seemed preoccupied by an inner obsession which brought him no visible expression of joy or even comfort. It was easy to imagine Harper in the arms of Ellen Donworth or Matilda Clover, and possible to think of Neill in such a situation. What of Bone?

He rarely joined their conversations and never joked. As a rule he spoke only when spoken to, though always with a cool and punctilious air. There were no women in his life, so far as Swain could make out. Yes, it was possible after all to imagine even Bone with such a girl. Bone going alone and secretly to his bitter pleasures. Bone leaving the girl, not with affection or good humour but a sour contempt for his own weakness and – still more – for the partner who had indulged it.

Twice the subject of women came up in conversation with consequences which caught Swain's attention.

'I wonder,' Miss Sleaper had said to Swain, 'I wonder you and Mr Bone don't plan your missionary medicine here in London. Heaven knows, there's plenty to do.'

Without looking up from his plate, Bone interrupted her.

'Heaven knows, Miss Sleaper' – there was no mistaking the reprimand for her use of such a term – 'Heaven knows all too well what there is to be done abroad.'

'Yes,' Miss Sleaper conceded the point amiably, 'but in Whitechapel and Lambeth you might save children's lives, you might aid the young women of the streets without going further than a few miles.'

Bone's fork stabbed at his boiled mutton.

'Children have no choice but suffering, Miss Sleaper. You are right in that. The women of the streets – or elsewhere – know God's right from Satan's wrong. There are other lands where such is not the case. No person here has to do the devil's work, except by choice.'

Swain waited and listened.

'What has the devil's work got to do with it, Mr Bone?' asked Neill. 'We talk of those who are unfortunate. Sick. Diseased. Whatever the cause.'

Bone saw that he had followed his own thoughts rather than the sense of the conversation and now tried to withdraw.

'Admirable work, Dr Neill. It is not, however, what I have chosen. Nor, you see, has Mr Swain.'

Harper, brushing back the dark sweep of hair from his forehead, relaxed in his chair and watched Bone apply the fork again.

'You might give your attention to Dolly Higgins or Lottie Maybury among the nurses, old Bone,' he said cheerfully. 'A man could wish for a worse life than curing the ills of such young charmers as they.'

Neill smiled politely at the others, as if he did not quite understand the references. Miss Sleaper looked ill at ease. Swain sensed that an old wound was being probed.

'Don't do it, Harper!' said Bone, warning without looking up.

'Do what, old Bone?'

'If you don't know by now...' The fork tapped Bone's plate in the silence.

'But I don't, old Bone!' Harper grinned, leaning back in his chair, plate cleared, thoroughly enjoying the game.

'Let's change the subject,' said Neill, light and helpful in his tone. But Bone was not to be stopped.

'Don't insult the house in which you are a guest, Harper! A gentleman does not use ladies' names in such a fashion at the dinner-table. In the same way he does not introduce politics or religion as matters of controversy. Those are

171

the fundamental rules of good conduct in any mess-room.'

'If this was a mess,' said Harper, 'we shouldn't talk shop either. Which you do more than most. I've been at mess dinners often enough, Bone. Which I daresay is more than you have.'

The casual insolence of his tormentor was more than the young man could endure. Bone put down his knife and fork. He looked not at Harper but at Miss Sleaper.

'Please,' he said, 'please excuse me. I mean no offence but I must decline to sit at table any longer this evening under such baiting as this. I beg your pardon. All of you.'

He looked round the table once, stood up, pushed his chair in and turned from the room. They heard him walking up the carpeted stairs. A door closed distantly, somewhere overhead. Miss Sleaper allowed her shoulders to fall in a long sigh.

'Oh, dear!' She turned in her chair to face the glowing countenance of Walter Harper. But she laid a hand gently on his, where he had rested it on the table. 'You *must* not treat him like this. Were it not for your father. . .'

'Dear father!' said the young man sardonically.

'Were it not for your father,' Miss Sleaper went on quietly, 'I should have to insist upon your making other arrangements.'

Young Harper assumed the easy contrite look of a decent fellow who meant no real harm.

'Very well, Miss Annie,' he said, taunting her by the familiarity, 'I shall go and apologise to old Bone after dinner. But he really is a dry old stick. Isn't he, though?'

He spread out his hands, appealing to the others.

'Mr Bone is a gentleman of manners and sensibility,' said the landlady firmly, 'and for the present, Mr Harper, I recommend you to study his example.'

There was a slyness in her dark eyes which belied the severity of her tone. Dr Neill sighed.

'What it is with these young fellows, ma'am and Mr Swain. We shall all have to keep our eyes upon them. Mark my words.'

Swain smiled, joining in the restoration of good humour as Natasha bustled round the table in a whisper of starched linen, removing dinner plates and setting down pink blancmange at every place. Bone, with his apparent hatred of sin and contempt for those who practised it, intrigued the inspector. But then so did Walter Harper with his determined and callous pursuit of pleasure. Even Dr Neill with his bizarre and laconic wit made a subject for suspicion. And Annie Sleaper? Well, Swain thought, there was a certain oddity about her. In a moment of wild conjecture he wondered if perhaps the entire household might be involved, if not in murder then in the blackmail which attended it.

The theory would not do. He knew that, as he undressed in his room the same night. The blackmail notes involved at least two women and a Spaniard. So he pulled the sheets and blankets round him, having leisure to feel, at last, a homesickness for the house near Clapham Common, for Edith Ryland and, most of all, for Rachel.

20

'Hello there!'

Without opening his eyes, Swain woke from a long sleep on the first Saturday morning of his residence at Miss Sleaper's. Even with lids closed he detected a golden flush of sunlight filling the room through the thin curtains.

'Hello there, Uncle Swain! Good morning!'

It was impossible that anyone could be in the room with him, he thought. Every night he had taken the precaution of sliding the little bolt across the inside of the door.

'Rise and shine, Uncle! Rise and shine!'

It was Harper's voice, full of energy and joviality. Though the difference in their ages was only a few years, Swain and Neill had become the two 'uncles' of Harper and his rowdier friends. Swain opened his eyes and realised that the younger man was talking to him through flimsy lath and plaster which served as a wall between their rooms.

'I say, Swain! Are you awake, old fellow? Are you there?'

Swain cleared his throat and swallowed.

'I am,' he said loudly, 'what's the trouble?'

'The trouble, Uncle, is that it's past nine o'clock and we're all going to Muttons. Remember? Do come on! The others are nearly ready!'

Swain pulled himself upright and looked at the clock. It was ten past nine. For the first time in years he had overslept.

'Breakfast is over,' Harper shouted cheerfully, 'and your shaving-can must be stone cold. Didn't you hear the skivvy knock?'

'I must have gone back to sleep.'

'I should say you did. Anyway, think of going to Muttons to get your greens, Uncle. If that won't make you shake a leg, we'll treat you for a dose of rigor mortis!'

'Muttons. . .' Swain tried to recall the passing reference in a conversation a couple of days earlier.

'Brighton, Uncle! It's Saturday and there's no classes worth going to. Down for lunch, back on the midnight train. You and Uncle Neill must keep order. . . .'

'Isn't Bone going?'

Harper laughed.

'Keep order, Uncle. Not turn the whole outing into an Evangelical meat-tea. Bone doesn't approve of Muttons. Nor greens, come to that.'

Cautiously, Swain opened the door and retrieved his can of tepid water. There was no post. According to pre-arranged signals, a letter from his auntie was a summons to report to the Criminal Investigation Department at once, whatever the consequences. In the absence of such a message he was to make a scheduled contact after the weekend. Shaving painfully, he recalled the conversation about Muttons. It was Neill's suggestion that he and Swain should go.

'Best make sure the younger fellows don't get into any scrapes. Harper has rather a way with the ladies.'

There was an uncharacteristic disquiet in Neill's amiability, as if Harper's 'scrapes' might be of a rather special kind. In that case, Swain decided, he must go. If there were to be a 'scrape' involving Harper, it was not to be missed.

A four-wheeled 'growler' called at the house just after ten, with three of Harper's cronies. Swain, Neill, and the younger

174

man joined them. Miss Sleaper marked their departure with a few words of knowing advice. Far from being a damper on their spirits, Uncle Neill sang and recited all the way to the station while the young men chattered and guffawed.

> A sweet Tuxedo girl you see,
> Queen of swell so-ci-e-ty...

They crowded into a compartment of the Brighton train, rattling over the shabby streets of south London brick in the sunshine of early spring. At this stage of the outing, there was everything to play for and the party was good-natured. Whether they would be as good-natured on the return journey was something which Swain waited to see with considerable interest. For the present, Uncle Neill sang them songs from American burlesque and Harper passed round what he called a 'flash' paper. Swain recognised it as the badly printed and luridly illustrated pulp which was sold in the grimy shops of Holywell Street near the Strand. Harper read them some choice extracts from a story called 'Lady Pokingham', and one of his companions, Charlie Chadwick, recited half a dozen of the limericks whose verbal caricatures of bowels and bladders might have turned all but the medical stomach.

They passed the paper to Neill, who looked a little awkward.

'Come on, Uncle!' shouted the younger men. 'Recitation! Speech! Speech!'

He turned the pages with a submissive smile, coming at last to a milder item.

'Come on, Uncle,' Harper said quietly, 'don't be a prig, now.'

Neill smiled again and began to read.

'A notice in the *Daily Telegraph* announcement of marriages. At the Parish Church, South Hackney, John Henry Bottomfeldt, of Hamburgh, to Sarah Jane Greens, of South Hackney. And now the verse:

> How lovely everything now seems
>   When joined in one by Hymen's belt,
> For now John Henry has his Greens
>   And Sarah Jane her Bottomfeldt.'

There was a shout of approval from the others and, as Swain had feared, the limp-bound volume was passed to him. He hesitated with it on his knee.

'Come on, Uncle Swain,' said Harper in the same quiet voice, 'you ain't a prig, are you? We thought only old Bone was a prig.'

Glancing across the carriage, Swain saw something like suspicion as well as mockery in Harper's eyes. It was impossible that the young man could have any idea of the truth. Surely?

'It's not my *forte*, I'm afraid. . .'

'Come on, Uncle Swain! Be a good uncle, now!'

'But I'll do my best.'

He opened the book at random, staring at the crude print without seeing it, and began his piece:

> 'A stick I found that weighed two pound:
> I sawed it up one day
> In pieces eight of equal weight!
> How much did each piece weigh?'

'Quarter of a pound,' said Neill quickly.

Swain shook his head.

'It must be a quarter of a pound,' Charlie Chadwick insisted. 'Divide two by eight and you get a quarter.'

'Listen,' said Swain and repeated the rhyme.

'Why can't it be a quarter?' Chadwick asked.

'Because,' said Swain, 'you can't saw wood without losing sawdust. Each piece would be less than a quarter of a pound.'

'Let me see that!' said Harper irritably. But Swain closed the book before he handed it back.

'That's good!' Neill slapped his knee and gave Swain a quick nod of admiration, 'I call that cute as mustard!'

'I call it dead lead,' Harper said. 'I don't believe it was ever in this paper.'

Swain shrugged.

'They put all sorts of pages from weekly journals in, just to make up the weight. It's only done for money.'

The affability of Harper's red face with its dark flick of hair was soured for the next half hour. He called Swain by his surname without the prefix of 'Uncle'. By the time they got to the pillared temple of Brighton Station and the long slope of Queen's Road to the cold and glittering sea, he had recovered his bonhomie.

'You may be a clever old fellow, Uncle Swain. But don't think I'm not up to every move!'

Once again Swain wondered if it was possible that Harper had guessed the true purpose of his stay at Miss Sleaper's. It was quite out of the question by any evident line of reasoning.

The young men and their two 'uncles' whiled away the afternoon with increasing impatience as they waited for Muttons to open and admit its dinner guests. In the brightness and the chill wind they walked the narrow deck of the Chain Pier, under the cast-iron suspension arches with their little booths open to sell sweets and souvenirs even in the cold March sunshine. Harper stared at the girls, as he smiled with the air of a libertine who weighed the pleasure of the conquest against the likely effort required to accomplish it. To judge from his conduct, he was saving himself for the evening.

When the clouds began to gather over Shoreham and the darkness came in with a Channel mist, they had tea at the Ship Inn and paid a visit to the aquarium. Already the day which had started with high spirits in the Lambeth sunshine was growing chill and morose.

Only when it was past seven o'clock and they made their way to Muttons, facing the sea near the incomplete skeleton of the new pier stretching out from the shore, did the morning's joviality return. By common consent they now regarded one another as jolly dogs and a desperate danger to the opposite sex. Alfred Swain thought of a book he had read long ago, in which Samuel Johnson described such 'sprees' as this. 'Their mirth was without images,' he recalled to himself, 'their laughter without motive; their pleasures were gross and sensual, in which the mind had no part; their conduct was at once wild and mean...'

He stopped, looking out where the dark surges of the incoming tide burst and rattled on the shingle below the promenade rail. Of course he was a prig. It was even possible to feel a certain pride in the realisation. However could he have doubted the truth of it?

Muttons, with its tables of wrought-iron and marble, its arcade of pillars hung with foliage and artificial fruit, its chandeliers and music, was more determinedly 'Parisian' than the Jardin Mabille or the Rue de la Paix whose pictures adorned its walls. At the far end of the long dining saloon was an open space for dancing and a raised platform where the orchestra played.

By pushing the tables together it was easy enough to accommodate a party of six or more. There were few couples. The clientele consisted of parties of men and women and, more often, groups of one sex eyeing groups of the other.

'This is the life!' Harper tilted his chair back and surveyed the menu. 'This is the life, what? Wouldn't you say, Uncle Neill?'

The American smiled, self-conscious but good-natured, at this appeal.

'It's what you young fellows say that counts, sir. We old folk must take things as we find 'em. . . .'

The mock modesty caused a general hooting from the others which drew the attention of several tables. Harper grinned.

'There's a couple over there, Uncle Swain. One of 'em's just the stuff for you. Daisies in her hat and passion in her heart. Will you look at the way that black silk goes so tight over her thighs. What a backside on her! Eh?'

'Perhaps,' said Swain lightly, 'you should go and tell her so.'

'Tell her?' Harper grinned hugely. 'Damned if I don't tell her more than that before the night's over.'

They ordered oysters and dry hock to begin with. It was the food which Swain enjoyed most. Having missed his breakfast and eaten little all day, he was ravenous. To hear the cold sea booming across the road and yet to sit in such warmth and eat food of such fragrance and taste seemed to him the height of sensuality.

'There's one,' said Charlie Chadwick softly, 'with ginger frizzy hair. Crack me if she won't go when you start her!'

178

'Cut that,' said one of the other young men, 'she's professional.'

'And what if she is?'

'And what if you get poxed, Charlie C.? They won't encore that at the deanery. Stick to home grown. There's plenty here.'

'Lou Harris was home grown, wasn't she? I heard she poxed two fellows from Bart's.'

'Gammon! She never did. . .'

Swain clutched his knife and fork, trying not to show the excitement which welled up inside him.

'A friend of mine knew Lou Harris,' he said casually. 'What happened to her? He was asking me that. Hadn't seen her for some time.'

The question sounded false and he knew it by Chadwick's reply.

'How should I know, Uncle? She was one of the bunters here at Muttons. Came with one or two other girls. We knew her by sight and nothing else. Not after hearing the story that she'd poxed a couple of Bart's men.'

Matilda Clover and Lou Harris. . .the names raced in Swain's thoughts. He tried to hold Chadwick to the conversation, as if it was natural.

'I must warn old Lumley then,' he said. 'You haven't seen her lately, I suppose?'

'I never saw her more than twice,' said Chadwick, irritated by Swain's persistence. 'I daresay six months or more ago. Still, I'd tell your friend Lumley to keep on examining himself just in case.'

There was a whoop of laughter round the table at this and Swain smiled, as if begging pardon for being so tiresome on the subject. It was little enough to have gathered, he thought. After all, Louisa Harris was a name that might be shared by a dozen girls in Brighton alone. And yet, he knew, this one was his Lou Harris.

Harper tore at a piece of bread, made a pellet of it, and flicked it hard in the direction of the young woman with the dark curls and the black silk tight over her thighs. It missed her and fell on the marbled floor beyond. Undeterred he took

179

the bread and rolled half a dozen pellets. The second one, with quite unmerited accuracy, plopped into the glass of wine she was holding. The girl looked up, startled, and blushed a little at the sight of six men from the other table staring at her. Harper sprang to his feet, walked across, and knelt down humbly at her chair. Like a pantomime suitor he made his apologies.

'Excuse me,' said Chadwick, turning away from the sight, 'I think I may have to vomit.'

The others gaped, except for Neill who watched the entire incident with a good-natured smile.

'Well, Uncle Swain,' he said genially, 'seems we never did manage to keep these young sparks out of trouble, after all.'

Swain helped himself to more oysters.

'Personally, I shan't lift a finger. I am ravenous. I don't believe I was ever so hungry in my life. Would you be good enough to. . .'

'Slaughter the loaf?' said Neill pleasantly. 'I shall deem it a privilege. I do believe that our young Mr Harper is making something of an impression on that saucy lady over there. I hope we shall be able to get him to the station in time for the train.'

Swain glanced across at the other table. Unlike the other girls who were besieged by male admirers, this one was regarding Harper with a tolerant smile. Conquest was never in doubt, Swain thought, only the sum of money to change hands. He was about to say something of the sort to Neill and then decided against it. Before long it was he and Neill alone who sat at the table. Chadwick and one of the others were dancing with girls whom they had chosen from groups at the other tables, while Harper and the final member of the party had taken their girls elsewhere.

'A walk along the promenade,' said Swain, replying to his companion's quizzical glance as Harper and the girl with the dark hair left them.

'Rooms,' said Neill quietly. 'In locales of this sort, there are rooms which may be hired for a very brief encounter. That's the attraction for our young men. He was right, though. Will you look at the rear view of her walking in that black silk!'

Swain looked and nodded. It occurred to him that there was a curious melancholy which afflicted such parties of pleasure as this. Harper had announced the expedition to Brighton as 'having some fun'. If appearances were any indication, it did not seem to Swain that the young man and his friends were having much fun at all. Polly Peach's wake for the two dead girls of Stamford Street had been more jolly. Neill interrupted these thoughts.

'You don't fancy something of the sort yourself, perhaps?'

He looked quickly at Neill as the question was put. But the older man was merely curious as to Swain's response. Swain thought of Rachel, the pressure of her arms about him, the soft intimacy of his lips brushing her ear in the golden half-light of the Canterbury auditorium. What was 'fun' compared with that?

'If it's all the same to you,' he said amiably, 'I think I'd rather have the cheese-board.'

Neill grinned at him, as if finding a particular satisfaction in the answer.

By eleven o'clock, all the others had returned except Harper, though Chadwick's girl was still hanging on his arm. She was a thin and fair-haired creature who clung to him among the chatter round the table.

'Let's go on the pier,' she murmured to him plaintively from time to time, 'there's still time to go on the pier.'

Swain had a very good idea of what going on the pier would involve, among the shadows of the cast-iron arches. But at length there was scarcely time even for that.

'Where's Harper?' he asked, looking round.

The young men stared at him, then grinned and shouted in chorus.

'On the pier! Ain't you slow, Uncle Swain?'

It was Neill who assumed responsibility for the group.

'In that case, we'd best go and find him. *Tempus edax rerum*, my young friends.'

There were vague protests but a few minutes later they made their way across the road and along the promenade, five of them with three girls still attending the younger men. Chadwick's girl clung coyly and whispered. Under its iron

181

suspension-arches the narrow deck of the Chain Pier was dimly lit by gas globes on either side. Harper and the dark-haired girl were now standing innocently together, staring out across the restless surge of water. To find them so easily was almost an anti-climax to the search.

'Where's Chadwick?' Harper said presently. But Chadwick and the thin fair girl had vanished. In a moment there came from the shadows a rising sequence of wordless exclamations, urgent and urging, from the fair girl's throat. The others, standing in a group, looked at one another significantly.

'That settles it,' said Neill firmly, 'I'm going for the train. Anyone else coming? You, Swain?'

Swain nodded, though waiting to see if Harper would follow.

He did, after kissing the dark girl in a prolonged simulation of passion, and waving back to her the length of the promenade. At the station they found the train waiting and almost empty. There was no sign of Chadwick. He arrived breathless and with his collar open a few minutes before it left, scrambling into their compartment.

'I'm surprised you had breath to run, Charlie,' said Harper pleasantly.

'Never known a fellow go at his greens like Chadwick...'

'Seems to me, some people don't know how to treat a lady...'

'And she's married too,' Harper said.

'No!'

'Yes, she is. You could see the mark where she'd had a ring on.'

'You're a devil, Charlie Chadwick! That's what you are!'

Chadwick grinned at them.

'Anyone else had his greens tonight?'

'Don't look at the two uncles,' Harper said. 'They might blush.'

Presently Chadwick tried to start the singing.

> 'Oh, there was a young surgeon at Bart's,
>   Whose patients all died of...'

'Not in front of the uncles!' said Harper solemnly. 'You

182

might shock them into fits.'

Swain raised a hand gently.

'I doubt it,' he said, 'please don't. . .'

But Chadwick had a better idea.

'Come on,' he said, 'into the next carriage. Leave the uncles to smoke a quiet pipe or two. I must tell you all about . . . you know. . .'

They scrambled out, leaving Swain and Neill alone. As the train began to pull out there was a guffaw beyond the partition and a few minutes later a raucous burst of singing.

> 'There is an old surgeon at Guy's,
> Whose major appendage won't rise. . .'

'Youth!' said Neill tolerantly. 'Were we like that ten years ago, Swain?'

'I wasn't.' Swain folded his hands and settled back against the padded seat. 'My friend Lumley was and is. Did you ever come across that girl of his, Lou? Lou Harris? She seems to have caught Charlie Chadwick's eye.'

Neill shook his head.

'I guess she must have been before my time. I've been down to Muttons on several outings but I don't recall anything of her.'

'Six months ago, he said.'

'I'd have been on the other side of the ocean, I expect, when he knew her.'

Swain nodded, as if that settled the matter. He was aware, however, that Neill was watching him, the tall dome of intelligence and the intense eyes reminding him a little of Walter de Grey Birch the palaeographer. Uncharacteristically, Swain felt obliged to say something.

'Don't you find it odd, Neill, that young men who know more about diseases than most live as they do?'

Neill's eyes held his. The expression did not alter.

'They don't. Bone certainly doesn't.'

'Chadwick and Harper.'

'Ah!' Neill turned his head at last and stared through the darkened window-glass. 'You mean that they frequent whores, or girls who are next thing to being whores?'

'Exactly.'

'Why not?' Neill looked at him again. 'Barristers and army officers have their doxies. Why not medical men?'

'You don't disapprove?'

Neill sighed at the question.

'Don't be a fool, Swain! Of course, I disapprove. Chadwick and Harper – most probably Harper – will land in a real scrape one day. Either the pox or his head broken by a footpad in Stamford Street.'

'Stamford Street? Where the two girls were murdered?'

'Yes,' said Neill shortly. It was clear that he had no intention of saying much more on the topic of Harper and his women.

Swain went for the important truth, straight and quick.

'Did he know them, do you think?'

Neill looked at him with genuine surprise.

'Of course he did! He was bound to. They used to be down at Muttons until a month or two ago. Our young medicals were one reason for them moving up to town, if you ask me. I don't say they knew Harper but he had his eye on them all right.'

'Does anyone else know?'

But Neill had had enough of it.

'I don't interfere,' he said firmly, 'I guess what Harper may be up to. A man that runs after women of that sort deserves what he gets. If it was my place to give it to him, I would. As it isn't my place, I leave him to others. I'm a guest in your country, Swain, and I don't intend to mark my stay by being prosecuted for slanderous statements about young Harper or anyone else. There was something between him and the two girls in Stamford Street. There was talk when he signed that other death certificate and put delirium tremens down. I was told he'd done something to her in the way of pleasure that killed her. It was said even then. But no one cares to stand up and make slanderous allegations with the risk of being prosecuted, I suppose. That young brute would cut her up for his pleasure and think nothing of it.'

If Swain was taken aback, it was only in part by these revelations. He was also intrigued by a new aspect of Dr Neill's own personality, a type of hard and vindictive puritanism which reminded him of Bone. It was not that Neill had altered in any way. He had always held back from the exuberance of Chadwick or Harper. Swain felt that everything he saw was consistent with the rest of the other personality. It was merely that he had seen one side, one profile of Dr Neill. Now, it seemed, he had gone full circle round the man.

They were halfway through the journey when Neill said, 'Will you do something for me, Swain?'

'If I can.'

Neill folded the paper he had been reading and put away his glasses.

'I should like you to refresh my memory. Would you be so kind as to list for me the bones of the human body?'

Swain laughed, though he felt the chill of one who hears the trap closing. For days he had meant to familiarise himself with the basic facts of anatomy and physiology, had indeed done so in a few details. What Neill asked was impossible to him.

'After a trip to Brighton and dinner at Muttons?' he asked facetiously. 'It will have to wait until tomorrow.'

Neill smiled gently and spread out a hand, insisting upon the invitation being accepted.

'Please,' he said, 'the bones of the human body. Even the major bones in their correct order. Or just the complete list of the bones in arms and legs.'

Swain gave a humorous sigh of self-mockery.

'Out of the question tonight. Why? Does it matter? You could look them up for yourself as soon as we get back.'

Neill touched the tips of his fingers together and looked at them as he spoke.

'I have no need to look them up, Mr Swain. I know them by heart. All the same, it strikes me as odd that you were accepted by our elders and betters, as a medical student, in such a state of extraordinary ignorance as you appear to be.'

Swain laughed again, easier in knowing the nature of the trap.

'I was a schoolmaster. They thought I should learn quickly.'

Neill shook his head.

'You misunderstand me. How, in such a state of ignorance, could you pass the necessary and preliminary examination?

185

Viva voce, that is.'

'I didn't,' Swain said simply. 'My acceptance is probation-ary and not by virtue of examination. A tribute to my advanced age and reputation as a pedant.'

Neill nodded, as if he might be satisfied after all.

'Curious, Mr Swain. I have never heard of such a provision. I shall enquire about it.'

'Why?' Swain felt the colour burn in his face. 'Unless you mean to call me a liar! Why?'

'Really, Mr Swain! In order that one or two people of my acquaintance may benefit from it. Why else?'

As he continued the conversation, Swain rehearsed in another compartment of his mind the number of those who would have to be warned to back up his story if Neill began to enquire. Only now did he realise how hastily and badly the surveillance had been prepared. Yet the deaths of four young women and the threat of more had left no leisure for meticulous planning.

'Even so, Mr Swain,' Neill was saying in his slow and tantalising manner, 'I find it odd that you did not prepare yourself in the rudiments of your study. I think that seems strange.'

'Then you may think what you please.'

There was no way out except by attack, Swain decided.

'May I, Mr Swain? In that case, I think you are not a medical student at all. That you never have been, you are not now, and that you never intend to be a medical man.'

'That's absurd!'

'Not to me, Mr Swain. To me it is entirely logical.'

'Just because the bones of the human body. . .'

'Not just that, Mr Swain. Let me see, what could you be? Most likely in hiding from someone or something. You might, of course, be a criminal hiding from the law. More likely, there is someone – a lady, perhaps? – by whom you do not wish to be found. You might be a private spy or a policeman. Please, I beg you! I would not suggest that you spy upon Miss Sleaper and her guests. But there may be someone else in the area.'

'This is becoming ridiculous. . .'

186

'Is it, Mr Swain? Did you not know that Mr Haynes, at the photographer's in Westminster Bridge Road, is a private enquiry agent who works much of the time for the British government? He will tell you so himself. My dear Swain, what you do and whom you have to do with is your concern. I shall not think the worse of you for it. But if you suppose that the world takes you for a medical student, you greatly deceive yourself.'

'Then the world is wrong,' said Swain sourly. He glanced aside and saw that they were crossing one of the bridges over a dark south London street. Turning again, he drew back a little as Neill leant forward and tapped him on the knee.

'If I seem forward in my observations, Mr Swain, it is only in order to tell you this. If I may be of any assistance to you in whatever it is you have to do, I shall be honoured to receive your instructions. I like you, Swain. You're all right.'

21

'It was bad luck, that's all,' Lumley said. 'Even now he can't be sure that you aren't what you say you are. Can he?'

Swain sat in his own chair again behind his own desk in his own little room.

'Oddly enough, he didn't seem to mind. Offered to help me!'

'He couldn't have followed you here?'

'Mr Lumley! I did take precautions.'

Lumley stared out at the chimney-pots of Parliament Street.

'I daresay, Mr Swain. Only funny things been happening this last week.'

'What sort of funny things?'

Lumley looked down at his thumbs.

'That Slater, the one threatening girls on the common . . .'

'Well?'

'Seen twice in the vicinity of your lodgings. Nothing suspicious as such. Just seen there. That's all. There's a watch being kept if he should go there again. Nothing heavy. Just discreet.'

'Perhaps he has something to tell.'

'I don't think it's quite that, Mr S. Still, the sooner we can get young Harper tidied away, the sooner you'll be home to look after the ladies.'

With an effort of will, Swain put Slater from his mind.

'Did you get anything at all on Louisa Harris?'

Lumley shook his head.

'There's nothing for six months past – nor for twelve months, come to that. The feeling upstairs is either she's dead and the body not found – or it's another Lou Harris.'

Swain got up and began to lock the drawer of his desk. In another hour, he had decided, he must put in an appearance at the lecture theatre of St Thomas's – at least to the extent of making sure that Harper and his cronies saw him.

'She's almost our only hope, Mr Lumley. Lou Harris. I'm at an end with everything else. Even Walter Harper. He may be the worst sort of villain but there's nothing I can prove. Bone keeps his mouth shut about everything. As for Neill, he knows too much to give any more away.'

'There's not a note come since we dug up Matilda Clover,' Lumley said. 'Not even a comic verse in printed capitals.'

Swain pulled on his coat.

'There won't be, Mr Lumley. I'm sitting right on top of this whole thing at the moment – for all the good it's likely to do.'

'And if nothing alters?' Lumley asked sceptically, 'What then?'

Swain shrugged.

'Arrest Walter Harper, I suppose. Confront him at least. If there's anything in what Neill says, Harper had something to do with three of the four girls who died.'

'And what about H. Bayne and his blackmail? There's no news of him nor W.H. Murray, nor A. O'Brien.'

Swain thought about this.

'They might all be lodging under the same roof, Mr Lumley. Lambeth Palace Road. Miss Annie Sleaper's. The idea keeps crossing my mind but I can't see how it fits. Not yet.'

'There'd have to be two women for a start,' Lumley said. 'You haven't got two there.'

'The maid, Mr Lumley. I'll take the maid if the worst comes to the worst.'

'And the Spanish or Portuguese?'

Swain ignored the question, having no answer for it. He walked down with Lumley to the side entrance of the building where a cab was waiting for him.

'You'll be back in two days, then?' Lumley asked.

'It may be quicker than that,' Swain said. 'If not, I'll need a sub from the commissary officer. Police expenses don't exactly run to Brighton and dinner at Muttons. You might pass that on.'

The cab bore him away through the rear entrance of the drive, into Northumberland Avenue. With the road clear behind him, he crossed Westminster Bridge, the river water chopping and gleaming in the bright chill, and then south to St George's Circus. By the time he paid the driver and got down, he was far enough away from Whitehall to approach Lambeth Palace Road as if from the opposite direction.

At the southern end of Westminster Bridge Road, the handsome terraced houses were quiet in the sun of the March morning. It was only when he came to the railway bridges and the shops that the tumult of iron-rimmed wheels and the crash of drays filled the air. This was the Lambeth of the doxies and their bullies, of the market traders and the penny showmen, whores and archbishops, surgeons and footpads. It was also the Lambeth of Annie Sleaper, Thomas Neill, Patrick Bone, Charlie Chadwick, and Walter Harper.

As if summoned from oblivion by this thought, Dr Neill made his appearance on the far side of the road as Swain attempted to cross by Orient Buildings. Though the inspector would have chosen to avoid him, it was impossible at such range. Neill called out to him with vigorous affability and Swain found himself cornered once more.

'Dear me, Mr Swain! I thought you fellows were all at your anatomy classes now. Learning the bones of the body and all that sort of nonsense. Except, of course, for you clever ones who know such items off by heart to begin with. Be patient a moment, if you will, my dear Swain. I have one more errand to complete before I go back to the hospital. Our young friend Harper asks me to call at Armstead's for his photographs.'

'Armstead's?'

Neill looked at Swain knowingly as they crossed Hercules Road.

'Dear fellow! You will hear the good Armstead much talked of among the fast young men. Harper and his kind will take a girl there and have her photographed in the most unusual poses – or else acquire photographs of a certain sort.'

Swain understood and nodded. It was a commonplace that many of the photographic studios in the shabbier areas of London provided a private service of this sort for their clientele. Their sideline was known, chauvinistically, as French photography.

'You know all this for yourself?'

Neill smiled at him.'

'It is the house where my acquaintance Mr Haynes lives. The private agent with his contract for the government.'

It made sense of a kind, Swain supposed.

'I won't keep you a moment,' Neill said. He left Swain standing on the pavement and disappeared through a doorway beside a small shop-window. A selection of portraits, staring or self-conscious, sometimes simpering, confronted Swain through the dusty glass. A cracked bell on the little door jangled as Neill closed it behind him.

Pretending not to watch, Swain saw the encounter between the shopkeeper and Neill. A few words, a nod, and the exchange of an envelope for money. While he waited, Swain glanced up at the floors of the building above him. Like so many of the little shops in Westminster Bridge Road, this was let out as tenements on its upper levels. Mr Armstead must have made a satisfactory living from his trade and his rents.

Neill came out again and took Swain by the arm.

'If you please, Mr Swain, you may see for yourself the nature of these little gems. I suspect they were not posed for Harper, merely printed from stock negatives somewhere. Obtained by Mr Armstead from the Leicester Square trade.'

Swain saw that the envelope which Neill took from his pocket, printed with Armstead's business address, was marked 'W. Harper, Esq.' Neill opened it carefully so that it might be sealed again and handed it to the inspector.

Swain shook the six cards into his hand and glanced at the images in turn. They showed a woman whose body, by a trick of the camera, appeared to be pierced by half a dozen bodkins as she lay tied to a wooden frame. It was a curious amalgam of martyrdom and erotic suggestion. She appeared to be undergoing the agonies of St Sebastian and yet the overtly sexual and voluptuous texture of her naked limbs urged the onlooker to delight in the scene.

He returned the cards to the envelope and handed it back to Neill, determined to conceal his interest in this aspect of Harper's conduct.

'It depends on how you see these things,' he said vaguely, waiting for a brewer's dray to pass before crossing the road again. 'I daresay you could put the same pictures up as paintings in southern European churches and no one would think it the least odd. A martyr. That's all.'

Neill slid the envelope into his pocket.

'A different matter in Lambeth Palace Road, however, in the possession of a young man like Harper. I don't care any more than you do, Swain, what he may choose to ogle at. But take this together with what you saw on Saturday. The bawdy paper in the train and the evening with the girl in black silk. It adds up to a different answer.'

'It may do,' said Swain carefully. 'It might just do. That's for others to say. I can't see that's any business of mine. You're the qualified medical man and if it disturbs you, I should think you ought to say something to the dean of the medical school. Wouldn't you?'

'It may come to that.' Neill turned the corner with him into Lambeth Palace Road, the hospital buildings rising tall and ornate opposite the houses. 'I don't like starting something I can't finish, however. I'll be going home in a few weeks. If I accuse Harper now, I shan't be here by the time they judge his case. Much as I care about these things, it's a long trip back from New York.'

There seemed no answer to that. Neill opened the front door of the house and Swain followed him in. To his surprise, the inspector saw a note addressed to him, lying on the polished mahogany of the hall-stand. He picked it up but before he could open it, Annie Sleaper appeared, dark and lynx-eyed as a demon.

'Your dear sister, Mr Swain!'

'Miss Sleaper?'

'Your dear sister called to see you about half an hour ago. I explained that you were out and she promised to call again later in the morning. My note was merely to explain the circumstances in case I should miss you.'

'Oh yes,' said Swain, as if absent-mindedly, 'thank you. That was very kind.'

'Were you expecting her today, Mr Swain?'

'I rather thought she might call on me while she was in town. This afternoon, I understood.'

'You should take more care of such a charming young lady, Mr Swain. I can't feel it's right for her to be walking alone in this area with things as they are.'

'That's true, Miss Sleaper. Very true.'

He made his way to the stairs, concealing his bewilderment by a look of indifference to Miss Sleaper's news. Alfred Swain had been his parents' only child. The appearance of a sister was an intriguing possibility.

He had scarcely closed the door of his room and begun to put his personal possessions tidy, when he heard the trill of the new electric bell and Miss Sleaper's voice.

'Mr Swain, dear! Are you there? Are you there, Mr Swain?'

'It's all right,' the girl's voice said peremptorily, 'I'll go up and see him. I mustn't stop long.'

'Second floor front, dear,' Miss Sleaper said. Hers was not the type of house where gentlemen were required to leave the doors open during a visit by a lady – relative or not.

Swain heard feet on the stairs, the steps carrying a vigour and enthusiasm which he found almost ominous. Had Lumley conscripted a bull-faced police matron to bring his messages? Could it be one of the girls from Muttons with the last item of evidence to put the noose round Walter Harper's neck?

He opened the door and saw her, hurrying towards him along the landing.

'You?' he said, bewildered. 'What the devil are you doing here?'

But Rachel Ryland brushed past him, with an almost contemptuous flick of the hand, and stood securely in the room itself. Swain followed her.

'This is preposterous,' he said, with more astonishment than anger. 'How could you come here masquerading as my *sister*? I haven't got a sister. And who told you I was here?'

'We were worried to death about you,' she said primly, pushing the door closed and invoking the presence of her mother to add moral weight to what she had done. 'For all we knew you might have been killed. Supposing you had been lying dead somewhere and no one knew. . . .'

Swain's anger failed him. Looking at the bob of Rachel's reddish hair and the slim elegant neck which it revealed, he felt a new pleasure in thinking that his life or death meant so much to one so young and whose very pallor seemed to vibrate now with an animal excitement.

'How did you know where I was? Who told you?'

'No one,' she said simply. 'You behaved so oddly that I followed you. It wasn't difficult. Anyone could have done it.'

Despite the injury to his pride, Swain loved her for her determination. The tilt of the chin, the prim little nose, defied him to reprimand her.

'Someone should . . .' he said and then stopped.

'Spank me, I suppose.'

'That wasn't what . . .'

'No,' said Rachel, flicking the bob of her hair to dislodge an awkward curl, 'I'm sure it wasn't. Such an idea wouldn't cross your mind.'

Having made a fool of himself, Swain tried to return to first principles.

'Why are you here?'

'To see you.'

'I'm well aware . . .'

'You haven't even kissed me. At least you kissed me when I told you about that poor girl.'

Rachel unbuttoned her blouse and shed it like the gauze casing of a chrysalis on to a chair.

'Stop that,' Swain said, dropping his voice to a murmur as he remembered how easily voices carried between his own room and that of Harper. Afterwards he knew that he should have bundled her out through the door at that moment. Before he could do so, Rachel had unhooked her outer skirt and drawn it off. To have ejected his 'sister' from the room in such a state would have destroyed the surveillance once and for all. Rachel watched him with an expression bordering on insolence as she dropped her underskirt and petticoat.

'Please stop this,' he said quietly enough not to be heard beyond the partition wall.

Rachel stared at him, caught between laughter and defiance, as she undid the strings of her drawers. Swain was no virgin. He remembered with gratitude Roxana Wilberforce, the chestnut-haired young widow who had been his landlady and mistress for several months. Roxana and half a dozen other women made up the sum of his sexual experience. The prospect which Rachel offered was quite different. It was indiscreet in the present circumstances, with Miss Sleaper still audible at the foot of the stairs and Harper likely to return to his room at any moment. It put his surveillance in jeopardy, even to the extent of bringing him before Sir Melville Macnaughten on charges of indiscipline. Far the worst thing was the emotional entanglement which would involve not only Rachel but Edith Ryland as well. He could not live with them as he had done. For a moment Swain was possessed by anger at the ease with which Rachel had destroyed the domestic comfort to which he had grown accustomed.

Now she was standing in a wine-red corselet and stockings, the reddish bob of her brown hair bowed while her hands went behind her to undo the fastenings. Swain knew that he had let the moment pass when he might have struggled with the girl to prevent the present state of her undress. The thought that she would be taken as his sister in such a situation alarmed him and yet left him resigned to what might happen. In his mind he heard again the young men's voices at Muttons, admiring the girl with the black silk tight on her thighs, the movement of her hips as she walked out with Harper. Rachel was naked now, turning to put her stockings on the bed, thighs of a greyhound slenderness, buttocks pale and slight. It was hard to say, he thought afterwards, whether they confronted one another as adults or as children in a game. Whichever it was, they were equals at last.

It was impossible that she had behaved like this with any other person. At the most, she knew only the theory of passion and desire, entering upon that moonlit terrain with no more than a map of it in her mind.

Rachel came across to him, placing one foot delicately in front of the other as if walking a tightrope. She folded her arms round Alfred Swain and, bowing her head again, pressed her forehead to his chest.

'You might at least say something,' she murmured. 'Something nice.'

The woollen cloth of his jacket pressed her bare back as his arms returned the embrace.

'Why here?' he said gently. 'Why today? And why like this?'

Rachel looked up at him.

'Because it's safe. . . .'

'It's nothing of the kind,' he said, misunderstanding. 'There's Miss Sleaper at the foot of the stairs and lodgers in every room.'

'With you,' she said, referring simply to the undressing and what would follow. 'There's no other man I wouldn't be afraid with. Don't you see? There's no other man I could . . .'

Swain drew her to sit down beside him. Rachel clung as if he might be saving her from drowning.

'And what of Cousin Henry and the proposal?'

Rachel tried to prevent a snigger and failed. It was the last trace of the girl whose hand he had held during their walks across the common.

'I'm sure Cousin Henry would be more afraid than I,' she said, still laughing quietly with her head pressed against him.

'Get dressed,' Swain whispered.

'No,' she said.

'You don't know what you're doing, what the consequences may be.'

'I don't *care*!' she said. 'I've made up my mind. You *know* that.'

'You didn't behave like this under your mother's roof. . . .'

'That was different. In any case, I'm not going to get dressed. You can't very well make me. Can you?'

Swain reminded himself that there had been occasions in his life when the most preposterous and injudicious decisions had turned miraculously to his favour. He might regret what Rachel offered him now. Yet it would be nothing like the regret, for the rest of his life, if he refused the opportunity. Of all the women in his world, she was *the* woman.

'Get up,' she said softly, 'we must turn the counterpane back.'

Every experience of making love, in Swain's experience, had been in part like a voyage of discovery, as if at the beginning his partner had become a stranger again. The face that one kissed, he thought, was a close geometry of physical beauty unlike the remembered image of the girl. Her body was a sequence of slopes and curves, cool or warm as the case might be, on which his hand moved as easily as a skate on ice. The restlessness of her breath touched him close as a kiss. A woman in her own right, Rachel gave herself for the first time with an assurance and a lack of reserve, as if it caused her neither apprehension nor the least difficulty. She did not pretend to more passion than she felt, her desire for him expressed gently and as a rule without words.

Afterwards they lay in one another's arms, talking of Edith Ryland, the house near Clapham High Street, and the years they had already passed together.

'I always supposed it would end like this,' Rachel said in her casual innocence, 'even when I was quite a little girl. I didn't know *how*, of course. One doesn't at that age. But I knew that whatever it was, it would be with you. Does that shock you, Mr Alfred Swain?'

Swain smiled at her.

'I don't think it even surprises me.'

'Conceit!' she said, and drew herself above him on one elbow. 'I thought you were safe. That's all.'

The great question lay unspoken between them. What of the future? Would Edith Ryland sanction the activities of her daughter's lover under her roof? Would they make love secretly while pretending, in her presence, to their former relationship? Swain knew the deception would fail. Edith Ryland was too perceptive and sympathetic to be deceived. Would a suggestion of marriage now sound like more than a chivalrous and condescending apology by a man trying to repair some harm that had been done?

It was Rachel who solved the problem for the time being.

'Miss Sleaper will wonder what we're up to,' she said knowingly, sliding her feet to the floor and standing up. 'I think you'd better do up this for me.'

It was the corselet whose fastenings were easier for the wearer to undo than to button into place again. Swain sat up and assisted her. Glancing at the clock he saw that it was a quarter past one. Less than an hour had passed since Rachel had entered that room. It was a commonplace of Swain's experience that weeks or months passed, causing so little change that they might as well never have been. Then in a day, or an hour, his world was altered fundamentally and for ever. In the past hour he had lost that individual world altogether, changing it for one which could only be shared with the young woman who stood before him.

'Must you go home now?' he asked.

'No,' said Rachel, examining her stockings as she sat on the bed's edge, and then drawing them up her graceful legs. 'Mama has gone to Streatham today. It is her day for Streatham. How easily you forget these things, Mr Alfred Swain.'

Her laconic affection for him. Would it always be that? Or would she, at some point, set her true feelings at liberty? He got up and began to dress. When he had put his jacket on, Swain dipped his hand into the pocket and felt there the folded paper of Miss Sleaper's note. He drew the paper out, wondering if it would at last be the only memento of his love for Rachel Ryland.

Mr Swain,

Your sister, Miss Rachel, called upon you at eleven this morning and was sorry to find you out. She proposes to call again in an hour. Please leave a message, if you are in.

A. Sleaper

Swain read it. He read it again, and then again, more slowly.

'Come on,' he said brusquely to the girl who was combing her hair into place, 'it's time to go.'

'Then you're sending me away?' Rachel murmured, teasing him. 'Am I to be abandoned already?'

'We're both going,' Swain said impatiently, 'I've got to see Mr Lumley.'

'So soon?'

'At once.'

In his excitement, he was not listening to her with his full attention. At last the long and humiliating months of the investigation into the Lambeth poisonings would be rewarded. He could not be sure, of course. But if there was any justice, it must be so.

Only when they were walking towards Westminster Bridge Road did Swain remember the most important thing of all.

'You'll be alone in the house today? Until your mother comes back?'

'Yes,' said Rachel. 'Why?'

Innocence, rather than pertness, Swain thought as she turned her face to him. In his mind he saw Slater, the man of the common.

'Has there been a person in the street? Standing there or walking about?'

'Yes,' she said primly. 'Quite often.'

'If you see him again,' Swain said, 'he must be given in charge. If he's there when you go home, turn round and report the matter to Wandsworth lock-up.'

'I can't do that!' she said enigmatically. 'He's such a nice man. I shall probably ask him for tea.'

'Oh?'

'In his smart blue uniform and helmet. He's a policeman, you goose, Alfred Swain! We thought you arranged for him to be there and look after us while you were away.'

The relief which he felt allowed Swain to indulge his irritation at her coyness. He glanced round and saw the road was empty. Then his hand moved round behind her and pinched hard through the folds of her skirt. Rachel caught her breath and hardly flinched.

'A gentleman wouldn't have done that,' she said thoughtfully.

Swain kissed her.

'A gentleman wouldn't have allowed you beyond the foot of the stairs this morning. Would he?'

Rachel sighed with an entirely selfish air of satisfaction at the thought.

22

'It must be!' Swain said impatiently. 'It can't be a coincidence!'

He was talking to the bald but impressive dome of Walter de Grey Birch's skull as the great palaeographer bowed his head over the two papers on his desk.

'Even I,' said Swain desperately, 'even I can see it.'

Birch raised his head and the eyes regarded Swain with the same dispassionate analytical stare.

'Then perhaps you were deceived, Inspector Swain. Appearances are deceptive, you understand.'

'Appearances are all you have to work on,' Swain said sourly.

Birch waved his hand.

'If you please, Mr Swain. I must be left to concentrate on the matter. Please!'

He resumed his scrutiny through the magnifying lens in his hand. Swain tried not to fidget. He looked round the room with its uniform rows of bindings in break-front bookcases of honeyed wood. Transactions of a dozen learned societies –

English, German, Scandinavian – which were proud to number Birch among their members. Outside in the warm March sunshine, pigeons cooed and growled under the stone eaves of the British Museum's colonnade. A fine case-clock on the wall ticked time away.

Swain sighed.

'If you *please*!' said Birch.

He made some notes on a piece of paper beside him and then resumed his inspection through the magnifying lens. Half an hour passed, the hands crawling ever slower on the clock-face, as it seemed to Swain. It was almost five when Birch put down the lens and looked up once more.

'In my opinion, Mr Swain, you were not deceived by appearances in this case. In my *opinion* only, the same hand wrote both of these messages.'

'Would you say so in court?'

'I would give it as my *opinion*, Mr Swain. I cannot be more certain as to the hand.'

A pigeon ducked its head and looked in through the long window.

'You mean you can't be certain?'

A pained look appeared briefly on the great palaeographer's face.

'I am quite *certain*, Mr Swain, that the same person wrote the two messages. I speak only as to the handwriting. There it is my *opinion*. However, the two notes are also written on the same type of paper. The watermark is identical. Dixon's Imperial Bond! A common enough blue writing-paper. There is also the matter of the pen. I have seen enough but you might, if you wished, submit the script to microscopic examination. It would show up slight characteristic variants of the nib. The same pen was used for both notes. It is my *opinion* that the handwriting is the same but that might easily be disputed in court. On the other hand – unless someone close to the author of the first note perpetrated a very skilful forgery – the identical pen and paper turn my opinion into a certainty.'

'Thank you,' said Swain, getting up, 'thank you very much indeed.'

He took the two sheets of paper which Birch handed him and restored them to their folder.

'You are to be congratulated, Mr Swain. I would not have expected anyone, without a trained eye for such things, to spot the resemblance so accurately. You could not be sure, of course, no one could. All the same, you brought the papers to me and that has now served the purpose equally well.'

Swain managed to swallow his anger and take a civil leave of the famous palaeographer.

'I hope I shan't need to bother you again, Mr Birch,' he said gently. 'In that case we can let any other little matters rest just where they are. Good afternoon.'

To his satisfaction, he saw rekindled the slight unease which filled the great man's eyes whenever Swain hinted – however ambiguously – at the details of his private life as having been known to the inspector.

Without yet returning the two papers to Sir Melville Macnaughten's files, Swain went straight to the lower floor of Scotland Yard with its drab rooms distempered in horizontal bands. A uniformed constable stood outside the first of these. Swain raised his eyebrows at the man and the constable nodded.

'With Mr Lumley?' asked the inspector.

'Sir,' said the constable with another dip of his chin.

Swain opened the door softly. The interview room was in silence, Lumley standing guard at one side and the prisoner looking up from the wooden chair at the plain table.

'Oh dear, Mr Swain,' said Annie Sleaper, a smile not far from her lips, 'I suppose I should have known that one day someone would find out about my little sideline. Do you think it was very wrong of me, Mr Swain?'

23

With her dark eyes and sharp olive-skinned features, Miss Sleaper became almost waggish with him. She shook her finger roguishly.

'There *was* something about you, Mr Swain. Something not quite in order. I had no idea, of course, that you were a policeman. Nothing of that sort. But there was something that gave you away. How exciting this all is!'

'Miss Sleaper!'

She looked at him and the smile died at last.

'Surely, Mr Swain, surely my little sideline won't get me into trouble?'

Murder and blackmail, Swain thought. What then would the sideline be? Thoughts of kitchen-table abortion and a bomb-factory in the cellar of Lambeth Palace Road crossed his mind.

'After all,' said Miss Sleaper soulfully, 'it's not as if I'd done anything really wrong. Is it?'

'At least four cases of murder, Miss Sleaper, and two of attempted blackmail.'

She waved them aside, as if they were nothing.

'I know *all* about those, Mr Swain. After all, I'm helping with them. Aren't I?'

'Helping with them?'

Just then, Swain was possessed by a dreadful conviction that Miss Sleaper would prove to be the agent of some other branch of the police service.

'Yes,' she said, 'helping.'

'Helping whom?'

'The coroner and the people who have to do with the inquests on those poor girls. If you're a policeman, Mr Swain, I'm surprised you don't know about it already.'

'I am a policeman, Miss Sleaper – and I don't know. Tell me.'

'Well,' she said self-consciously, 'I suppose you know that

when they have courts of that kind, they need copies of the main documents in the case? So that everyone has a copy?'

'Yes, Miss Sleaper.'

'Well,' she said again, 'I'm the copyist – or one of them.'

'For the coroner?'

Annie Sleaper sighed.

'I suppose I shouldn't be telling you all this,' she said, 'but I expect it doesn't matter. There's been talk about young Mr Harper. Dr Neill who lodges with me was asked to keep a watching brief in the cases of the murdered girls for one of their families. Only with Mr Harper under suspicion, it wasn't something that could be talked about openly. You see?'

'Perfectly,' said Swain. 'What then?'

'Dr Neill needed copies of two or three documents that were in the case. He asked if I'd do them, seeing that I write a good clear hand. Medical gentlemen do scrawl so, Mr Swain.'

'And you wrote a copy of a letter to Mr Frederick Smith, after the death of Matilda Clover?'

'Yes,' she said, 'that's right. That and several others. But they were all in the papers at the time of the inquests. I copied letters and papers for Dr Neill even before that. There's a lot do it for medical gentlemen, Mr Swain. Especially when the papers are confidential.'

'Have you copied many papers for Dr Neill?'

'Ever so many,' she said proudly, 'all sorts of things.'

'When was the first one?'

'Oh,' Miss Sleaper looked up at the ceiling, 'I think it was ages ago. Then Dr Neill was asked to help, retained by those who had doubts over the death of Matilda Clover. I copied the papers to do with that, including the letter to Mr Smith the bookseller. Of course, I didn't know then that young Mr Harper was the doctor with the girl when she died. I never dreamt I'd have both him and Dr Neill under my roof. I don't expect Mr Harper murdered her, though. Do you?'

Swain ignored the question. Now that he had uncovered the origins of the blackmail, it remained to be decided whether Miss Sleaper was a party to it or merely a dupe.

'Did you ever copy letters for Dr Neill signed by A. O'Brien or W.H. Murray? Letters addressed to the police?'

'Oh, no,' she said, 'I'm sure there was nothing like that. It was mostly copies of medical papers and notes, only one or two letters.'

Swain nodded and went outside to speak to the uniformed constable.

'Send for two of the police matrons. I want a watch kept on Miss Sleaper. She must stay here while Mr Lumley and I go to make enquiries.'

Fifteen minutes later, in company with his sergeant, Swain walked quickly across Westminster Bridge towards Lambeth.

'It's blackmail, at least,' he said vindictively, 'and it might be murder.'

Lumley breathed heavily, racing to keep up.

'And where's that leave Miss Sleaper?'

'Perhaps it leaves her out of it – and perhaps it leaves her with a hand in the blackmail. What I fancy at the moment is young Harper being responsible for the death of at least one girl. Neill – probably Neill – discovering this and using it as a means of blackmail or tricking money out of others.'

'Perhaps Harper gave the girls something which he thought would liven them up – and killed them instead. It doesn't even have to be murder.'

They had reached the southern shore now, the junction of Lambeth Palace Road and Westminster Bridge Road, just beyond the Albert Embankment.

'It's murder all right, Mr Lumley. No two ways about that.'

Swain opened the front door with his key and led the way up to Neill's room on the first landing.

'Wait out here,' he said to Lumley. 'Wait but listen.'

He knocked, heard Neill's voice, and went in.

'A word with you, Neill,' he said, 'if you please.'

Neill had taken off his jacket and was sitting in waistcoat and shirtsleeves at the table, which was covered by books and papers.

'Sure,' he said, 'sit down, if you like.'

Swain ignored the padded chair which Neill had indicated.

'Before we go any further,' he said, 'I think it right to tell you that I am a police officer. Inspector Swain.'

Neill seemed pleasantly surprised.

'Is that so? I guessed you were probably that. Close enough. I'm something of the sort myself. In a medical way.'

Again Swain ignored the distraction.

'Have you employed Miss Sleaper to copy documents for you?'

'Certainly.'

'Including the letters of a blackmailer?'

Neill stretched back, put his feet on the table and folded his arms behind his head.

'You'd much better sit down, Swain. You'll have to hear me out.'

'I can do that standing.'

'All right.' Neill tilted his chair on to its back legs, rocking gently. 'I will say just this and then I can say no more at present. I was retained on behalf of certain persons – not by them but on their behalf. They are names I am sure you would recognise. It had to do with certain women in Lambeth and with the deaths of a few of them. There were hints of blackmail. I had already asked Miss Sleaper to copy medical papers for me in the ordinary way. I also asked her to copy one or two relating to the other business. I ceased doing so when I realised that she was indiscreet – or worse.'

'In what way?'

'I suspected she might make use of the knowledge for some purpose of her own.'

'Blackmail?'

'I hope not. At the same time, it became clear that I was very close to the source of the trouble. Walter Harper. By now I imagine he suspects you and me for what we are. There was a time, though, when he used to confide in me. He said that he got an abortion for one of his girls at Muttons. That girl had two friends, Marsh and Shrivell, who came to London. Apparently they thought he was the son of a rich father and that they could put the bite on him. Either he must pay blood-money or else they would tell the story of the Brighton abortion. How long might he get in prison for that, Mr Swain? You know better than I do.'

'Several years.'

205

'Exactly,' said Neill. 'I guess you know the sequel, then. Marsh and Shrivell died of poison before they could talk.'

'And Ellen Donworth and Matilda Clover?'

Neill brought his chair to rest on four legs.

'I don't know about Donworth. He was with Clover when she died. He signed the certificate. And then there's Lou Harris.'

'Tell me,' said Swain quietly.

Neill shrugged again, as if he did not much care whether Swain believed him or not.

'After our trip to Brighton, Harper got rather drunk the next evening. He remembered talk of Lou Harris. If one believes his story, he met the girl at the Oxford Music Hall and gave her poison in a drink. She fell down dead soon after they left. If the story is true, you can check quite easily. He says the girl was kept by a businessman in a house at 55 Townshend Road, St John's Wood.'

'Tell me about W.H. Murray and A. O'Brien, the detectives,' Swain said.

Neill shook his head.

'The names mean nothing.'

'Nor H. Bayne, the barrister?'

'No.'

'But surely you are employed by those people? Are they not the men who "instruct" you on behalf of their clients? If not, from whom does the instruction come?'

Neill gave a short, repeated laugh. It rang like a quack of glee.

'Oh no, Swain! Oh no! You don't try your policeman's trick on me! Keep to logic, old fellow. Murray and Bayne must be my masters if you can't find any others who are? Poor stuff, Swain! Not worthy of you!'

Swain stared at him. It was true, the logic was flawed. And yet its effect on Dr Neill was most remarkable. After a certain period of resilience, during which he had answered questions coherently and convincingly, it seemed as if his rationality was about to give way to hysteria.

'Oh no, Swain,' he guffawed, 'you don't get away with that! Believe me, you don't!'

He had turned his face away and was shaking his head in disapproval as if for the benefit of someone else in the room who was invisible to Swain.

The inspector sat down at last.

'You must tell me, please. Are Murray and O'Brien responsible for instructing you? Or Bayne? If not, then who is? You are engaged upon surveillance of the most important kind. Life and death may depend upon it for some young woman. I must know upon what authority you act.'

'No!' Now the voice was a peevish squall. 'I'm damned if I tell. I'm not saying if they instruct me or if they don't. There's an end of it.'

'Oh no,' said Swain quietly, 'there's the beginning of it. Until you produce those whom you say are instructing you, I cannot believe in their existence. Which leaves you, Dr Neill, and Miss Annie Sleaper as principals in the blackmail. You claim that the letter to Frederick Smith was all her own doing. She maintains it was yours.'

'I know nothing of a letter to any Frederick Smith.'

The self-confidence had returned again, as suddenly as it had lapsed. Swain guessed his opportunity was gone.

'And Lord and Lady Russell?'

'I know nothing of them. Nor any letter.'

Swain relaxed, then sprang the bluff upon his prey.

'The original of that letter is already identified as in your own hand, Dr Neill. By admitting its existence, you might have explained it as a copy purloined and sent by Miss Sleaper. By denying its existence, you convict yourself of blackmail.'

But Dr Neill laughed.

'I shall not deny its existence, Swain. When there are other ears than yours to hear me, I shall admit it in the very terms you recommend.'

He was getting up from his chair as the burly figure of Sergeant Lumley came through the doorway, as apologetically as a messenger at an agreeable social gathering. He looked towards Swain and Swain nodded.

'Thomas Neill,' Lumley said, and paused. 'That's all, is it? Just Thomas Neill? Thomas Neill, then. I charge you that at various dates between the 13th of October 1891 and 31st

March 1892, you did maliciously and feloniously utter and issue letters demanding money upon threat of blackmail to Mabel Edith, Countess Russell, to Frederick William Smith, Esquire...'

Swain listened, staring beyond the other two men at the limpid blue of river sky through the window. In every respect, he thought, it had been a truly surprising day.

24

The van, bringing the prisoners from the magistrates' court back to the cells of Bow Street police station, clattered over the stones of the courtyard. Lumley, who had sat handcuffed to Dr Neill in the back of it, got down with his prisoner in tow. Swain was waiting for him by the courtyard door.

'Remand in custody,' Lumley said with a backward nod at his prisoner. 'He won't be going very far.'

Two uniformed constables came up and removed Dr Neill from the sergeant's charge. They led him away across the sunlit yard towards the cell. Swain turned to them.

'Don't put him away yet. I shall want him in a minute or two.'

Lumley took off his bowler hat and wiped his brow on the back of his hand. The spring morning promised the warmest day of the year as yet.

'Opposed bail,' he said. 'No argument from his brief, not to speak of. I thought our man would never end. Every one of those notes was read out in court. H. Bayne and W.H. Murray, A. O'Brien and the rest. He shouldn't have done that. After all, we haven't got the killer yet – not as far as we know.'

But Swain turned and led him towards the door through which the uniformed men had taken Dr Neill.

'We might know soon enough,' Swain said. 'It's got to be a chance that Neill did the murders himself. In that case he can be identified.'

'Not by Ellen Donworth nor Matilda Clover, not by Lou Harris nor the Stamford Street girls. The girls that saw him, died of it.'

'Masters and May,' Swain said as they went through the doorway and the door swung to and fro behind them with a hollow boom until it closed at last.

'Who?' said Lumley sceptically.

'Masters and May. A pair of young women from Hercules Road who were with Nellie Donworth and the Stamford Street pair the nights they died. *And* who remember seeing the men they picked up.'

Lumley turned, his mouth open in simple admiration.

'How d'you do that, then, Mr Swain? Just how?'

The inspector shrugged modestly.

'Miss Peach – Miss Polly Peach. She's been good to me these last few days. You've no idea how good, Mr Lumley. When it came to the point of fitting blackmail and murder in the picture, she chattered away as if her life depended on it. Which it might have done, Mr Lumley. An accessory can hang as easily as the principal in these matters. Miss Peach had a sudden attack of memory. Swore that young Masters and May must have been at the music hall with the very girls that night. Gatti's in one case and the Oxford in the other. So it proves to be. They were at Gatti's on the night Ellen Donworth was killed, saw a man she picked up there and took across to the York Hotel. They were at the Oxford Music Hall before that. Both of 'em saw the man that Matilda Clover went off with. The same one that was with Donworth the night she died. Both girls called him "Fred".'

'And Lou Harris?'

Swain looked indulgently at his sergeant.

'While you were relaxing with the Bow Street magistrates, Mr Lumley, I took Constable McGouran out to 55 Townshend Road in St John's Wood. Yes – Miss Louisa Harris used to live there, kept by a bully called Harvey. No – she doesn't live there any more. About six months ago Lou Harris went out and never came back. No one knows where nor why.'

'Then where's her body?'

Swain shrugged again.

'Buried under another name or "found drowned", perhaps. It's close enough to the river, the Oxford Music Hall. Perhaps she's still there, in the water. A bloated mass wedged between the piles of a wharf, under the boarding, swelling and rotting further with every tide. Perhaps he buried her in waste ground, somewhere out at Hammersmith or Wimbledon. It might be years before anyone finds her – if they ever do. Much as I hope the file can be closed, I'd as soon not be the man who finds Miss Harris in her present state.'

A uniformed man, just going off duty, came down the distempered passageway towards the yard door, whistling to himself in the anticipation of leisure. He looked at Swain and the tune faded from his lips.

Twenty minutes later, Betty Masters and Eliza May entered the ground-floor office at Bow Street, looking out on to the police station yard. Swain had erected the usual board with eyeholes on the inside of one window. The witnesses had a view of the line of men, standing about three feet beyond the glass, without revealing themselves. The two young women were dressed as like as sisters in their mauve gowns and hats that were top-heavy with red and green feathers. To Swain they looked grotesque, no more glamorous than pantomime dames.

'Take your time,' he said gently. 'Mr Lumley will keep you company in the next room. Then you shall look through the eyeholes one after the other. There will be about a dozen men standing there. Remember that the man you saw with Nellie Donworth and the others may not be there at at all. If you see him – or think you recognise him – tell me which he is.'

It was not merely a sense of justice which led Swain to be scrupulously fair on such occasions as this. He knew from experience that any attempt to coax the girls into a wrong identification would guarantee waste of time, frustration, and failure at a later stage of the case.

'Miss Masters the first, if you please.'

Lumley led the other girl into the adjoining room and Betty Masters applied her eyes to the holes in the wooden screen. Outside in the barrack-like yard stood a line of a dozen men. They were dressed alike in dark clothes, frock coats and tall

210

hats, for all the world as if they might have been waiting for the orchestra to strike up a song-and-dance number. Dr Neill was second from the left. Just to one side of the line stood a uniformed police sergeant.

'Take your time,' Swain said gently. 'Take all the time you like. Look at each man carefully. See if there is one who might have been the person in company with Nellie Donworth – or with Matilda Clover. Is there one who might have been with the girls on both occasions?'

The feather in her hat quivered as she pressed her face to the partition.

'I dunno,' she said plaintively after a few minutes. 'They look all the same with their hats on.'

Swain concealed his fury by a bland mask of understanding.

'Was the man – or were the men – hatted when you saw them?'

''Course!' she said peevishly. 'But gentlemen like that all looks the same with hats on.'

Swain decided to take a risk with the evidence.

'Could you tell better with their hats off?'

'I might,' she said woefully. ''E could a-took his hat off in the bar to mop his face. It being hot in there. To see 'em without hats might make a difference.'

Swain went out for a moment and then returned. In the yard, the sergeant gave a precise, shouted order.

'Hats off!'

There was an uneven ripple of black silk in the spring sunlight as the line of men obeyed him.

'And now?' Swain asked the girl expectantly.

'Oh lor',' she said desperately. 'I dunno. Honest I don't! I can't swear I ever did see him without his hat. That's jist the trouble, you see. I'm sorry. Really I am.'

The neat solution of the case – Dr Neill as blackmailer and murderer in one – vanished from before Swain's sight. In his frustration he managed to treat the girl with courtesy.

'Never mind,' he said, touching her upper arm gently to draw her from the partition, 'it's better than picking out the wrong one. Much better to be honest.'

She turned round to him.

'I'm so sorry,' she said, 'really I am. Nellie was my friend. She was.'

An easy tear glimmered in her eye at the memory of such distant grief. The hat-feather quivered dangerously.

'We'll find him,' he said, offering her a reassurance he no longer felt himself. 'I promise you that. The best way you can help us is by being truthful.'

He opened the door to let her through and watched Eliza May take her place. It was useless, of course. Swain had expected that after the first failure. Months had passed since the crimes. Now the two girls were confronted by men in a costume which made them as indistinguishable from one another as soldiers on parade.

Unlike Betty Masters, Eliza May was brisk and self-confident.

'That all you got?' She turned to Swain from her survey of the line of men in the yard.

'All? Of course it's all.'

'Then you ain't got him!' she said. 'He ain't any of those out there. I'd take a Bible oath on that.'

'You're perfectly certain?'

'I don't take a Bible oath on things I'm not certain of,' she said scathingly. 'What's your game anyway? You trying to put up some poor bugger for what he never done? Wouldn't be the first time you'd done that. Would it?'

Inveterate contempt for the law – probably imbibed with her mother's milk – showed in Eliza May's eyes.

'Listen,' said Swain, 'I'm talking of murder. Slow and cruel killing. Not soliciting nor obstructing the footpath!'

Eliza May shrugged and then set her hat at its correct angle.

'I never seen any of them men with Nellie nor Mattie Clover. Murder or not makes no odds. You want me to tell lies for you in court, then you put the request in writing. All right?'

Swain turned away from her, went out into the yard and ordered the sergeant to dismiss the officers from the identity parade.

'Dr Neill for blackmail, then,' Lumley said ten minutes later, 'and young Harper for murder. Is that how it looks?'

'It might,' Swain said, gazing gloomily across the granite parapet of the embankment towards the cold river as the cab took them back to Whitehall. 'It might even be worse than that.'

'What's worse?'

The inspector looked at his sergeant, as if unable to believe that Lumley had missed the point.

'How long was the remand for today?'

'A week,' Lumley said. 'Why?'

'In seven days' time, Neill will be back with a *proper* lawyer. A Queen's Counsel. As things stand now, he'll have a strong case for release on bail. And that might be the end of that. As for Harper, all we've got as yet is words.'

But this deficiency was remedied soon after. Waiting for Swain was a courier with two messages. One was a packet from Armstead the photographer addressed to Walter Harper but intercepted by the private-clothes surveillance. Swain tipped the photographic cards from it while Lumley watched. The first showed a plump young woman sitting in a small lean-to privy. She was naked. There was a wash-bag over her head and a dark bottle lying on the ground. Her head had fallen forward and it was only the support of the walls, close on either side, which kept her from toppling over.

'She could have been posed,' said Lumley hopefully over Swain's shoulder.

'And she could be dead, Mr Lumley. What woman would choose to pose like that? And what man would want her so? A memento, Mr Lumley. A memento mori.'

He opened the second envelope. It had been posted the day before and its handwriting was familiar. There was a single unfolded sheet of paper.

The man you have in your power, Dr Neill, is as innocent as you are. I gave the girls those pills to cure them of their earthly miseries. Mr P. Harvey might also follow Lou Harris out of this world of care and woe. Lady Russell is quite right about the letter, and so am I. Lord Russell had a hand in the poisoning of Clover. If I were you, I would release Dr T. Neill, or you might get

213

into trouble. Yours respectfully, Juan Pollen, alias, Jack the Ripper. – BEWARE ALL! I WARN BUT ONCE!

Swain turned the envelope over.

'Yesterday's postmark,' Lumley said, still over the inspector's shoulder. 'Three days too late for Neill to send it. He'd been in custody that long.'

Swain lifted the letter by its corner.

'The Spaniard's handwriting,' he said. 'I don't need Birch to tell me that. This could be the end of our case, if we're unlucky. A good defence counsel can make mincemeat of the blackmail case against Neill if the notes keep on coming in days or weeks after he's been locked up. This is one of them. The handwriting is identical. The paper and watermark too.'

'Miss Sleaper?'

Swain shook his head.

'The wrong handwriting. I don't *think* she'd risk anything now, even if she was involved. The rest of the gang would lie low until Neill's case was settled.'

'It'll be settled all right at the next hearing,' said Lumley folding the papers again. 'There'll be an application for bail. And this time he'll have a QC briefed and waiting. You might just have to drop the charges. Even if Harper is the man who killed the girls, he's been warned off by all this. You'd be lucky to make a case against him now.'

Alfred Swain nodded. He noticed how, in Lumley's prophecy, the sergeant spoke of 'you' and 'your case', rather than 'us' and 'our case'. With his usual plump caution, Lumley had begun to distance himself prudently from Swain's handling of the murder enquiry.

25

Swain and Lumley sat behind Treasury Counsel in the well of Bow Street magistrates' court at the second remand hearing. From time to time Swain glanced at the dock, compelled by the image of Dr Neill, earnest and attentive in the rimless spectacles which made his eyes seem wider and staring. The heavy moustache, the hard and high crown of his bald head, gave the prisoner an aggressive or resentful air. Yet his expression was one of composure and self-possession. He *looked* like a man who had been wronged. That was the worst of it, Swain thought. In the battle of legal technicalities, Neill had the poise of a man who was going to win.

Luxmoore Drew, counsel for the defence, ruffled his gown a little like a dark brooding hawk arranging its plumage. He touched his wig lightly, as if fearing that it might fall off, and launched into the main drift of his argument. As he spoke directly to the three justices sitting at their bench above him, it seemed that he dared them to disagree with his appeal for fairness and decency.

'I shall not comment here, your worships, on the propriety of a police inspector disguising himself in order to live under the same roof as his suspect. Whether it be tolerable for a police spy to entrap a man in conversation, seeking to provoke words which may be given a sinister connotation when wrenched from their context, is a matter to be decided elsewhere.'

No one looked at Swain. Luxmoore Drew kept his back to the inspector as he continued.

'That Dr Neill suspected a certain other person of a crime is admitted by the counsel for the crown. That he tried to warn those whom he thought to be in danger is not disputed. That he arranged for the copying – the innocent copying – of papers relevant to the case and his own investigations is not in doubt. But, your worships, that any action of Dr Neill's is open to a criminal interpretation remains wholly in doubt. The case against him – the charge of blackmail – rests almost entirely on the report of a single alleged conversation. For that reason alone I have no hesitation in asking the court to order my client's release upon bail. That he should be held in custody pending trial is justified neither by the evidence against him nor as a matter of law.'

Swain's heart sank as Luxmoore Drew continued, with casual persuasiveness, to explain that the charges – of which his client was innocent – constituted little more than a public nuisance.

'Is it credible, your worships, that a note offering to help the police can be construed as blackmail? Can the other letter to Mr Frederick Smith, offering the services of a barrister, be called blackmail? The charges, against whomsoever they be laid, are ill-conceived and ill-founded. The crime alleged cannot by any process of law or logic be derived from the evidence which has been presented to your worships by the crown.'

Sergeant Lumley sighed into Swain's ear.

'He'll be out of here and on his way back to New York by tonight!'

Swain grunted and stared malevolently at Luxmoore Drew's back, a great black avian in full persuasive song. He recalled the remark which had once landed Benjamin Disraeli in court on a libel charge. The principle of a barrister's vocation is that he may say anything, true or false, provided he is paid for it.

Lumley was right. Swain watched in oppressive gloom as bail was set and arrangements made for Dr Neill's release. The court began to clear for lunch, Swain and Lumley walking out through the vestibule in the wake of the others. Outside in the sunlit street, two hostile groups stood several yards apart waiting for their cabs. Swain and Lumley were in conversation with the Treasury Solicitor's man, while Dr Neill and Luxmoore Drew waited in silence.

Each group went through the legal pantomime of pretending that the other was not there. When Swain looked up he was surprised to see Dr Neill looking directly at him. What surprised him more was that all the earnest attention and self-possession had gone from Neill's face. Now he stared at Swain, white-faced and with his eyes large in fear and indignation. He took a step backwards and shook his finger at the inspector, shouting defiance even in defeat.

'You set a rip after me, Swain! You did! I'll see you damned for this. By God, I will!'

Swain stared at him in astonishment as Neill turned and began to run. Even before the inspector could look at Lumley

216

and ask for an explanation, he heard what Neill had seen. It was the cause of the man's terror and sudden flight. A girl's voice just behind Swain said, 'It's me, Mr Swain. It's me he was looking at. I'm a ghost, Mr Swain. Back from the dead. I'm a voice from the grave. See?'

The words were spoken so quietly and feebly that, despite the warmth of the morning, Swain felt his spine turn to ice. Her voice had that simple childish quality of a medium in spiritualistic trance.

'I'm Lou Harris, Mr Swain. I was with Mattie Clover when he killed her.'

Swain turned and saw the frail vision of a girl of twenty in a black mourning-gown with white trimming. Under the dark bonnet was a fringe of ginger curls, the thin and freckled face of the consumptive.

'Stop that man!'

It was Lumley's shout, a roar which seemed to fill the street. Now the sergeant set off heavy-footed in pursuit of the suspect. Neill was far ahead of him, running towards a hansom which had just set down its passengers. Fright gave him such energy that he was well ahead of Lumley, snatching for the door of the cab. He missed his foot on the step, dragged himself up and pulled himself into the cab. While Swain and Lumley were still fifty yards away, Neill had shouted his instructions to the driver. The whip cracked and the wheels began to turn.

'Keep your eye on that cab, Mr Lumley! Don't lose it! Get the number if you can!'

But Swain was already taking the lead from his sergeant and was soon in the better position to carry out his own orders.

Ahead of him in the busy street the hansom shone black and sleek in the sun. With tantalising skill, it manoeuvred through the heavier traffic approaching the Strand, gaining easily as it pulled away from the pursuers. If Neill should get clear now, Swain knew that he would never be found again. Such a man would hang himself before he allowed the law to do it.

For a moment the cab slowed down as it came to the Strand, opposite Waterloo Bridge. By the time Swain reached the junction he had lost sight of it for half a minute or more. It had slipped into the main stream of the traffic. The inspector stood at the corner of the Strand where the glass of the shop windows shimmered in strong light and the wide avenue was packed with slow-moving vehicles. In the immediate area he guessed there were between fifty and a hundred hansoms, most of them nearly identical.

Dodging into the traffic, ignoring the shouts of the drivers and riders, Swain leapt at each cab, drawing himself up on the step and looking into the buttoned leather interior. There was no sign of Dr Neill. By this time his cab might have turned from the Strand into one of the streets running north, doubling back the way he had come. Perhaps it had somehow got across Waterloo Bridge to the south or else along the Embankment.

'Mr Lumley! Mr Lumley!'

Swain glanced about him as he ran from one cab to the next but there was no sign of Sergeant Lumley.

Once again, Swain felt the familiar despair at this investigation of a proven case slipping away from him. Then, just beyond the Aldwych, his reward came at last. Dr Neill had seen the search getting closer to his own cab. He burst from its door, ignoring the cabman's shout. His silk hat rolled away as he scrambled between the vehicles, reaching the south side of the Strand and going at a hobbling gallop towards Waterloo Bridge. Swain saw no sign of Lumley, but the unpaid cabman flourishing his whip had joined the chase.

'Stop that man!'

It was useless, of course. The pavements of the Strand were so busy that it was hard to see which man was being chased. Was Neill the fugitive or merely the first of the pursuers? The strollers paused and stared. One of them, misunderstanding, tried to stop Swain. The inspector threw him off and plunged on through the crowd.

Waterloo Bridge! Neill was going to throw himself off the parapet! To cheat the hangman. The coincidence with Montague Druitt, the Ripper suspect, was too plain to miss.

'Stop that man!'

No one stopped him. Dr Neill, his coat-tails flying absurdly behind him like fins, had turned on to the bridge.

Then, to Swain's astonishment, Lumley appeared at the far end of the bridge, running back towards them. Neill paused, seeing himself caught on the wide span which rose across the glittering water of the river and the panorama of Westminster to the north. Now he was almost in Swain's grasp as they raced towards the parapet of the bridge on that side. It would be all right after all.

At that moment Swain's feet went from under him, his shoe skidding on a perilous smear of horse-dung. For a moment he was in the air with time for an instant of wholehearted fury at the unfairness of it all before he came down on his back with a bruising thump. By the time he had rolled on to his knees, Neill was at the parapet, scrambling up. Swain looked for Lumley and saw him still twenty or thirty yards away.

'Stop him!'

He was like a child crying for the unattainable. Dr Neill hesitated only a moment, then gathered himself to jump. At that moment, something seemed to fizz past above Swain's head. A streak of black light circled the London sky. It clutched Dr Neill in its grasp and snatched him back from the parapet so that he fell to the pavement with Sergeant Lumley standing over him.

Swain looked round in amazement and saw the cabman standing beside him, drawing in his whip again. There was a look of profound grievance in the man's eyes.

''E bilked me of me fare!' the cabman said. ''Oo's 'e think he is?'

26

'She was my friend, Mattie was,' said Louisa Harris quietly. 'Why'd he want to do such a thing to her?'

'That's what we must find out.' Swain put a hand on her shoulder, feeling bone sharp and prominent under the skin. Then he went round to his own side of the desk and sat down opposite to her. 'Just tell me the whole story from the beginning.'

Louisa shrugged.

'I saw him that night in October, when I was with Mattie in the promenade of the Alhambra. He came up and spoke to us – but we didn't make an agreement. Then me and Mattie went to the St James's Bar in Piccadilly to see if we could do any good – and there he was again. Come up and put his hand on my arm, just there. This time was different. We made our arrangements with him and spent the night with him at a hotel in Berwick Street. Next morning he talked about the pills that could be had for all sorts of things. They could get rid of spots on the face – which I had just then – or stop a girl getting in the family way – or even just make her feel more lively.'

'Did he tell you he was a doctor?'

She nodded eagerly.

'An American doctor that was working at St Thomas's Hospital. Anyway, he promised to meet us the following night on the Embankment – the bit by Charing Cross Station – at eight o'clock. And he said he'd bring some of the pills for getting rid of spots, for me. Mattie wanted some of the others.'

'Were there just the two of you – you and Mattie?'

She thought about this for a moment, as if unwilling to reply.

'Please,' said Swain, 'I promise you have nothing to fear.'

Lou Harris made up her mind.

'There was Charlie Harvey that I lived with in St John's Wood.'

'The businessman who kept you?'

'He just kept me,' she said miserably, 'he's no businessman. Charlie takes the money I earn. That's all. He didn't come all the way with us. We left him in Northumberland Avenue under the trees.'

'Could he see the man you met?'

'Oh, yes,' she said, 'plain as day. Anyway, along we go and find Fred standing there. He took us to the bar of the Northumberland and bought us wine – and some roses from a flower-girl that came in selling them.'

220

'The pills,' said Swain gently. 'What about them?'

'He showed us the pills. They were oblong capsules wrapped in tissue. Two of them for each of us – different colours. I asked him if I should take them straight away and he said no, after the wine. Mattie Clover was going to meet a man and so she took both the pills. Then this man – Fred – put her in a cab and paid the fare. I walked with him down to the Embankment and he said it would be best if I took the pills then. He promised to meet me later at the St James's Bar and we was to spend the night together in a hotel. I was to take the pills now and try and eat some figs before I met him again, as the fruit would make the pills work better.'

'The pills,' Swain insisted. 'When did he give them to you?'

'Then,' she said. 'Straight away. He took them from his waistcoat pocket and gave them to me. He undid his silver flask so that I could swallow them down with a little drink. I was to swallow them and not bite.'

'Did you?'

Lou Harris shook her head and smiled for the first time, at her own cleverness.

'I never. I put my hand to my mouth – my right hand – and pretended to swallow them. But I thought there was something rum about it all – that he meant to harm me. It was his look just then. I passed the pills into my other hand – the left. He seemed concerned that I might not have swallowed them and he made me open my right hand to show him. It was empty. But while he was looking at it, I dropped the pills behind me from my left hand. So when he made me open that, it was empty as well.'

'Did he leave you then?'

'He put me in a cab and paid the fare. He said he had an appointment at St Thomas's Hospital first but he'd meet me at the St James's Bar at eleven o'clock. He never showed up. Of course, by then he must have thought I was dead.'

'Why did you leave St John's Wood after that?'

Lou Harris stared at him as if astonished by his stupidity. The first hint of antipathy to his kind entered her voice.

'I had an offer of work down at Muttons, didn't I? And Mattie Clover dying of drink, as was said, shook me up. Only when I got down to Brighton I was poorly. So that was the end of that.'

'Where did you hear about the arrest and the trial?'

'It was read to me,' she said triumphantly, 'by one of the other girls. Not that I can't read for myself. And there was my name along with Mattie's as having been murdered. The only person that thought I was dead must have been the one who gave me the pills. Me and poor Mattie. Charlie Harvey could see an advantage in that. The money that might be made if it was a startling thing. The papers 'd pay to hear my story. So I come up and sat in the public gallery. The minute they put him up in the dock I recognised him. So did Charlie Harvey, though he'd only seen him across the road.'

'Thomas Neill?'

She looked at him again as if Swain was deliberately acting dense.

''Course not!' Lou Harris brushed a stray ginger curl from her forehead. 'That's not his real name. He's called Fred.'

'Anyone could be called Fred.'

'Not just Fred,' she assured him. 'He showed me a letter once. Written to him in America. He's not just Fred. He's Dr Frederick Cream.'

27

'Frederick Cream?' Rachel looked up from the comfort of Swain's bare arm about the smooth nudity of her back and shoulders as they lay together on his sofa, 'Frederick *Cream*? No one's got a name like that. He sounds more like a patent medicine than a doctor.'

Swain kissed her mouth and the youthful scorn vanished in relaxed contentment. It was Mrs Ryland's day for visiting her married sister at Streatham where the last hope of Cousin Henry as Rachel Ryland's bridegroom died among the cakestands and the teacups.

Swain kissed her again and stroked the warm living marble of her flank.

'I don't really care what he's called. We've got him. Six more weeks and his trial should come on at the Central

Criminal Court. Luxmoore Drew won't talk his client out of this one. They find him guilty and give him three clear Sundays.'

Rachel brushed a troublesome hair clear of her eyes.

'What's that?'

'Three clear Sundays.' Swain explained, 'When a man is sentenced to be hanged, they give him three clear Sundays before they do it. Tradition, I suppose. Time to repent. I don't know.'

Rachel sat up, hugged her bare knees, and stared out through the window at the light rain falling on apple leaves.

'Would you poison me?'

'No,' said Swain reasonably, 'I'm a knife man myself. Or perhaps even a gun.'

'They'd hang you!' Rachel tugged gently at his hair.

'You forget,' he said, 'I know all the mistakes not to make.'

Rachel sighed.

'I shan't marry you,' she said thoughtfully, and then became suddenly intense.

'This!' She pointed at the disordered sofa. 'This doesn't mean you have to marry me. That isn't the point.'

Not a line deepened in Swain's long, intelligent face.

'I wouldn't dream of marrying you,' he said blandly. 'Wild horses wouldn't drag ... That *hurts*! Damn you, you little witch!'

With both hands he freed his hair from Rachel's fingers which were tugging upon it with nonchalant energy.

'There!' she said triumphantly. 'You'd poison me, after all. Wouldn't you? If you could have forced strychnine down my throat just then, while I was pulling your hair, you'd have done it!'

'I'm a policeman,' Swain said, blinking involuntary tears from his eyes. 'The law has proper remedies ...'

Before she could evade him he administered a slap to Rachel's bottom which made the walls of the room sing. Clutching herself she gasped as if to release the effect of the reprimand.

'You brute,' she said at last, 'that wasn't *funny*!'

'It depends,' said Swain evenly, 'upon one's sense of humour.'

They stared at one another, as if in silent hostility, for several minutes. Swain's mouth quivered presently but it was Rachel who began laughing first. The game of 'straight faces' was one which they had played, with variations, since her childhood. She threw herself upon him, as if in attack, forcing him down on his back with her legs splayed either side of his hips.

'I wonder,' she said a moment later, 'I wonder what the law feels about *this*. . . .'

It was still only five o'clock when a door slammed somewhere on the ground floor. Rachel shot upright and jumped from the sofa.

'It must be mama,' she said, snatching for her clothes, 'but it's too early.'

'Perhaps Cousin Henry has thrown you over,' Swain said, gazing absently at the girl as she dressed. 'He must be tired of waiting for an answer.'

He stroked the slim quivering leg as she pulled her stockings on.

'Oh bother Cousin Henry and the lot of you!' Rachel, in a panic at her mother's voice, threw on the rest of her clothes.

As she opened the door softly, Swain said, 'I shall speak to your mama about you. All this must be put upon a regular footing.'

She turned and saw the amusement in his eyes.

'No!' Swain heard the whisper as a violent hiss. 'Don't you dare do any such thing, Alfred Swain!'

A single stair creaked as she made her way down quietly to her own bedroom on the floor below. Swain got up and straightened his clothes. Throughout his life he had found that the best things happened quickly and certainly. With his hair combed and his tie immaculate, he went down to the drawing room. Edith Ryland had taken off her coat and unpinned her hat, which lay on a side table like a trophy of lacquered basketwork.

'Mr Swain?' Edith Ryland turned with a smile. 'I thought it was your late duty this evening.'

He nodded. 'I wondered if I might have a word before I go . . .'

224

'As many as you like, Mr Swain.'

He sat down opposite her and looked at the slight smugness of her pale face, behind which kindness lingered. Drawing breath he wondered how best to enter the cold reality before him. For better or worse, it was to be a plunge.

'I love Rachel,' he said. The ticks of the ormolu clock came slow as minute guns in the silence of the room as he watched and awaited her response.

Half an hour later, Mrs Ryland was saying, 'Of course, you know, some of our more distant cousins have been quite in the public eye. My husband's family was descended from Edward Ryland, the engraver, who came from Wales to London at the end of the last century. One of his own cousins was Mr Henry Ryland who painted *The Young Orpheus*. . . .'

Swain tried politely to make his point.

'I ask only your leave to speak to Rachel upon the subject. The decision must be hers. Whatever it may be, I shall accept it.'

It was time for him to go.

'I had not thought,' said Mrs Ryland, 'I had not thought of such a thing happening so soon in her life. All the same, you know her better than any man alive. I hope, Mr Swain, that will not prove a disadvantage.'

She turned and went back into the drawing room, as if to meditate alone on this difficulty. Swain hurried up the stairs to get his coat and hat. Rachel was on the landing, in a sulk.

'I told you not to!' she whispered bitterly.

'You don't know what it was I did.'

For a moment she looked at his invincible stupidity.

'Doors have ears,' she said meaningly. 'Keyholes! I won't marry you just because of . . . because of *that!*'

Swain understood.

'I hope you won't refuse me because of it either,' he said lightly. 'I should feel hard done by.'

When he came down again with his hat and coat, she had gone into her room and closed the door. All the way to Whitehall Place in the horse-tram, Swain wondered whether he had done a wise or a very foolish thing that day.

There was no sign of Sergeant Lumley. On the little desk in

his room Swain found a single envelope. It was the dull blue of a telegraphic message. Only when he opened it did he see that it had come from the office of the District Attorney in Joliet, Illinois.

Identify subject as Thomas Neill Cream, released from Joliet Penitentiary, Illinois, 14 August 1891

Born: Glasgow, Scotland, 27 May 1850
Entered Canada with father: 1854
McGill University: 1872
Graduate, Faculty of Medicine: 1876
Practice in London, Ontario: 1877
Suspected of causing death of Rosie Barnes by pills given to procure an abortion: 1878
Licensed medical practitioner, 434 West Madison Street, Chicago: 1879
Acquitted of murdering Arabel Julia Faulkner by the administration of poison to procure an abortion: 1880
Charges of murdering Helena Stack by poison not proceeded with: 1880
Bailed on charges of sending scurrilous matter through the United States mails: 1881
Charged and convicted of second degree murder – i.e. the poisoning by strychnine of Daniel Stott, husband of Julia Stott, mistress of the accused: 1881
Sentenced to life imprisonment: October 1881
Upon his father's death, Cream's sentence was commuted to seventeen years. He was released on parole in August 1891.
Cream was married in Canada, in 1876, to Flora Eliza Brooks who died in unusual circumstances the following year.

Swain put the blue paper on his desk again with mixed feelings of gratitude to America and the Atlantic cable coupled with an astonishment amounting to awe at the criminal endeavours of Dr Neill Cream, *alias* Dr Neill, *alias* Fred Cream, *alias* H. Bayne, barrister, *alias* W.H. Murray, *alias* A.

O'Brien, detective, and in the case of the wreaths sent to the graves of the Stamford Street girls, *alias* Wattie.

The greater awe was reserved for the doctor's public performance. At least eight young women and one old man had died in agony from his poisons. How many more had gone to their deaths unavenged? Yet this was the same Dr Neill who had been Annie Sleaper's conscientious lodger, the genial 'uncle' of the younger medical men; the man of financial integrity and honest citizenship. Swain tried to imagine the private hell of death and torment behind this earnest appearance. What images of martyrdom had there been in the animal shrieks of his victims? What cackling delight in their convulsions? Could it be that the glint in the doctor's eye signified a mission from on high to rid the world of its human corruption, the girls who clustered outside Orient Buildings and a thousand other tenements, plucking at the sleeves of the men who passed by?

For the greater part of the evening, Swain sat at his desk and thought of the man who was to be brought to justice. Now the people would have their revenge. True, they lacked the laws to put the murderer to death by means as cruel as he had employed upon his victims. All the same, they would find tortures for him. The public glee of the trial at the Central Criminal Court. Then the three clear Sundays in the condemned cell. The agony of lying down each night in the knowledge of his coming destruction, finding a respite in sleep only to wake with a start of terror more intense as the end came one day closer.

Swain pitied him. There was time for that now that the killer had been caught and the world was safe again.

Like the bright colours of a child's kaleidoscope the mirrored fragments of truth formed a final pattern. With his access to Canada and the United States, it would have been the easiest thing for Neill Cream to have the Metropole Hotel circular printed by men who thought it part of a fiction of some kind. To incriminate Walter Harper, Cream had only to order photographs under that name and, perhaps, masquerade as the young man in Stamford Street.

By ten o'clock, Swain had unravelled the last corner of the

web by which the murderer had protected himself at the expense of an innocent man. Sooner or later, Harper would have been proved guiltless. By then, however, Dr Cream's shadow must have passed, falling instead upon New York or Melbourne, Paris or Chicago. For a little while, Swain felt so pleased with his meticulous skill that he almost forgot the riddle of the blackmail notes.

28

'Engaged? Engaged to the prisoner?'

Swain was at the same desk looking at the expensively dressed vision of Laura Sabbatini who sat in the chair on the far side. She had that slim and high-boned prettiness which went with eyes of a violet hue, a light blush on velveteen cheeks, and a chignon of chestnut-red hair.

'He is somewhat older than I,' she said in a charmingly pedantic manner, 'seventeen years older. But, yes, we are engaged.'

'The difference in age was not what . . .'

'As soon as this wretched business is over we shall be married. It is all decided. I hope it will be soon, so that we may go away together while the Italian lakes are still warm.'

'Married?' Swain looked in disbelief at her beauty in its lavender-blue gown and bonnet.

'Mr Swain!' Now there was scholastic authority in the young voice. 'I beg you to remember that I know Dr Cream. You do not. Oh, I suppose you *think* you do, Mr Swain! *You* the finder-out of other people's secrets. But you are quite mistaken.'

'In what way?' Swain was impressed and intrigued by her.

'You do not know him,' Laura Sabbatini said with a simple shrug. 'In the months I have known him, I have received nothing but kindness, courtesy, and devotion. The man I know, Mr Swain, is no murderer, though you may wish him so.'

'He served ten years in Joliet for murder, Miss Sabbatini.'

'Yes,' she said, her voice almost a sneer for his idiocy, 'to protect the woman he loved! She who had killed her husband!'

Swain sighed and then played a careful and meditated shot.

'When did you first come to England, Miss Sabbatini?'

The blood rose to her cheeks as if the detection of her alien birth might be a matter for shame.

'I was a few weeks old. My father was of an Italian family in the service of Queen Isabella of Spain. My mother was Spanish. When the Queen was deposed in 1868, we came to England, to the Old Rectory near Tring. But we are not beggars, Mr Swain. We ask charity from no one. My father brought with us all the family treasure, the carriages and those servants who chose to accompany their master and mistress. My position in England is quite as legitimate as your own, Mr Swain.'

'I have no doubt of it,' said Swain chivalrously, his heart beating fast with anticipation of her next answer. 'Was it only to you that Dr Cream entrusted the copying of papers in the case he was working upon?'

'I copied papers for him, Mr Swain. It is common practice in such circumstances.'

'And your father, perhaps?'

'My father is dead, Mr Swain.'

Swain's confidence faltered, seeing the way ahead of him blocked. It was Laura Sabbatini who saved him.

'Two of the servants, Luis and Manuel, made copies. They speak English and write Spanish. They could not compose well in English but they copied easily enough.'

So that was it! The preposterous simplicity of the blackmail mystery left Swain silent and marvelling at it. He might have searched all London but without penetrating the closed expatriate world of the Sabbatini family. A 'gang' of extortioners – the Spaniards and women – would have eluded him. As for 'Dr Neill', he was unknown at the Old Rectory near Tring. In that house he went by his true name of Thomas Neill Cream. Before Swain could ask his next question Laura Sabbatini answered it for him, unaware that she was doing so.

'You are not to blame Luis and Manuel, Mr Swain. They do

not read English well enough to be sure of what they were writing. Yet each of them has a fine clear script. I knew that they copied for Dr Cream and that he gave them little presents for it. As I made no objection, the fault cannot be theirs.'

Swain nodded.

'They have nothing to fear, ma'am. I promise you that.'

She seemed content with this, as he prepared himself for the last question of all.

'Did you ever post Dr Cream's letters for him?'

'Sometimes,' she said, shrugging her graceful shoulders to indicate the triviality of the assistance to her lover. 'When he was not to be in London, I would bring them up and post them a few days later. I attend life-classes once a week at the Royal College of Art in South Kensington. Several times I posted letters for him on my way. But they were letters of every kind, Mr Swain. Not merely the copies for the coroner's court or the police. There was one letter he left with Manuel in a sealed envelope – to be posted if ever he failed to keep our rendezvous.'

'With Manuel?'

Laura Sabbatini looked at him steadily, as if he should have understood her.

'My fiancé believed that the criminals against whom he worked might discover the assistance he was giving to the authorities. In that case, they might try to kill or injure him. Because he did not wish to alarm me, he gave his instructions to Manuel. Was that wrong?'

'No,' said Swain quickly, 'no, of course not.'

The last thread of the blackmail tangle was clear. Though the note had been posted after the suspect's arrest, Juan Pollen, *alias* Jack the Ripper, was Neill Cream himself.

'You are wrong, Mr Swain. Wrong in your suspicions and your conclusions.'

He returned the steady gaze of the violet eyes, fascinated by the shift of light upon them.

'Fortunately, Miss Sabbatini, there is a court of law which will show me to be wrong, if I am so.'

'It will,' she said, pitying him quietly. 'To be sure, it will.'

He got up and opened the door for her. As she passed,

Laura Sabbatini turned her face to him, pale but composed.

'My fiancé wishes you to know, Mr Swain, that he bears you no grudge.'

'I am glad to hear it.'

'He asks only that you should visit him so that he may talk to you in a capacity other than that of a policeman. I believe he likes you, Mr Swain. Despite everything.'

The lunacy of the Lambeth poisoner suddenly invaded the warm room. Its effect on Swain's nerves was as if someone had drawn fingernails down a slate. Regaining his equanimity with an effort he answered her.

'Until the trial, I can only talk to him as a policeman. He will understand that. Afterwards, we shall see.'

Afterwards. In the next few hours all Swain's thoughts were penetrated to some degree by speculation on what 'afterwards' might be. The Director of Public Prosecutions had ordered the prisoner to be charged as 'Thomas Neill' with the murders of all four women in Lambeth and with blackmail. Swain disapproved. It was all or nothing, this way. If by some madness of courtroom logic, it was held that Dr Neill was not Dr Neill Cream, then Cream must go free. The House of Lords had ruled in favour of just such nonsense when Lord Cardigan shot Captain Tuckett on Wimbledon Common.

A more probable outcome was that the defence might succeed by putting in a plea of insanity. Swain wondered if anyone who had witnessed the deaths of the victims or read the jubilant taunting and nonsensical threats of the blackmail notes could believe that Thomas Neill Cream was sane. The amiability and ease of manner which he exhibited turned suddenly to a savage and vindictive lust for pleasure and murder. Several of the papers had already hinted at the story of Jekyll and Hyde, which had taken the bookstalls by storm six years earlier.

At last the oppression lifted from Swain's thoughts. In the dock, Neill Cream would appear only as the amiable and rational Jekyll. It was that which would hang him.

Even so, the four days of the trial at the Central Criminal Court did little to reassure Inspector Swain. In the streets outside the newsboys bawled the fame of the Lambeth murders whose ghastly story was told in thick-lettered headlines and column after column of close print. Inside the court, there was quietness and anti-climax as the facts of life and death were rehearsed with unreal calm. Neill Cream sat polite and attentive in the dock between the two warders. No reproach was uttered against him, there was no anger or indignation yet. Each afternoon he was taken back behind the massive walls of Newgate gaol nearby.

By the end of the third day, Swain decided, there was only one course open to the defence. Admit the facts and plead insanity. To his astonishment, on the following morning, the defence called no witnesses who might have supported such a view of mental alienation. Mr Geoghegan rose and addressed the jury. To Swain's bewilderment the defence counsel began to attack the prosecution evidence. The murderer was never seen except by lamplight. Might the girls not have been mistaken? Thirty or forty thousand men in London wore similar hats and moustaches. The analysis of human entrails for poison was an uncertain science, still susceptible of error. Even if strychnine had been found, which Mr Geoghegan disputed, the time of its administration could not be proved. As for the references to Matilda Clover and Louisa Harris in the blackmail notes, was this not proof of innocence of murder? The fact that one girl was dead and the other alive made it certain that the names had been cited at random by a man who knew of the young women but was unaware, in truth, whether they were alive or dead. If Neill Cream were truly the murderer, why did he not name Ellen Donworth at the time?

Swain supposed that it was impossible for a barrister to stand up in a murder trial and explain to the jury that his client had no defence. Mr Geoghegan had done the next thing to it, however.

'Dr Neill,' said Geoghegan firmly, 'was a stranger in London. He was thrown upon his own resources for amusement. Unfortunately for him, he did not make the acquaintance at first of a modest woman. But my client is not being tried for immorality, gentlemen of the jury. That is not the issue here. Fearful mistakes have been made in the past.

Identification in police courts is nothing more than a mockery. Identification in such circumstances as obtained in Bow Street is the most dangerous of all.'

Swain relaxed at last. It was all over. Mr Geoghegan knew it, even if his client did not.

On the fifth day, the jury retired after lunch to consider their verdict. Ten minutes later there was a stir in the court at the news that they were returning. In that case, Swain knew, there could only be one verdict.

Presently, Mr Justice Hawkins, for all the world like a little old lady in his red robe and white wig, was speaking slowly and precisely to the figure in the dock. Thomas Neill Cream was a mere body now in which, as an act of grace, the law permitted life to continue for 'three clear Sundays'.

'Thomas Neill Cream . . .'

Swain winced. Could they hang a man called Cream if he had been tried as Neill?

'. . . the jury have found you guilty of the crime of murder. Those murders are so diabolical, fraught with such cold-blooded cruelty, that one dare hardly trust oneself to speak of your wickedness.'

Swain glanced round the court. Lou Harris and Annie Sleaper watched pale and ghastly. For whom was their horror treasured up? The girls who had died in such agony, or the man now condemned to the cold early walk to the execution shed at Newgate?

'. . . What motive you had to take the lives of these girls, and with so much torture, I know not. The crimes you have committed are of an unparalleled atrocity. For those murders, our law knows but one penalty. When you descend the steps from the spot where you now stand, the world will be no more to you. The sentence of the law is that you be taken hence to a place of lawful execution, and that there you be hanged by the neck until you be dead. And may the Lord have mercy upon your soul.'

The chaplain's 'Amen', the judge's removal of the black triangular cap from his wig, were followed by a split second of total stillness. It was the prisoner who ended it. Light shone on the hard bald dome of his skull as he turned his face to the judge, rimless spectacles a-glint and a pleasant smile on his lips.

'That's all right,' he said easily, as if accepting an apology from Baron Hawkins, 'no one's going to hang Mrs Cream's boy!'

Stillness in the court became a murmur of shock at the man's irreverence. The warders took him down the steps to the cells below the court to await the Newgate van. Swain stood and watched the judge leave with his chaplain and clerk. Then the inspector stood in his place while the court emptied. Either the murderer had lost all touch with reality or some grotesque development lay in wait for the world during the next three weeks. What? What else could there be?

He was alone in the courtroom now, except for an assistant clerk gathering up papers from the judicial bench. At that moment he became more fully aware of a sound which had been growing in his consciousness for a minute or two. It seemed to come from the empty dock.

> Oh, an egg and some ham and an onion!
> As a dish it seems rather a funny 'un!

The song came, shrill and jubilant up the steps to the court, accompanied by a pattering of shoes on stone and hands clapping.

> What did Charlie Peace ask for the day he was 'ung?
> Oh, an egg and some ham and an on-i-i-on!

The song began again, higher and shriller with excitement and release. Swain mastered his incredulity and shivered as he stood there. Below him, Thomas Neill Cream sang and danced himself to exhaustion in his cell.

29

'No hard feelings, then?' Neill Cream grinned at Swain in a myopic unfocused leer. His rimless spectacles had been taken away from him for fear that his remarks in the dock were a promise that he would cheat the hangman by suicide. This had caused him great hilarity.

'No.' Swain ignored the outstretched hand and sat down on the little wooden chair, the table between him and the condemned man. At one end of the cell with its barred windows high in the blank wall, the two warders of the death-watch stood at ease, as if hearing no word of the conversation.

'No hard feelings!' Neill Cream sat down, as if that settled the matter. 'You tried, though! Oh boy, did you try!'

'It's over,' Swain said earnestly. 'Please, for your own sake, face that while you have time.'

Neill Cream chuckled.

'I'll be out of here in a day or two. I'll have all the time I need.'

Swain sighed helplessly.

'Believe me, you won't. By this time tomorrow, you will be dead.'

Neill Cream smiled again. They had taken away his tie and collar, as well as his boots. In his smart black jacket and trousers he looked like a man caught in the middle of dressing for a formal occasion.

'Have I got a surprise!' He grinned at Swain again. 'Have I got a surprise for you! When the British Government hears what it is, they won't be able to get me out of this fast enough.'

'They'll hang you, anyway,' said Swain monotonously. Whatever compassion he had felt for the condemned man was frustrated by this truculent lunacy. 'If you have fresh evidence, anything at all, now is the time . . .'

Cream wagged a finger at him for his naughtiness.

'Oh no, old fellow! They'd take it and hang me just the same. I intend to keep you on your toes. All of you. I'm in charge now.'

Swain tried not to shout at the man's stupidity.

'You have less than twenty-four hours . . .'

Cream nodded, as if conceding the point for the sake of argument.

'Suppose they string me up. You think the little pranks are going to stop? You think there's not a girlie or so walking the Lambeth streets with a capsule or two in her reticule, to be taken when she feels she might have got into the family way? There's a couple of dozen of them yet, Swain. Oh, won't you be a busy fellow from now on!'

'I don't believe you,' Swain said simply. 'Whether I did or not – whether it's true or not – it wouldn't save you. If that's your surprise . . .'

Cream grinned at him again.

'It's not even part of my surprise, old fellow. It's just a little something extra. Mind you, I don't promise they'll all take their little capsules. Perhaps half of them . . . a dozen or so.'

There was nothing for it but a plain appeal. Swain tried it.

'If you have any humanity, give me their names. Let them live.'

Cream laughed at the unfairness of the suggestion.

'And would you then let me live, Swain? Damned if you would! What's sauce for the goose . . .'

'Is there anything else you want?'

Cream thought about this.

'Chewing-gum,' he said finally, 'I used chewing-gum a lot in Chicago. A soothing habit, Swain. That's what I'd like.'

'I'll see what I can do.'

Cream rubbed his hands.

'In any case,' he said, 'you'll be here tomorrow morning, won't you? For the surprise?'

'I have to be a witness.'

'Oh good!' Cream said. 'You'll be here for the surprise!'

Swain got up and the prisoner followed his example, courteously.

'By the way,' Cream said, 'how is Miss Rachel Ryland?'

The shock took the breath from Swain's throat and fastened on his heart like ice.

'Why?' He turned and looked at the dark squinting eyes, the myopic stare.

'Because,' said Cream, 'you know her very well, don't you? You know her intimately, Mr Swain. I had to make certain enquiries when you came to Lambeth Palace Road. Though I was never privileged to meet her, they tell me she is a charming young lady.'

'What has she got to do with you?'

'Nothing,' said Cream hastily, 'not a thing. Except that I *do* have a friend or two, despite what was said in court. Men of like mind to myself. I hope you will believe that if anything should – go wrong – tomorrow morning, Miss Rachel Ryland will meet one of those friends. Alas, the pleasure of that encounter will be entirely on his side and not at all on the young lady's.'

Swain looked at the two warders who stared ahead of them, seeing and hearing nothing.

'I believe they will hang you tomorrow at eight,' he said quietly. 'Nothing you say or do will alter that.'

Cream smiled at him.

'The chewing-gum,' he said, 'if you would be so kind. Just enough for tonight. I shall be able to get all I need after tomorrow.'

Swain walked away from the sparse death cell with its bare and minimal wooden furnishings. He tried to collect his thoughts in the passageway outside where the escort warder waited. Even this was frustrated by the high and taunting song which came from within, celebrating the murderer Samuel Hall.

> Oh, my name it is Sam Hall, Samuel Hall,
> Oh, my name it is Sam Hall
> And I hate you one and all . . .

'He's mad,' Swain said to the warder, 'mad and evil in equal proportions. They shouldn't hang him. We don't yet know the half of what he's done . . .'

'Tomorrow's the day.' The warder chose a key from the bunch on his ring and shouted, 'One off! Death cells! Tomorrow or never, Mr Swain.'

They waited for the second iron-barred gate to open on the other side. Behind him, Swain heard the shrill arpeggios of lunacy.

Oh, the chaplain he did come, he did come,
Oh, the chaplain he did come, he did come,
Oh, the chaplain he did come,
And he talked of Kingdom Come!
He can kiss my bloody bum,
Blast his eyes!

Swain walked through the cold afternoon to Ludgate Circus and began to look for chewing-gum in the confectioners' shops.

On the following morning at six o'clock the air was colder still. Outside the main gate of Newgate prison, like the entrance to a great Florentine palace, Sergeant Lumley said, 'I brought this. If it was me I'd want a good stiff drink to start with.'

He went back to the cab, opened the door and took out a quarter bottle of whisky and a glass.

'Here you go,' he said, handing them to Swain.

The inspector took them, shivered in the cold, then handed them back.

'It won't do, Mr Lumley. I can't go to the governor with drink on my breath.'

Lumley looked at him in astonishment.

'*They* won't smell it. Not with what they'll have had already.'

'And if you're wrong, Mr Lumley, I'll be done for drinking on duty.'

All the same he took back the glass and bottle and poured himself a tot.

'Good luck, then,' said Lumley at last. 'I'll be waiting out here. Just keep thinking of them poor girls. He deserves what's coming to him. It's not half what those young creatures suffered. Not to mention the ones in America. They should have hung him in Chicago in the first place.'

Swain nodded. He turned and presented himself to the warder at the prison gate, offering the letter with the high sheriff's authority upon it. The escort led him to an ante-room near the governor's office. It was long after seven o'clock when Swain was admitted to the company of the governor, the high sheriff, the commissioner of police and the medical officer. Each of them received him with a nod.

The governor, a bantam-weight with bandy legs, checked his watch with the clock on the wall.

'How is he?' he asked, looking up at the doctor.

'He slept until just before six. The chaplain went in to him about ten minutes ago. No breakfast. It was offered but he refused it. Quite calm, though. He seems confident of the success of his surprise, as he calls it.'

The governor sighed.

'Men will create hope for themselves where none exists. Does anyone else know what this surprise may be?'

Swain waited politely but saw that no one else was going to reply beyond a negative murmur.

'Deaths still to come, sir,' he said quietly. 'He gave the same capsules to two dozen other women with instructions to take them when they choose to avoid pregnancy or precipitate menstruation. That's part of it. He also claims to have an associate, prepared to kill a young woman in Clapham as an act of revenge if we hang Neill. To save these lives, we must spare his.'

'Fiddlesticks,' said the high sheriff irritably. 'Any man might cheat the gallows by inventing such a threat.'

'I have the name of one young woman from him, sir,' said Swain mournfully. 'To my knowledge she has been watched by a man whom we suspect of criminal assaults upon women.'

'I have no instructions in the matter . . . The Home Office has kept its own counsel but the telegraph line is open for any message. Even at the last minute.'

Swain took a step forward.

'With respect, sir. If the prisoner begins to tell us the names of women who may take strychnine unawares, are we to proceed with the execution?'

The governor looked at him, eyes narrowed and suspicion growing in the set of his face.

'What else? The warrant is signed . . .'

'By the high sheriff of London who is here and might intervene.'

The governor's fingers played upon his watch-chain in fresh irritation.

'For how long? Until Scotland Yard has checked the well-being of every young woman whom the prisoner cares to name – or whose name he invents? Are we to keep him standing on the gallows-trap while this is done? Or return him to the deathcell? Is the notice of execution to be posted outside while the man is still alive? There will be a big enough crowd waiting to see it by eight o'clock!'

'It would be necessary to reprieve him, sir.'

The governor looked at Swain as if the inspector himself might be the villain of the plot.

'Then any murderer can escape hanging by pretending something of the sort!'

'With respect, sir,' Swain said in the same dispassionate tone, 'the facts will be different. In other cases there can be no credence given to threats of such a kind. In this case, where he has killed nine or ten women to our knowledge, a posthumous vengeance is quite possible.'

'The Home Secretary thinks not.'

With that, the governor turned his back and spoke no more to Swain until his general invitation to the others at ten minutes to eight.

'If you're ready, gentlemen.'

He had heard or seen a signal unnoticed by the others. Almost at once there was a tap at the door. It was the chief warder, his assistant and Billington, the hangman, who appeared as a modest-looking man with the air of a neatly dressed clerk.

They formed an untidy procession, the governor and the warder at the head, Swain and the commissioner at the rear. The door of the death cell was already open, Cream standing rather sheepishly with his two guardians.

'Already?' he said brightly. 'Well, the sooner the better, I suppose.'

They had given him back his glasses, his collar and tie, his boots. With the glasses on, the squint in his dark eyes was less noticeable. His confidence contrasted with the pallid look of the chaplain in his cassock and bands. One of the warders held out a mug of rum to him while the governor read the death warrant, stumbling over several of the words in his agitation.

240

'Man that is born of a woman hath but a short time to live . . .'

Muddling his words in confusion the chaplain began that strangest of all liturgies, the burial service of a man who was still alive to hear its opening words. Alive and in perfect health, Swain thought.

Billington had strapped Cream's arms behind his back and the untidy procession formed up again, the prisoner at its centre. He began to talk, his voice drowning the chaplain's prayers. The warders of the death-watch moved aside a tall cupboard and revealed a door in the wall of the cell, leading directly out on to the yard. It had been opened from outside and two men stood guard upon it.

'The first,' said Cream loudly, 'was Martha Turner near the Angel and Crown in Limehouse. Only a surgeon could have cut her up that small. Then there was Mary Nicolls. I did her throat easily in two gashes . . .'

Every one of them was pretending not to hear him, pretending that his existence had already ceased. Only Swain tried to keep a record of the words in his memory as they crossed the prison yard with its blank walls towards the execution shed a little distance away. The chaplain's cadences faltered and almost stopped entirely.

'Annie Chapman was a good one – and would have been better if I'd had a little more time. Still, her entrails were all out, steaming hot, by the time they found her . . .'

They entered the shadow of the execution shed, where the floor had been marked with a cross in chalk. Billington stood the prisoner gently upon it. Though there was a beam overhead, there was no sign of the coiled rope.

'The double was best of all!' Cream shouted. 'Elizabeth Stride with her windpipe slit and Catherine Eddowes ripped up, stem to stern! Ah, you know me now, do you?'

The assistant hangman pinioned Cream's legs while the prisoner's head twisted triumphantly, side to side, to look at them all. They watched him in silence and horror – as they might an animal hurt beyond repair, who must be destroyed as an act of mercy.

'You know me, do you? You know the story I must tell?'

241

'I think we'd better have this on, Dr Cream,' said Billington gently.

He drew the white canvas hood over Cream's head, the noose hidden in its lower fold. Still the terrible voice was not silenced.

'And Mary Kelly! I cut her up and stacked her, just like a post-mortem exhibition. Do you know me yet – you fools?'

Billington clipped the noose to the rope which his assistant had uncoiled from the beam. Then the hangman stood back to take hold of the lever for the trap.

'I am the man who has cheated you all!' Now the voice was almost a scream, as if sensing that the surprise had failed, 'I am the man you could not find! Listen to me! Answer me!'

Swain longed only for the rasping, shrieking voice to be still.

'I am Juan Pollen!' shouted Cream. 'I am—'

The governor, white-faced and red-eyed, roared his command.

'Mr Billington!'

'Jack the—'

There was a crash of wood on wood. Cream dropped straight and silent through the hole that opened in the floor of the shed. The rope juddered and hummed briefly. It swung to and fro through a six-inch arc for a few moments, creaking against the wooden beam.

There was silence at last. Swain never knew whether the governor's shout had been intended to precipitate the execution or to stop Billington with his hand already on the lever. It no longer mattered.

30

'If there's one thing he couldn't have been, it's Jack the Ripper,' Lumley said comfortingly.

All day he had fussed over Swain, as if caring for one who had been bereaved.

'I suppose not.'

'Cream was in Joliet prison seven years by the time of the Whitechapel killings, and he was there for three years more. If that's the best surprise he could manage, I don't think much of it. How could it have saved him?'

'It might have done,' Swain said. 'I think it might have done, if they'd believed him. He was far gone. He wasn't in that execution shed at all. You wouldn't think he could see us. He'd gone off into a world of his own – a world where he really believed he was Jack the Ripper – and proud of it. Don't you see? He'd rather be believed and hung than respited and called a liar.'

'I heard they never let him have the chewing-gum after all,' Lumley said laconically, 'in case he should accidentally choke on it before the hangman could do the job for him. Did you ever hear anything so daft?'

He went out and, for the first time since his ordeal that morning, Swain found himself alone. Sitting on the edge of his desk, the inspector stared at the familiar skyline of chimney-pots and roofs, across Parliament Street and Northumberland Avenue. The Thames shone warm and tranquil again. It seemed like a fading nightmare, the ghastly scene in the execution shed enacted a few hundred yards from all this normality. Men and women ate, talked, made love, while others hung in the hangman's noose a few streets away.

His thoughts were interrupted by lowered voices in the corridor outside. There was murmuring and whispering. Swain knew that something was wrong. He thought of Cream's threat, of the women who walked the streets with their capsules of strychnine. The coincidence was too great that one of them had taken her 'medicine' and died this very day. He opened the door and found Lumley standing there with several other officers from the division behind him. Lumley held out a sheet of paper. Swain recognised it as a telegraphic message.

'There's this from Wandsworth,' Lumley said. 'They got Slater. Caught him.'

'Good,' said Swain absent-mindedly.

'No it ain't!' Lumley directed his attention to the paper.

'They found him on the common. Standing over the body of a girl. Knife in his hand. She'd been dead some time. Seems as if he might be the "friend" that was doing Dr Cream a posthumous favour.'

Satisfaction in Swain's heart gave way to dread. He knew more than Lumley about the posthumous vengeance, enough to know that the promised victim was Rachel Ryland.

'You go,' he said, thinking of her rather than his own words. 'I'll follow . . .'

'There's no need yet,' Lumley said. 'They got Slater in the cells. Bang to rights. There's no need . . .'

'I'll be there!'

Even his anger was of a kind to which he could not give his full attention. Without waiting to see what Lumley would do, Swain ran down the stairs and out through Whitehall Place into Northumberland Avenue. Rachel! Her name went through his mind mechanically and her image rose before him. Let it not be her! Let it not be Rachel! Whatever doubts he felt before about their relationship vanished in the apprehension of losing her. Let it not be Rachel! Let it be Sally Petts rather than her!

In his panic he knew no charity for others.

Across Westminster Bridge, the sound of his own breath sawing in his head as he ran, he passed the hospital and the music halls, down the shabby sunlit length of Westminster Bridge Road. Once he slowed to a walk to regain his wind and then began to run again. Faces moved past him quickly, like the passengers on a platform when the train passed through. He saw their curiosity and apprehension at the sight of him.

Past Orient Buildings and Hercules Road. Why not a cab or a horse-tram? The tram would stick in the traffic, the cab would be held up. In his present state, Swain could not bear the thought of sitting motionless, waiting.

Yet in Kennington Road, he could run no more. Walking and stumbling by turns he sprinted suddenly after a horse-tram and swung himself aboard. At Clapham Road he jumped down quickly, stumbling and twisting his ankle. The long thoroughfare stretched ahead of him and he counted the house-numbers to mark his progress. Let it not be Rachel. . . .

244

Let it be any woman but Rachel. . . . One of them is dead. . . . Why need it be her? The litany of obsession possessed his thoughts. He wished harm to the rest of her sex, if only Rachel could be saved, as earnestly as Dr Cream had done to his victims. The knowledge of this failed to shock him.

His anguish was supremely comic to others. A group of urchins ran after him down Clapham Road, at a prudent distance, shouting 'Stop, thief!' with all their power. Among the faces in Clapham High Street, by the smart little shops, were several he knew.

A voice said, 'Why, Mr Swain!'

He ran on, turned the corner and saw the house ahead of him. How long had it taken him? How far had he run? Snatching the key from his pocket, he sprang up the steps and fumbled at the door.

Edith Ryland stood alone in the hall, watching him doubtfully.

'Rachel! Where is she?'

In his despair, the words came like a shout of anger. For that moment he could have wished Edith Ryland dead, rather than that he should watch her grief breaking at the news and should endure her misery so close to his own.

'Where is she?'

Mrs Ryland hesitated, the doubt growing deeper in her eyes.

'Why, here I am, of course,' said Rachel's voice, as she came from the drawing room and put her hand in his. 'Shall we always have such impatience from you, Mr Alfred Swain?'